A new light shon
Thatcham bent his head
away. She begged her　　　　　．．．ınstead, it
leaned closer as though a magnet pulled the two together. She could not resist.

"Philomena," Lord Thatcham murmured. "Is that name real? Who are you? What brought you here to make me—" He stopped abruptly and straightened a little, searching Philomena's face. He lingered on the black curls, the blue eyes, and then his gaze slid down to rest on her mouth. His lips parted. "You are very beautiful."

Philomena could not speak. Her body, responding to the hitherto unknown power of male magnetism, yearned for the first touch. Lord Thatcham's breath escaped in a rough gasp. He surrounded her, his arms gentle, and eased her body forward until Philomena felt his heart beat in time with her own.

Her eyes were half closed. His lips brushed gently, soft and warm, over her mouth. For an endless moment, she stayed quite still, beguiled by the spicy sharp taste of his lips. A charge electrified her body.

Then her head cleared. She gasped. Was she mad? This was Lord Thatcham, and she was nothing but a penniless waif in his power. He meant to have his way with her, just as Joseph had tried to do.

She tore herself away from the embrace. "How dare you." Her voice shook with fury. "How dare you treat me so?"

Lord Thatcham's arms fell away. Blood drained from his countenance, leaving the dark eyes aglow in a white face. He said not a word.

An Independent Woman

by

Frances Evesham

An Independent Woman

Cover Art by Debbie Taylor

The Wild Rose Press, Inc.
PO Box 708
Adams Basin, NY 14410-0708
Visit us at www.thewildrosepress.com

Publishing History
First English Tea Rose Edition, 2014
Print ISBN 978-1-62830-390-2
Digital ISBN 978-1-62830-391-9

Published in the United States of America

Dedication

For David, with all my love.

Chapter One

Philomena crept up the twisted stairs. A rat scuttled past and disappeared into the early morning fog of the London alleyway. She shuddered and pulled her shawl closer, stepping lightly to soften the clink of patten on wood as she climbed, head pounding and legs trembling.

Last week, dark curls bouncing, she'd skipped up the same stairs in happy anticipation of breakfast with Samuel, her guardian and employer. Since his death, Philomena lived in dread of Joseph, Samuel's son. So far, she had come to no harm for Joseph fell into bed each night, drunk and incapable. During the day, though, as she moved around the workshop, Philomena felt her tormentor's black eyes on her body. Whenever she looked up, Joseph licked wet lips and winked.

Philomena stole up the last few stairs, biting her lip at each protesting creak. All was quiet outside the room. Joseph still slept.

"You see," she murmured. "There's nothing to worry about." She turned the key in the lock and pushed the door open.

Joseph shot out from behind the door, grabbed her arm, and dragged Philomena into the room. She stumbled and dropped the basket. Wiry fingers bit into her flesh. Joseph jerked her closer. She recoiled from the rancid stink of last night's beer and held her breath as he sniggered.

Philomena twisted her head from side to side, searching for a weapon, but the dingy room, like thousands of similar tiny rooms in the teeming stews of the city, held little but a rough table and chairs. Neighbours hearing screams through the paper-thin walls would make no move to help. Quarrels and fights in the building were too common to raise more than an eyebrow.

Joseph forced his lips onto hers. Teeth clenched, Philomena took a deep breath, stood tall, and drove her knee into his groin. Joseph doubled up, grunting. A two-handed thrust launched him across the room. He crashed into the flimsy wall and lay still, shocked and gasping. A grey snow of loose plaster rained down, speckling the head and shoulders of his fustian waistcoat.

Triumphant, Philomena laughed. "Don't you dare touch me again or you'll be sorry."

Joseph stumbled to his feet and sneered, lips curled over a jungle of mismatched yellow teeth and a single black stump. "Little fool. You'll give in soon enough. Make no mistake about that." Blobs of congealed fat from last night's dinner fell from his coarse cotton shirt as he lurched out of the room. The door crashed shut.

Philomena's mind raced, sharp and clear. She'd managed to get the upper hand this once, but next time would be another matter. The city she called home offered precious little protection to a lone woman. The time had come to leave. Her chin lifted. "Tomorrow," she whispered, "I'll be in Bristol."

Skilful with a needle and thrifty enough to have saved a few sovereigns over the years, she could build a new life. The new Great Western Railway would whisk her to the other side of the country in less time than a cab took to cross London. Joseph would come after her, of course. He needed her expertise in the tailor shop, for he lacked any talent. Philomena must take care to draw no attention.

She snatched his Sunday best clothes from a hook. Lord, the smell was terrible. The clothing hadn't had the benefit of the laundress's tub for many a month. She breathed through her mouth and dressed in the heavy fustian trousers, tightening a length of string around her waist to prevent them falling off. Fastening the jacket snugly with a pin across the chest, she turned back the sleeves. A flat cap led to a struggle. No sooner was one handful of raven-black curls tucked inside than another escaped. Philomena's fingers fumbled, as fat and lazy as slugs.

She pulled a pair of Samuel's scissors from a table, took a deep breath, grasped a heavy lock of curls, and chopped hard. Hair tumbled to the floor. She worked fast, wasting no energy on regrets until a heap of curls lay on the wooden floor.

Goodbye, Philomena. A grin spread from ear to ear as she slammed the door of the lodgings.

Night closed in before she reached Bishop's Bridge Road Station, tired and footsore, to clamber aboard the train. Heavy rain plummeted down. She shivered in the open wagon. For more than an hour, the train rattled onward. Philomena's weary eyes closed, lulled by the regular rhythm of the wheels. At last, head nodding and chin resting on her chest, she slept.

The train lurched, pitching her awake. A cry, so shrill with fright that it was impossible to tell if it came from a man or a woman, pierced the night. "Gawd 'elp us all, it's a landslide."

Philomena lost her grip on the slippery side of the wagon as it pitched and bounced. For a heart-stopping moment of silence, the world held its breath. The front of the wagon tilted, flew into the air, and flipped backwards. She soared high into the dark, as weightless as a bird. *I'm going to die.* She knew a brief stab of sorrow that the adventure had ended so abruptly. Then the ground rose up to deal a blow that squeezed all the breath from her lungs.

****

Deep sleep enveloped the inhabitants of Thatcham Hall, rewarding the servants for long hours of toil with a brief respite before the first maid rose to set fires. Wind and rain howled through cracks and down chimneys. Only Hugh—Lord Thatcham—was still awake, hunched over the oak desk in the silent library, long legs cramped as the embers of the fire died away and the night chilled his bones.

His gaze sped down a column of figures. He added them once and then again. Finally, satisfied, he scrawled a signature below the total. He drew a deep breath and released it in a sigh, the knot in his stomach easing a little. The Hall, with its debts and its crumbling East Wing, so often swallowed every penny of profit raised, but, slowly, Hugh was turning things around. The improvements planned for the farms would help. Next year, barley yields should be up, thanks to the new thresher. He yawned and stretched, then turned again to the pile of papers.

Hugh pulled the next document near and read it, eyes narrowed, pen poised. Old Walden's cottage needed work. Could it wait a while? That would save a few pounds. His hesitation lasted only a moment. Old Walden, long-serving butler to both his father and grandfather, deserved some comforts. The roof of the retirement cottage must be a priority.

So many priorities crowded round that sometimes Hugh could hardly breathe.

He strode to the window and squinted into the darkness that shrouded the land. The night stars hid behind scudding clouds, but even in the pitch black, Hugh visualised each cottage, tree, or fence on the estate. This was his land. He knew and loved every stone, leaf, and blade of grass of it. The Dainty family had lived there since Tudor times, through good years and bad, and three hundred years of ancestors weighed heavy on Hugh's shoulders. If he achieved nothing else, he would make sure the Hall and its estates passed, intact, to his son, John.

If only Beatrice had shared some of Hugh's love for Thatcham Hall. Maybe, then, they would have managed better together. Restless, he turned from the window. The brief marriage had ended in disaster, leaving a bitter legacy of guilt and remorse. Nevertheless, Hugh would forever be grateful to Beatrice for giving him a son. John, now four years old and the image of his dead mother, enjoyed robust health and vast stores of energy. As mischievous as a puppy, he romped each day through the nursery, leaving torn books, broken ornaments, and a succession of frantic nursemaids in his wake.

Hugh bit his lip. He had kept busy all day, far from the nursery, but tomorrow he could avoid his responsibilities no longer. He must deal with John's latest misdemeanour. Could he avoid punishing the boy? He remembered the painful punishments that followed his own wild behaviour as a child. No. He must check John's worst excesses, even though each wide-eyed stare from eyes as round and green as Beatrice's, and just as quick to tears, twisted the knife of guilt in Hugh's heart. Easing his legs back beneath the desk, he concentrated on the stack of documents.

Finally, the day's work completed, he threw his pen aside and tossed down the last dregs of claret. A foot crunched on the gravel. His head jerked up. A voice called and another answered, loud and urgent. A fist hammered on the door, insistent. Hugh's heart lurched.

He hurried to the window and flung open the shutters. A dozen or so labourers, lanterns held aloft, jostled one another on the front drive. Hugh took the stairs, two at a time. The butler threw open the front door and a noisy cacophony exploded into the Hall.

Hugh spoke steadily, hiding his agitation. "What's amiss?"

"Oh, begging your pardon, my lord. There's been a terrible accident over yonder. One of them there new-fangled steam trains has come off its tracks, and all the people are dead, my lord. Dead, or dying."

"Good God." Ice slid down Hugh's spine, and he shivered. It seemed that death and disaster had returned to Thatcham Hall. "Tell the coachman to send a horse and cart at once, and saddle Thunder for me. I'll ride over and see what can be done."

The rain still fell and the night was cold, with the wind blowing in gusts from the east. At the railway cutting, amid swirls of smoke and arrows of rain, shapes shifted and stumbled, indistinct in the flickering light of lanterns. Oil lamps threw shadows that hid as much as their glow illuminated. Hugh squinted into the gloom.

The whole village, it seemed, had turned out to help. He urged Thunder on to where a carriage lay overturned on the ground, wheels in the air. Broken planks littered the mud. Here and there, twisted bodies lay quite still. Dead bodies.

Hugh leaped down, took a pace forward, stumbled, and almost fell over a bundle on the ground. He fought for balance, boots sticking in the mud that reached to his ankles. The bundle moved, rubbed its head, rested a moment on its elbows, then fell back and lay still. Hugh bent nearer, and the bundle opened its eyes. Startling, bright blue pools stared up from a face caked in dirt. The bundle coughed and sat up. "What happened?"

It was a boy's high voice. Hugh let out the breath he had not even known he held. "You're not dead yet, then."

Chapter Two

Hugh peered more closely at the boy. "Of course, you're not dead. I meant to say, are you hurt?" A crimson streak on the boy's temple shimmered in the ghostly lantern light. "You are bleeding." He touched the boy's head. The lad jerked as though Hugh had struck him and scrambled to his feet. Hugh, surprised, grabbed his arm.

"Oh, sir." The boy seemed no older than fourteen or fifteen. His arm shook in Hugh's grasp, and he gazed around with unfocused eyes. "Sir, will you help us? There are people trapped under there."

He shook Hugh's hand away, scrambled to his feet and ran, slipping and sliding in the mud, to tear at the upturned carriage.

"Wait," Hugh called. "That won't work." He peered through the murk. Where was the coachman? "Ince!"

"Sir." The voice came from Hugh's right. The coachman was struggling to restrain a carthorse so that bodies could be loaded on board the wagon. The poor beast, terrified by human screams and the smell of smoke, snorted and stamped.

"Ince," Hugh shouted. "Throw me a rope."

"Sir," the boy piped up, his voice shrill. He still pushed and pulled at the carriage, his efforts hopeless. "If you can only help me lift this wagon a little, there's a woman and her child caught below."

"Are they alive?"

"I can't tell, sir, I can't hear them anymore."

"Hold a moment. We can't lift that weight by ourselves. We need my horse."

Hugh ran back to Thunder, who shivered and fidgeted nearby. He untied the black stallion and pulled him across to the upturned carriage. Thunder relaxed in his master's hands, snorting gently.

Ince relinquished the wagon to others and came running, a rope coiled over his shoulder. "My lord," he panted. "What should we do?"

"Tie one end of your rope to Thunder and lead him on to higher ground. Be quick about it. God knows how many poor souls are trapped underneath."

Hugh turned and shouted to the boy, his voice cutting through the chaos. "Come away. You won't lift it by yourself. Let the horse do the job."

The boy fell back. The coachman led the horse a few steps, but Thunder resisted, terrified of the lights and noise. His eyes swivelled, whites gleaming. He pulled away from Ince and reared, hooves flailing and thrashing, threatening to add Ince to the tally of injured.

"He's not used to this kind of work, my lord," gasped the coachman.

"No more are the rest of us." Hugh took the horse's reins in his own hands. "Come, now." He kept his voice low and steady. The horse skipped sideways. "Now then. This is no time to be foolish. Just follow me."

Thunder, settling to the sound of his master's voice, took a few steps. The carriage creaked.

"That's better," Hugh said.

Thunder responded with a few hesitant steps and

then, as nothing dreadful happened, pulled harder. The railway wagon creaked, groaned, and lurched. For a moment, it seemed it would not budge, but at last, with a loud suck and gurgle, the mud released its hold and the wagon flew, upside down, a foot in the air.

The boy darted forward. He put out his hand to a woman who sprawled, spread-eagled in the mud. A little girl lay motionless beside her. The woman bawled and screamed, bellowing language ripe enough to shock the costermongers of London.

"Madam," Hugh barked. "Be still at once." At the voice of authority, the woman stopped wailing. She scrambled up, clutching a basket to her breast.

Hugh ran to help the child, but the boy was there first. "She's breathing, sir." His high-pitched laugh bordered on hysteria.

The woman smoothed her skirts and resettled the mud-spattered bonnet that, by a miracle, remained securely in place on her head. She retied the ribbon. "I give Betsy a good mouthful o' gin not half an hour gone, so she'll be fast asleep for a while, bless her." The woman brimmed with pride at her own prudence.

"All's well with the child, sir, so far as I can tell," said the boy.

"If that's the child's mother, the poor thing's likely used to misadventure." Hugh's lips twitched. The boy glanced up, an answering grin cracking the mask of mud over his face.

One of Hugh's farm workers stepped out from the gloom. "It's a bad thing, my lord, and no mistake. At least six dead and a good couple dying as I speak. I knew no good would come of these 'ere iron horses." He shook his head. "We're taking all the rest to find beds for the night in the village, and there's a couple on the last cart that need to get to the hospital. The inn's full to bursting."

Hugh nodded. "Take the good lady and her child as well. I don't think there's anything broken that won't mend when they're sober, but it's as well to be sure." He looked at the boy. "You should go with them."

The boy shook his head and took a step backwards. "There's no need, sir." His voice was husky. "I mean to continue on my way. The sun will be up shortly."

Hugh shrugged. The hospital would be busy enough. If the lad chose not to go, that was his affair.

The boy recovered his cap from a puddle. Covered in mud and soaking wet, it was a sorry sight. He turned it over once or twice, fingers shaky, and then set it back on his head. Strands of short, raven black hair curled around the peak. His blue eyes met Hugh's dark grey ones for a second and then flickered away. His cheeks glowed pink.

Hugh looked more closely. The lad was older than he seemed at first; closer to seventeen perhaps, though his cheeks were smooth and hairless and his frame slender. Hugh frowned. "Nonsense. You can't go further now. In any case, you've done good work this night, and you've earned some rest and a decent meal before you move on." He gestured to the fat lady. "That this good woman and her child have escaped with their lives today is to your credit. Come, we'll make our way to Thatcham Hall. It's little more than fifteen minute's walk. Can you manage that?"

He signalled to the coachman to leave. The fat woman's eyes widened. "Thatcham Hall? Bless me, you must be Lord Thatcham." She clasped her hands to her cheeks and curtsied. "We don't know how to thank you, me and Betsy, my lord. If it weren't for you and that fine horse, and this lad, of course, well, we wouldn't be here now. It don't bear thinking about."

Dawn turned the sky yellow as the small procession finally reached the hall. A tiny figure wearing nightclothes shot out from the door, with the housekeeper, Mrs. Rivers, gasping in hot pursuit. "Now, you come back here, Master John."

"What are you doing out here in your night clothes?" Hugh was stern.

John stopped in his tracks. Tears filled his eyes. "But Papa, I could not sleep after the men came to get you. They said there was a train. Was there a..." He paused, thinking. "A accident?" He articulated the word with great concentration. "A accident, like before?" His voice tailed off in a sob.

Hugh knelt to gather John close. His coat muffled the boy's tears. "There was indeed an accident, I am sorry to say, but everyone from the Hall is safe and well. There is no need to be afraid." Gently, he wiped the boy's nose with his own handkerchief, until the tears dried. He held John at arm's length. "Now then, what do you mean by running around in the dark when Mrs. Rivers is calling you? You know you must obey her."

"Well my lord, I'm sorry he got away from me." The housekeeper's face was red with exertion. "But with Abigail gone, it's hard to keep him from mischief, what with the preparations for Christmas and all."

"Yes, yes," said Hugh. "I'm sure you're doing your best. John, I will take you to bed myself to make sure there will be no more running away." Surprised by a pang of affection, he cleared his throat. "There is nothing to see here, but we do have an unexpected visitor tonight."

The distraction worked. John stared with unashamed curiosity and an open mouth at the stranger, who swayed a little on his feet.

"We'd better call the doctor in to have a look at you, I think," Hugh said.

The lad started. "Oh no." His voice was light and musical: a young boy's tones. "Not me, I mean, I'm sure there's nothing amiss."

Hugh tired of the argument. "Very well, if you're sure there's no damage." He tossed John onto his shoulders and set off towards the Hall. John clung to his hair. "Just let Mrs. Rivers—or perhaps one of the maids—look at your head." Mrs. Rivers' bosom heaved with indignation at the very suggestion. "Yes, that would be best. Ask one of the maids to put something on that cut." He peered once more at the youth, and his nose wrinkled. "I suggest a bath, as well." He strode into the house without another word.

Chapter Three

Philomena leaned back on a wooden settle in the vast kitchen of Thatcham Hall. Her bones ached, but her mind raced. A range stretched the length of one wall, its heat reaching into every corner of the room. London had not offered such delightful comfort in summer, never mind in the middle of winter. A muddle of pots towered nearby, scraped clean of their breakfast contents, awaiting attention from the scullery maid. Philomena's body, confused by lack of sleep and stoked with more food than she normally ate in a week, hovered on the edge of slumber.

The kitchen throbbed with activity. Philomena felt distant, as though she watched from outside a pane of glass. The cook clattered spoons in a bowl, cracked eggs, and weighed out flour, engrossed in preparations for the next meal. A parlour maid trotted past the doorway to the stairs and peered over an armful of bed linen and tablecloths, blushing and giggling at a footman. The footman, tall and dark, a boot in one hand, a brush in the other and his mouth a little open, watched the maid wiggle up the stairs.

Philomena's head spun with the change that just twenty-four hours had brought. Yesterday, at home in London, she had fought off Joseph's unwelcome advances. The triumph seemed a distant memory now. She'd already be in Bristol had fortune not taken a hand. Fate, it seemed, had other plans for her that depended upon tossing her, cold, wet and terrified, into the mud of the railway cutting.

She let her eyes close but did not sleep. Her thoughts whirled back to the cutting. Noise and chaos rang again in her ears and for a second, fear returned, sharp in her stomach. She covered her ears, trying in vain to shut out the cries of the injured.

Worst of all had been the dreadful silence of the dead. She would never forget the sight of bodies in the mud. She shuddered and took a deep, shaky breath. *You're safe, here.* Her fear drained away in the warmth of the kitchen. *You're not dead.*

One other memory returned to Philomena. Disoriented by her fall, she'd opened her eyes to see the face of a stranger. There was harshness in the lines around the man's mouth and eyes, and a fierce frown had etched itself into her memory. Lord Thatcham, the stranger, had been calm, as though he considered it no out of the way occurrence to hurtle to the ground from a speeding train. In the turmoil and disaster of the night, as he took control of the chaos, the steady gaze of his grey eyes had calmed Philomena.

She shook her head, trying to clear it, but the impression of his face remained, obstinately bright. Lord Thatcham was rich. His Hall was grand. He was aristocratic. Why, most likely, he even had a seat in the House of Lords, where he helped shape the law and influenced matters of importance to the whole nation. No wonder every gesture he made spoke of confidence, and his voice resonated with infuriating tones of authority.

Philomena sat straighter. Here was yet another

aggravating man, enjoying easy power. Why did all men think themselves superior? She wished to have nothing to do with them. She tried to dispel Lord Thatcham's image and focus instead on her plan. Neither the luxurious comfort of the Hall, nor its intriguing, arrogant owner, would distract her from her purpose. This was her adventure. She had defeated Joseph. She could find her own way in the world. A pair of grey eyes and a severe face would not deflect her from her purpose, no matter how fascinating.

Thatcham Hall, despite its grandeur, was just a short stop on Philomena's quest for independence. Soon, she would pick herself up, resume her travels, complete the journey to the other side of the country, and become a woman of business. For many years, she had cherished that dream. She would let nothing stop her.

She looked around the kitchen. The warmth made her toes tingle. Philomena drew a deep breath and drank in the savoury cooking smells that had seeped into the stone walls of the room, over years of use. She detected hints of roast mutton, spices, dried fruits, and honey. Of course, today was Christmas Eve. The activity in the kitchen must be preparations for the next day's feast.

Philomena's mouth watered despite her full stomach as she thought of tables, groaning with more food than she had ever seen in one place. She licked her lips.

The cook broke into her reverie and she jumped, guilty as a kitten. Short and square in build, Mrs. Bramble flopped heavily into her special chair by the range, wiping drops of sweat from her face with a large grey handkerchief. She poked strands of hair back under her cap with floury fingers.

She was breathing hard. "I'll just put my feet up for a moment." She rested swollen ankles on a small wooden stool. She placed a steaming china cup and saucer on the table and nodded to Philomena while keeping one eye on the kitchen staff. "Alice, you get that tray up to Master John in the nursery, and be quick about it," she called.

Alice tossed her head. "How I'm supposed to finish tidying the dining room while I'm playing nursery maid, I'm sure I don't know."

"Be off with you," said Mrs. Bramble, "and stop complaining. Master John can't eat breakfast all alone, not at his age, so you get along up there. You should think yourself lucky, my girl. You'll have a chance to sit down while he eats."

"Yes, and spend an hour cleaning up afterwards when Master John takes one of his tantrums and throws food all around the room." Alice pouted.

"We'll have a bit less cheek from you," snapped Mrs. Bramble.

Alice flounced away, the starched white ribbons on her white cap flicking jauntily. Mrs. Bramble took a gulp of tea and sighed with pleasure. She raised her voice again, calling for James, the footman, to carry the tin bath into the scullery.

She spoke to the scullery maid. "Heat some more water and fill up the bath, Ivy. This young man could do with a nice long soak after all that scrambling about in the mud, I'll be bound."

She turned back to Philomena, satisfied that the lesser servants were attending to her instructions. "Now then, young man, let's get those clothes off you and into the wash and find you something decent to wear. I'm sure some of the master's old clothes will suit, though you're naught but a willow-wand compared to him."

Philomena, tempted by the luxury of deep, hot water, smiled. "I'm afraid these clothes are past cleaning." She brushed at the mud drying on Joseph's best trousers and fingered a tear in the jacket.

"Nonsense," Mrs. Rivers, the housekeeper, poked her head into the kitchen, checking to see that all the servants were about their business. "We've known worse when the weather's bad like this. You hand them over, after your bath, and we'll see what we can do."

Philomena opened her mouth to protest that she could perfectly well mend the tear herself. Just in time, she caught the words. She'd forgotten about her disguise. *I'm a boy. Boys don't sew.* She'd nearly given the game away. She gulped and coughed. "No maids, mind," she said, her voice as deep and gruff as she could manage. She headed for the scullery with long strides.

Mrs. Rivers laughed. "None of the girls will disturb you. I'll get James, the footman, to bring the hot water in when Ivy finishes heating it up."

Philomena shuddered. "No, I beg you." Her voice squeaked, and she dropped an octave, hoping no one had noticed the slip. "I've no wish to be a trouble in the house. Indeed, I'll take the water in now and be on my way as soon as I can."

Mrs. Rivers and the cook shook their heads, eyebrows raised, and agreed there was no accounting for the strange ways of young men. "I'll warrant you can use a good day's sleep before you continue on your way. That's if there's a train today, after that dreadful accident. A pretty penny your journey must be costing you. On your way to Bristol, you said?"

Philomena hesitated. "I was on my way to make my living in Bristol." She struggled to keep her voice deep and think at the same time."My uncle lives there, and he wrote to say there's plenty of work to be had, more pleasant than that to be found in London, where we live all on top of each other." She ran out of steam. Surely, the story would convince no one. After all, most young men ran away towards London, not in the other direction. Philomena prayed for inspiration and took a slow breath. "I want to work with Mr. Brunel, building railways and bridges." *That's better.* She watched for the reaction.

Mrs. Rivers nodded. "I see you are looking to the future. The steam train is a wonderful invention, so I hear."

Mrs. Bramble shuddered. "Oh, no, mercy me, just think of the noise and the danger. Look what happened last night. Why, who knows how many more poor souls will end up in the mud. Nasty, new-fangled things, trains. I won't have no part in them. Give me a pony and trap, now, and I'm happy." She fell to muttering under her breath, and Philomena's breathing settled. The story had passed its first test. In any case, she would soon be gone, long before Joseph could track her down.

****

Hugh spurred Thunder to a gallop. Blood pumped fast through his veins. Last night's emergency in the cutting had chased away the fatigue of the evening before, leaving him alert.

Such action was rare within the confines and

estates of Thatcham Hall. Frustrated by the sterile decorum of such a Great House, Hugh could sometimes almost envy the farm hands as they toiled in the fields, hands black with the fertile soil. He'd far rather spend an hour chopping wood alongside the forester than engage in the gentleman's pastimes of hunting, boxing, and fencing.

Thunder showed no sign of fatigue. Hugh felt the power of the horse's muscles as the creature galloped ever faster across the fields, leaping fords and brooks. A boundary hedge rose steeply in view, bushy and tall, challenging to any animal.

"Thunder," Hugh called, as the hedge towered before them. "Let's see what we can do."

He urged the horse forward and felt the animal gather its hind legs in preparation for the jump. A gust of wind rocked the hedge towards horse and rider and the branches loomed as high as Hugh's shoulders. Laughing into the wind, he leaned his weight forward until he touched the horse's neck. Thunder responded with a leap that cleared the hedge by almost a foot, landing smoothly on the grass at the other side as though the huge obstacle was no more than a chicken coop.

Exhilarated by the ride and panting from the exertion, Hugh allowed the horse to slow to a canter. "Well done," he gasped, breathless, his spirits high.

He tried to close his ears to the voice in his head. *Beatrice died from a fall. What would become of John if he should lose his father as well?* Hugh sighed. Must guilt contaminate even the pleasure of the gallop?

It was time to return to the Hall and shoulder once more the mantle of responsibilities for the estate and all who lived there. Hugh wheeled Thunder round and turned for home. He had no choice in the matter. He must remain reliable, trustworthy, and dependable at all times, for the sake of his son's inheritance.

As his pulse slowed, his thoughts turned to the boy from the train. The lad intrigued him. He'd been brave, last night. There was a streak of maturity and fortitude that belied the light voice and slight build. For a working lad of no more than fourteen or fifteen, the boy was sure of himself. His speech was clear and he seemed educated.

Hugh sensed a mystery. It piqued his interest. He would enjoy unravelling it. It might offer some respite from the ennui of the next few days. He groaned at the thought of the imminent Christmas visit by his mother, the Dowager Lady Thatcham, and his sister, newly out of the schoolroom. There was little enough amusement at the Hall.

He had only himself to blame, of course. As a young man, well aware of his position in life as the head of Thatcham Hall and keen to fulfil his duty, he had set out with enthusiasm to find an appropriate, well-born, well-brought-up lady to be a wife and the mother of many children.

Beatrice seemed perfect. He had let the fact that she was lovely as well as suitable cloud his judgement. Blinded by the beauty of her face and her tiny, feminine figure, he overlooked her frivolity, ignored the rapid shifts of her temper, and disregarded her need for constant attention. Hugh discovered, within a very short space of time, that Beatrice shared none of his tastes or opinions. Conversation withered between them, and Hugh's initial admiration and love slowly died, shrivelling into cool affection and, at last, exasperation and dislike.

Beatrice brought a little much-needed wealth to the Hall, for which Hugh would always remain grateful. In exchange, the Hall offered her status and a superior position in society, but married contentment eluded them. Hugh gave her all the freedom he could afford, to entertain friends and buy dresses, but he could not make her happy. As his wife grew more discontented, he spent less time with her. Instead, he poured every ounce of energy into managing the land, struggling to pay off the mortgage that hung around his neck like an albatross.

His efforts were finally beginning to bear fruit, and the estates were in better shape than they had been while his father lived. The late Lord Thatcham had not understood that change must come to ancient estates. Mechanisation sent wealth flooding into the wool factories of the North and made old-fashioned farming methods uneconomical.

Hugh read widely, eager to join the march of progress. Beatrice laughed at him. "I cannot imagine, my dear Hugh, why you waste your time on these ridiculous new machines. Horses and labourers have always tilled the ground, and I am sure they always will."

She tossed his latest journal aside. "In any case, these matters should be left for the farmers."

"No." He tried to stay patient. "The world is changing."

He took her hand. Surely, she would love, like him, to travel. They could see the world and shape the future. He tried to convey his excitement. "Why not travel with me to the Americas? I hear the country is enormous, with fields stretching out as far as the eye can see. Would you not love to see a New World?"

Beatrice removed her hand from his and waved her fan, languidly. "Really, Hugh, why would I wish to travel amongst foreigners? We have everything we need, here in England."

Beatrice adored parties, gaiety, jewels, and comfort. She regarded Hugh's love of the outdoors, his desire to spend as little time as possible in London, and the hours he enjoyed drawing plans for new machines, as a bore. She was jealous of the time her husband spent with his agent, and she disliked the servants at the Hall who adored Hugh and mistrusted her.

Still, a year had now passed since Beatrice's death. Hugh could make a new start in life. He would spend more time with John, show him the ways of the farm, and arrange for them both to visit the Americas. His spirits rose. He was a young man. Why should he not find happiness at last?

He would take care. He must learn from his mistakes in the past and guard against repeating them, for John and the army of workers who relied upon the estate for food, shelter, and work all depended upon him. He must restrict himself to the status of a solitary widower. He would not risk making another foray into marriage, for his judgment had failed him before. He would throw himself into his responsibilities. Perhaps, by subduing selfish frustrations and engaging all his energies in duties, he could begin to find some kind of peace.

Chapter Four

The enormous breakfast of bacon and sausages lay reassuringly in Philomena's stomach, floating in a sea of hot chocolate. She would sit here for just a while longer, enjoy a hot bath and then beg for a ride back to the station to continue the interrupted journey to the West Country. Her purse held sufficient for another ticket to Bristol. All would be well.

Automatically, Philomena felt for the purse in the pocket of Joseph's trousers. She gasped. It had gone. Struggling to stay calm, she tried again, wriggling her fingers into the corner of the pocket. Perhaps she had misremembered. The purse must be in the other side. She tried the other pocket. Her fingers went straight through a hole, deep in the pocket on the right side of the trousers. Philomena felt sick. The purse was gone, and with it the only sovereign she owned. "Oh no," she cried, forgetting in her panic to disguise her voice. "All my money's gone!"

The cook, kneading bread nearby, raised her head and glared. "Well, no one here's been anywhere near your money, so don't you go accusing us."

"No, no, I'm sure no one here has touched it." Dread constricted Philomena's throat. The missing purse meant all the money was gone, and with it, her only chance of a future. Her plans crumbled once more. She swallowed hard, her lips trembling. "I must have dropped the purse in the cutting. It's all I have. Everything. I must go back at once." She leapt to her feet, ready to run out of the kitchen.

Mrs. Rivers, the housekeeper, raised her hand. "Now, then." She could be sympathetic so long as no servant was in trouble. "You rest a while before running back there. Wait a bit, and we'll inform the master. Maybe he will send the coachman to look for it."

Philomena was in no mood to wait. She shook Mrs. Rivers' hand off her arm. "You don't know what it means! It's all I have. How will I get to Bristol without it?" She fled from the kitchen, deaf to the pleas from Mrs. Bramble and Mrs. Rivers as they promised assistance from half a dozen members of the household.

Oblivious to the ache of weariness in her body and forgetting her longing for a hot bath, Philomena scurried outside, heading for the path that led back to the railway cutting. Her tired legs could hardly support her. She gasped for air as panic took hold. Every plan was going wrong. She should be in Bristol by now, finding lodgings, not stranded here without a penny to her name and only a set of Joseph's clothes to wear. Sobs rose in her throat, threatening to overwhelm her. She tried to keep running, but the gravel slowed her progress. She stumbled to a stop, legs shaking with weariness. Tears of despair prickled her eyes.

Hooves thundered close behind. Startled, she turned to see Lord Thatcham's stallion skid to a halt, so close that the heat from his breath condensed on her face.

"What's this?" Lord Thatcham's voice cut through her misery. He looked down from far above, shaking his head. "Where are you off to so soon? Do you think the devil resides at Thatcham Hall, that you must run away as soon as you arrive?"

He clicked his tongue and rode Thunder in a circle around Philomena. She fought an impulse to run as the horse snorted, nostrils flared. Lord Thatcham's lips twitched as though he were on the verge of suppressed laughter. She would stand her ground. She straightened her back, raising herself to her full five feet and seven inches.

Neither Lord Thatcham nor the horse appeared in the least tired or disarranged by their night time exertions at the railway cutting. The man's hands lay relaxed on the horse's shoulders, controlling the powerful animal with light touches of the rein. Thunder snickered quietly, obedient to his master.

Lord Thatcham's dark blue coat stretched over broad shoulders and fitted tight to the waist. His cravat lay in a careless knot, as though he wasted little time or thought on dress. Philomena clenched her fists. She hated the shabby, ill-fitting fustian that drooped from her shoulders. Her fingers itched to pull at the waist of Joseph's voluminous trousers, and she blushed at the contrast between her ragged costume and Lord Thatcham's casual elegance.

Mud splashes defiled his otherwise gleaming boots, and sweat glistened on the horse's neck. Lord Thatcham must have spent the hours since his return from the cutting in riding through the fields, rather than seeking sleep. He must have endless stores of vitality, while Philomena longed to give in to the almost overwhelming desire for sleep. Every muscle in her body ached with weariness, but Lord Thatcham showed no symptoms of tiredness, beyond a few tiny lines around eyes and mouth. Even the horse shifted from one foot to another, as though keen for another outing.

Lord Thatcham's eyes glinted in the winter light, as grey as the sky. "By God, you have yet to change out of those undesirable breeches, I see. Could Mrs. Rivers find nothing to fit you among my old clothes? Surely, James the footman could offer you something to wear." He regarded her from on high, eyebrows raised.

Philomena's neck ached from staring upwards. Fury threatened to overcome her. How dare he look down his nose, as though she was a less than satisfactory toy, put on this earth for nothing but his amusement? She had long feared that all men except her dead guardian must be like Joseph, selfish and cruel. It seemed she was right. Philomena's hackles rose at this man laughing at her. It was bad enough that she was in this predicament, alone and penniless, with not a friend in the world, without a rich, supercilious man, no matter how unnervingly attractive, looking down an aristocratic nose at her.

She swallowed the anger that threatened to choke her. "Is it your business if I wish to return to the train? I am not your servant to treat as you wish."

A smile flitted across the arrogant face, and Philomena blushed under such scrutiny and disdain. She was even less than a servant. She was a vagabond: nobody. Anger dissolved into despair. In a moment of clarity, she saw herself through Lord Thatcham's eyes. He had rescued a waif from disaster and provided food and shelter, yet she was behaving just like one of the street urchins.

"Indeed, I'm grateful to you for rescuing me," she gabbled, hardly aware of the jumbled words that fell from her lips into the silence. "I'm glad you rescued Betsy and her mother, though I'm sure I never met them before last night, and they're no business of mine, and I'm obliged to you for helping me, but I have to go now and... Oh, I don't know what I'm to do..." Her words made no sense. As the heat of anger ebbed away, hot tears of weariness and fear threatened to overwhelm Philomena. She gasped and dashed a single tear from her cheek, struggling for control. Perhaps he had not noticed. She glanced up.

The silence lingered. Lord Thatcham's smile faded, leaving his face stern, the lines from nose to mouth more deeply etched. He looked suddenly older. He frowned. The horse snorted and pawed the ground.

Philomena's breathing slowed. She turned, glancing along the path towards the road. She should just run away—run until she was too tired to think. She should forget all about the accident and this man with grey eyes. Perhaps she should have stayed in London after all. Her shoulders slumped.

Lord Thatcham swung his right leg over his saddle and dismounted, landing lightly beside her. She blinked. She would not cry. He stretched out a hand and rested it on her shoulder. It warmed her skin through the cotton shirt, for Joseph's jacket lay abandoned in a heap on the kitchen floor. She shivered and gulped, turning away to hide unshed tears.

"Now," he said, suddenly kind. "Explain why you're in such a hurry to get away, and we'll see what can be done."

Her cheeks flamed. She hung her head.

"Look at me." He turned her round. "What do you seek to escape?" The words struck near the mark. Her

28

head jerked up. "Ah," he breathed. He dropped his hand. "I thought as much. Take care what you say." He leaned away to stroke Thunder's nose, speaking quietly over his shoulder. "I would not want to be obliged to take action against you. Boys will be boys, of course, but I have responsibilities as a magistrate and must uphold the law. If you have committed a crime, you must be prepared to face the consequences."

He turned back. "If there is some other difficulty, however?" He smiled. "If there is the matter of some debt, for example, that you hope to escape, do not be afraid to say so. Your adventures last night have entitled you to some leniency. "

Philomena shook her head. At least she was not on the run from the law or from creditors. "I've committed no crime, and I owe no one a single penny."

"Hmm." He looked into her face for a long moment, as though debating inwardly whether to believe her. "Very well," he said at last. Ice glimmered in his grey eyes. "If you say so." He brushed mud from his coat.

Philomena's stomach lurched. How could she make him trust her, while in disguise?

"I really think I ought to know your name, before we proceed, don't you?" Lord Thatcham continued. His voice was lazy, now. "Are you not running away from the peelers in London?" His eyes searched her face.

"I can assure you I'm not in the least trouble with the law. My name's Phil—" Her hand flew to her lips. How nearly she'd given it all away. No female of virtue would take the train unescorted. She would not confirm this arrogant man's low opinion of her. She had some pride. He must not think her someone's light o' love. It would be easy to believe that, or worse, of a lone female.

She tried again. "I'm Philip."

"Delighted to make your acquaintance, er— Philip." His eyes narrowed. "As you will have doubtless been informed already, I'm Hugh Dainty. Lord Thatcham." He nodded once. "Hmm. Philip, now. That must be Greek. Would that not be so? It means something about horses, if my time at Oxford serves correctly. Your father must be a scholar." Was he sneering? His eyes glittered.

"My father is dead, my lord." Philomena felt herself blushing again. In truth, she had no idea whether her real father was alive or dead. Samuel was her guardian, no more. Her own parents were lost.

All she had of her mother was a likeness on a brooch that Samuel had given her. Was it even her mother? The woman in the portrait was beautiful, with long, blonde hair teased into elaborate ringlets. She wore a blue gown and jewels glinted around a long neck. A diamond sparkled on one finger. She was wealthy. She was hardly likely to be related to Philomena, whose own hair was black, curly, and wayward and who owned nothing but the clothes she stood up in. Even these belonged, strictly speaking, to Joseph.

Philomena had no family name. She had adopted Samuel's surname, Tailor. She did not even know her place of birth. Lack of family set her free to build the life she chose. She smiled. She would not worry about the past. She had escaped Joseph, and that must be enough for now. So long as Lord Thatcham believed her honest, he would not care about her history. She would move on soon and he would sigh with relief.

"Well," said Lord Thatcham. "The thought of a dead parent seems to have revived your spirits. Shall we continue our discussion? You claim to have no fear of the law. Pray explain, then, why you were rushing away from the Hall at such speed. Has someone harmed you?"

"Oh, no. Everyone is so kind. It is just that I lost something when the train overturned, that was all. It was a coin. But it doesn't matter." She could manage somehow.

"Indeed, it does. Tell me, young man. What did you lose?" Lord Thatcham patted Thunder's neck as the horse snickered, impatient to be off. His expression softened. "Wait a moment, Thunder."

"Oh, a sovereign or so." She waved one hand in the air as though a sovereign was of small account. Lord Thatcham reached into his pocket and brought out her worn velvet purse.

He held it aloft, between finger and thumb. "Would that be the sovereign in this purse?" he asked, one eyebrow raised. "Where did you get it? And where were you going?"

Philomena lifted her chin. She must sound honest. "Indeed, my lord." She hoped her voice carried the ring of truth. "Truly, I did not steal it. My adopted father died recently and left me this purse and I—well—I needed to make my fortune elsewhere than London. May I ask how…" She hesitated as Lord Thatcham's eyes flashed.

He laughed, but the sound held little amusement. "Do you imagine I stole your money?" His voice purred, as soft as silk.

Philomena shivered. She would not want to cross this man. She said no more.

Lord Thatcham shook his head, as though tired of the subject. "I hardly recall how I came by it, if the truth be told. I suppose I picked it up by the train, thrust it in my pocket, and thought no more of it until I emptied my pockets to change my clothes.

"I planned to ride into the village this morning to search for the owner. The loss of such a sum is a serious matter for any one of the villagers. However, in the circumstances, I am pleased to return your money to you." He held out the purse.

She didn't know what to say. There was too much to explain, and every time her mouth opened, the wrong thing came out. Philomena took the purse and stuffed it in her pocket. "Thank you," she muttered, at last, knowing she sounded ungracious. She tried again, speaking the truth. "I really am grateful, my lord."

She fiddled with Joseph's shirt collar. Several inches too large, it chafed her neck. Lord Thatcham's eyes burned into her. Embarrassed, she thrust her hands into her pockets. "I do not know what would have become of me if you had not brought me here last night," she confessed. For the first time, the stern lines of his face relaxed. She smiled in turn.

"I trust you will remain at the Hall, at least until after our festivities. Tomorrow, of course, is Christmas Day, and Mrs. Bramble has been preparing a feast such as, I believe Shakespeare would say, dreams are made on."

Philomena laughed. "I do not believe Mr. Shakespeare was talking about food."

Lord Thatcham laughed too. The edges of his eyes

crinkled. "So you are a scholar, as well, like your adopted father."

She blushed. "No, my lord, I am no scholar. I do not remember when I first learned to read. Samuel, my guardian, was a tailor. Sometimes, his patrons gave me their old books to read. I believe, my lord, they found my interest in reading something of a joke."

"Amusing, no doubt," said Lord Thatcham. He smiled, and the years fell from his face. A thrill chased down Philomena's back.

"But enough talk for now." He spoke abruptly. "Return to the kitchens and change your clothes. Remember to ask Mrs. Bramble for a new set." He paused, looking her up and down once more. This time, though, real humour lit his face. "Tell her to choose the breeches with care."

He nodded, swung himself effortlessly into the saddle, gave the horse its head, and disappeared in a crunch of hooves on gravel.

Philomena flipped her purse from hand to hand, waiting for her rapid heartbeat to slow. The shiver that ran through her body had little to do with the cold and damp of this December morning and everything to do with Lord Thatcham's sudden smile. Had he noticed her reactions? What did he think of her? He was a strange man.

At least she had maintained the disguise. The thought gave her little pleasure. She spun on her heel and hurried back to the kitchen.

The servants of the Hall soon found better things to do than worry about an unknown young man when there was work awaiting their attention. Had they been the only people in the kitchen, she would have slipped away to enjoy a bath. All would have been well.

However, Lord Thatcham's young son, last seen in nightclothes, now sat in the comfort of the kitchen. He must be a favourite of the cook. He looked older, now, in a velvet jacket with breeches and a cravat. He sat at ease, rosy cheeked, on a stool at the far end of the table, one hand in an earthenware jar, the other clutching a fistful of raisins. He beamed. "Why are you dressed like a boy?"

Chapter Five

Hugh strode through the passageway to the kitchen. His boots clanged on the flagstones, the sound echoing through the hall. The youth from the train left him at a loss. Perhaps his unease stemmed from guilt at the postponement of parental duty. He should have punished John for misbehaviour yesterday but had deferred the unpleasant interview.

His own father would never have allowed such a duty to remain incomplete. "Spare the rod and spoil the child," he liked to say.

Hugh recalled this morning's resolution to put responsibilities before pleasure and straightened his shoulders. "John, where are you hiding, you young scoundrel?" he bellowed. "I wish to have a serious conversation with you. Be sure you will not escape by hiding in the kitchen."

He flung the door wide and noted, satisfied, the loud thud it made as it crashed against the wall. He leaned his shoulder on the doorpost, flicking a riding whip against the tall hat he cradled. "You are already in enough trouble..."

The kitchen had fallen silent. Perplexed, Hugh looked from face to face. The normal bustle of the kitchen was frozen into a tableau, as though the room was a stage. Mrs. Bramble's jaw hung open, her hand stretched out, motionless, halfway to a mixing bowl, eyes fixed on that strange boy, Philip. The little scullery maid stood still, only her nose twitching with excitement. A passing footman had skidded to a halt, leaving boot black in a stripe across the floor.

Hugh was accustomed for the servants to stop work at the entry of the master. They would acknowledge his presence with bows and curtsies, tug at their aprons, straighten their caps, and wait to hear and carry out his orders. Today, though, they all appeared to have taken leave of their senses. They gaped, open-mouthed, not at the master, but at that strange, untrustworthy new arrival, Philip.

Hugh glared. "Is aught amiss?" His voice was harsh.

Mrs. Bramble cleared her throat, but no one ventured to speak.

He lost patience. "Mrs. Bramble, perhaps you would be so good as to explain why the entire staff is staring at this young man rather than continuing with the preparations for the Christmas celebrations?" Hugh looked at every face. No one moved.

Impatient, he continued, his voice firm. "My mother and sister will arrive later today and expect all to be in hand for the Christmas celebrations. I am sure you will not wish to disappoint. Get on with your work, everyone."

To his surprise, no one moved. He glared. This must be John's doing. What had the boy been about, now? "John, I can see you perfectly well behind that table. Take your finger out of the honey pot and come with me."

"Can the lady come too?" asked John.

The kitchen held its breath once more. Hugh's

whip tapped a brisk rhythm on the hat. "Lady? What lady?" He spoke as quietly as a sense of rising irritation allowed. Really, John tried his patience, with one piece of nonsense after another.

John pointed. "That one."

Hugh's gaze followed the direction of John's hand. A sticky blob of honey dripped off his son's finger on to the floor. Hugh ignored it. He looked at Philip and frowned. The boy's face had turned ghostly white. Hugh blinked and looked again, the frown deepening. Slowly, he took in every detail of the lad's appearance as realisation dawned. Hugh finally saw why the lad had struck him as strange.

He was of medium height, for a young boy. A tousled mass of black hair framed a white face. The curls, badly trimmed, stuck out in random wisps. A tiny, upturned nose twitched above a mouth that was a little too wide. Pale lips, clamped together in a straight line, trembled. A pair of blue eyes gazed at Hugh, wide and shocked, fringed by long, dark lashes. Hugh recognised with a jolt that the young boy, Philip, was in fact a tall and pretty woman. She was very young.

A heartbeat of wonder turned to shock. The shock soon escalated to anger. Hugh had taken the lad to be an unformed boy, vulnerable and in need of help. Why, he had felt sympathy for the boy's plight: had even vowed to direct Mrs. Bramble to supply a good meal before the lad moved on. What was the reward for such concern?

In return, the boy had deceived everyone. He—no, she—was an accomplished liar who had set out to hoodwink everybody at the Hall. Hugh was at a loss for words. He grasped his whip with stiff hands as he strove to remain calm.

This woman—a very pretty one, at that, no doubt about it—this female had tricked him. Blue eyes gazed at him, wide with horror. Of course, the woman feared the consequences now that he had uncovered the deception. The back of his neck tingled. She had taken him in completely. How could he have been such a fool? He closed his eyes.

He had brought her into his house, offered food, shelter, and Christmas cheer, and in return, she had lied to him. With more lies and more deceit, yet another woman had made him ridiculous. A wave of disgust broke over Hugh, bringing the colour to his face. He closed his ears to the tiny nagging voice. *You knew all the time. You would not have taken such trouble with a lad. You would not have cared so much.*

Hugh took a long, steady breath. When he spoke, his voice cut the air, as sharp as a whip crack. "I see. You are not who you say? Perhaps your protestation that you have committed no crime is also false?"

The woman flushed scarlet. The blush soon faded, and her cheeks turned dead white. She opened her mouth to speak, but Hugh was too angry to listen. "I will hear no more lies." He flicked his whip against his boots. "John, come with me. We have business to discuss, pertaining to yesterday's behaviour."

John jumped down from the kitchen table, licking sticky fingers. He seemed to be the only one in the room unperturbed at his father's anger.

Hugh spoke through clenched teeth. "Where is Mrs. Rivers?"

The housekeeper stepped forward.

"We seem to have a strange female person in the house, Mrs. Rivers," Hugh continued, controlling his fury and speaking quietly. "I suggest you put her to good use in the kitchen."

The woman started. So, she considered herself above performing the duties of a maid. He let his eyes slide slowly, insultingly, from the tip of the young woman's heavy boots, up to the unruly curls.

Her face was a picture of dismay. The blue eyes had clouded, and a lip quivered between her teeth. How could he ever have mistaken this young woman for a boy?

She lifted her head high, chin thrust out bravely. Hugh's anger melted. The horror on her face struck him, suddenly, as ridiculous. He bit his lip and took refuge in as fierce a frown as he could contrive. "Tell me, Miss, what do you truly call yourself? I imagine Philip cannot be your name." Her blue eyes, huge behind their lashes, glared at him. Her lip quivered again.

Hugh felt a pang at the sight of such distress. He must harden his heart. He gripped the whip more tightly, annoyed to feel his hand shake. Women find it so easy to cry. Beatrice had perfected the art. She had fooled and then betrayed him. He would not be taken in now. No woman would hoodwink him again.

"My name, my lord, is Philomena." She stood straighter. "I have done nothing wrong except to pretend I was not a female, and that deception was intended only for protection from the dangers of a long journey alone. I meant no harm by it." The young woman looked Hugh full in the face, every trace of fear gone. "Perhaps you are not aware of the threat to females who travel alone."

He heard challenge in her voice. What sort of

scrape had she fallen into, that had forced her to travel alone and unprotected on the night train? He hesitated. Was he being unfair?

No. He must not bow to sympathy. Not this time. He must rely on good sense. After all, no young person of virtue would parade around the country alone. He shrugged, turned away and spoke over his shoulder. "Thatcham Hall has always opened its doors to those who seek help. We prefer honesty." He paused, letting the bitter words do the damage. "However, at this time of the year, we turn no one away. You are welcome to remain with the servants. Whether you choose to help or simply benefit from others' efforts is a matter for your conscience. Come, John."

John, only slightly subdued, scuttled behind his father. Philomena brushed at her cheek. Her head was high. At least the woman had not wept. Beatrice never showed such self-control.

Hugh marched John directly upstairs to the nursery. He motioned to the boy to sit on a hard wooden chair and frowned. He flicked his whip from one hand to the other. How should he punish yesterday's escapade?

John's big blue eyes filled with tears. *He has learned his mother's tricks.* "Well," Hugh said, his voice languid. "We must deal with yesterday's misdemeanours, must we not? We cannot overlook such behaviour, simply because there was a train accident during the night. Perhaps you would care to explain just what you did to the nursemaid, this time?"

Hugh leaned on the fireplace, suddenly weary. "Please do not waste my time with tears. Weeping is for girls."

"I am sorry, Papa." John sniffed and wiped his nose energetically on a sleeve. Hugh handed him a clean kerchief. "I never meant to upset water onto Abigail. I was just sliding down the banister, and I slipped off."

John stopped a moment, thinking. His face lit up. "Why did she not move out of the way?" He snatched at the possibility of resting the blame elsewhere. "She should not be carrying water on the main staircase, anyway."

Startled, Hugh recalled an incident from his youth. He had been just such a small boy, trying to explain away some mischief, while his father stood nearby, flicking a whip. The crime had involved frogs and the nursemaid's clothes. It had not ended well, for his father had made good use of the whip. Surely, John deserved similar treatment. It was the duty of a father to punish a child, as his father had so often done.

Still, Hugh hesitated. The case differed. John had no mother. There was no one to soothe away tears and offer sugarplums after a well-earned chastisement. Hugh wavered, looked at John's eyes wide with hope, and saw defeat. He sighed. "That is not the point, my boy. Mrs. Rivers spoke to Abigail on the matter. She feels no longer able to remain at the Hall. She believes life would be more restful, as she puts it, 'scrubbing floors in a—' he coughed—'a house of, that is to say, less good standing—'" He floundered, recalling the exact words relayed by the housekeeper.

John's eyes sparkled. "Has she really gone forever, then?" Hope spread across his face. His tears had dried.

Hugh wracked his brain for a suitable punishment, but could think of nothing. "Early to bed, tonight." He would be more severe another time.

"Very well, Papa. I'm sorry."

Hugh ruffled the boy's hair. "Now, I suppose, I must find someone to keep you from mischief for the rest of the day." He took a few paces around the room, glancing at well-remembered pictures and books. He ran his finger along John's battered desk, where he had sat, many years ago. He leaned against the mantelpiece and picked up a familiar, chipped china horse. The animal had suffered many falls, and one of its legs was missing.

Hugh stroked its mane. "Perhaps the kitchen is the best place, after all. Mrs. Bramble will doubtless fill you full of sweet things, so that you will be sick all night, and the maids will neglect their duties in playing childish games, but at least you will be safe. Do not," he added, remembering a previous occasion, "under any circumstances, attempt to persuade Ince the coachman to take you out in the carriage."

John looked up, his eyes wide and innocent. "What are circumstances?"

"Ask Mrs. Bramble," Hugh said, vanquished. "Now go."

John left him no time to change his mind. He scampered away, high spirits fully restored. Hugh rested an elbow on the mantelpiece and leaned his chin on his hand. A small fire in the grate kept the worst of the winter's gloom from invading the nursery. The room was pretty and bright. Beatrice had chosen new wall coverings and hangings, full of excitement at the birth of a first child. Little more than a child herself, exasperating with a string of foolish, selfish demands, Hugh's wife had nevertheless given birth to a precious son.

Her death was sudden. Hugh could never forget it. One year ago, in the early morning, Beatrice had ridden out, alone. Her absence went unnoticed for hours, for she enjoyed early morning rest and habitually refused to allow a maid to bring morning chocolate until late in the day.

At last, a servant raised the alarm. The household spent the day searching, finding Beatrice's body a few miles from the Hall. She had never been an expert rider, and the horse had thrown her to the ground. A heavy frost the night before had left the earth rock hard: solid enough to crack her skull. Hugh carried her into the Hall, but she never recovered consciousness. She died the next day—Christmas Day.

Hugh pulled his watch from a waistcoat pocket. It was not yet noon. Today would be a long day, but tomorrow would be even worse. He dreaded the Christmas celebrations. The Dowager's presence would send the Hall into a spin and Selena, Hugh's sister, would chatter ceaselessly, not noticing how her brother's head ached or how deeply he longed for solitude. She would seek to cheer the day with games and jests, unaware of a heart heavy with secret guilt, or the strain of each cold smile. Hugh must lay aside horror at the responsibility for Beatrice's death and play the part of host.

Damn that nursemaid. She deserted John, just when he had most need of care. *Damn the woman from the train…*but Hugh knew not why. He knew so little about her, except that she lied. Nothing in the world angered him more than dishonesty.

Frustration overcame restraint. *There will be no*

more deception in this house. Teeth clenched, Hugh flicked the whip along the mantelshelf. Candles clattered to the floor. He kicked them across the room. *And no more lies.*

Chapter Six

Philomena faced the ranks of Thatcham Hall household servants who stared, confusion written on every face. Ivy, the scullery maid, was the first to find a voice. "So you're a girl, not a boy." She drew the words out, trying to understand. Her lower lip stuck out. "Leading us on."

Mrs. Rivers waved a bunch of keys aloft. "That's enough, my girl. Now, get back to work, all of you."

The maids turned away, disappointed that the spectacle had finished for the moment.

"Now," the housekeeper continued, "I'm sure we're all too busy to stand around gossiping, today of all days. Mrs. Bramble, we are all looking forward very much to the treats you have planned for us to eat over the next few days. While you continue the good work, I will take this young person into my sitting room and establish what to do. We do not wish to cause more trouble for Lord Thatcham at this sad time, now do we?"

Without another word, she shooed Philomena towards her sitting room and shot a glare at each member of the household, until each one returned to his or her duty. She led Philomena into the tiny, spotlessly clean sitting room that marked out the housekeeper as the senior female member of the household servants.

Once away from the rows of accusing eyes,

Philomena struggled to keep tears at bay. She sniffed twice and dashed a hand across aching eyes. A few deep breaths helped to steady jangling nerves. Mrs. Rivers doubtless wanted a full explanation but, just at the moment, that was too much. Philomena would not embark on her life story today. Her eyes were heavy and sore from lack of sleep, and a headache raged round her skull.

Mrs. Rivers stood in silence for a long moment. She handed Philomena a glass of water and motioned to a chair. "You seem," she said with a faint smile, "to be a young woman of resource. This world is not always easy for women alone. Men, I am afraid, do not always understand our difficulties. Lord Thatcham, the master here, has a good heart. Occasionally, appearances can be deceptive." She smiled, repositioned a cushion neatly on a tiny armchair and settled down comfortably. "Many a master would have turned a soul away for such behaviour. Lady Beatrice would certainly have done so." She blinked. "Poor Lady Beatrice," she added, as though guilty of disloyalty.

Lady Beatrice must be Lord Thatcham's wife, then. Philomena sat a little straighter. She could hardly breathe, let alone talk. Lord Thatcham had a wife, not to mention a son. How could she have imagined otherwise? In any case, the master's opinion mattered not at all.

She fought to remain calm while the housekeeper chattered. "Lord Thatcham is willing for you to remain here a while. Naturally, you will want to show gratitude. There is a way for you to repay such kindness. I am sure you will wish to help out where possible in the Hall: that is no misjudgement, I hope?"

Philomena shook her head. "No, indeed, and I can assure you I am honest…" Her voice tailed away.

Mrs. Rivers smiled. "Except for the little matter of pretending to be a boy?"

Philomena giggled. There was a funny side to all this, after all.

"In any case," the housekeeper pointed out, "it does no good to be idle. Whatever troubles may come, hard work is the best way to overcome them." Samuel would have shared Mrs. Rivers' sentiments. Philomena began to like Mrs. Rivers.

"Now, Master John is without a nurse," the housekeeper said. "They come and go, I am afraid, and Master John can be a handful. Perhaps you would help to watch over the boy while the maids go about their business?"

Philomena nodded. She would agree to anything if it meant a few hours rest. Her arms and legs throbbed with weariness, and both eyelids drooped. At last, the tears that had threatened all morning bubbled up. Mrs. Rivers' kindness was the final straw. Philomena pulled out a handkerchief, scrubbed at both eyes, and blew her nose.

"You get off to Ivy's room and have a sleep," Mrs. Rivers said. "I'm sure things will seem better when you are less tired, my dear. In any case, you will need to be fresh as a daisy to keep up with Master John. He has energy enough and to spare—but a dear child all the same. I cannot think why Abigail left the house, with no thought of loyalty to the family at such a sad time." She sniffed.

What did she mean? Why should Christmas be a sad time in the Hall? Philomena longed to understand

47

but was far too exhausted to bother with questions. Instead, she accepted the offer of a bed in Ivy's room and the promise of more appropriate garments when she awoke, and in return, agreed to present herself in the kitchen at 6 o'clock that evening. Her first duty would be to take Master John's tea upstairs and sit while he ate. "Of course, I'll help in any way I can." She struggled to swallow down the lump in her throat.

Sleep arrived at once, within seconds of lying down on Ivy's bed, but no longed-for peace came with it. Philomena dreamed. The screams and shrieks of the train accident returned to haunt her. In her imagination, she smelled fumes from the engine and remembered the pull and suck of sticky mud as she tried to scramble back to the overturned carriage. The chaos of light and dark as lanterns wove through the night had burned images into her memory. She tossed and turned, restless and frightened; the dream more horrifying than the reality, for no rescue came in her sleep. No handsome, severe Lord Thatcham arrived on a black horse, with a haughty frown, dark grey eyes and sardonic smile. Philomena cried out in her sleep, but no one came.

Then, the dream changed. Cold green eyes bored into hers from a hidden face. A hood shrouded the stranger, revealing only a pale, thin countenance, with mean, narrow lips compressed in a straight line. In the dream, Philomena heard Samuel, her guardian, speaking quietly, telling her not to be afraid, but her fear was real. Something terrible was happening.

She awoke with a start. She shivered, cold, shaken and bathed in sweat and knew the dream was not the figment of a tired mind. It was a true memory, from long, long ago when she lived with Samuel. Over the years, it had haunted her at night. During the day, she could hold it at bay, and she'd fought so hard against it that now, it only rarely returned.

Philomena had always known she must make a lonely way in the world, with no man by her side, and no hope of love. The stranger with the green eyes at the centre of her terrible secret made any other dream impossible. She shuddered. One day, the stranger would return to destroy any life she made. Her escape to Bristol had been more than just a flight from Joseph. No, she prayed that the man with the green eyes could never find her, hidden on the other side of England.

The man's existence, somewhere unknown, blighted all her hopes and dreams. Philomena could never find a man to love. She must live alone in the world that could be so cruel to a woman, bound forever to the furtive stranger with eyes full of menace, by ties that could not be broken.

He was her husband. Philomena did not know his name, nor why she had been married to him while still a child, barely eleven years of age. She had hardly understood what happened on the day Samuel gave her a new dress and took her to the cold, unwelcoming church. She shivered with terror beside the hooded stranger, trying not to look up into those green eyes, as Samuel made half-understood vows on her behalf. The man with the cold green eyes, now her husband, disappeared as soon as the short, surreptitious ceremony ended. She never saw or heard of the man again.

That day changed her life forever. Philomena trembled at the memory. She prayed she would never meet the man again, for she feared the cold of those green, cat-like eyes. Growing up, safe under Samuel's kindly protection, she learned that one day only skills as a dressmaker would keep her from penury. She must build a life as a single, lone woman.

She'd dreamed today of the green eyed stranger, her husband. The dream was a warning. She must put away any ridiculous notions about Lord Thatcham, who in any case was as far above Philomena as the moon. He felt only mistrust and dislike for the newcomer who arrived in foolish disguise. By the by, he had a wife. Philomena was determined to care for no man. She would think no more at all about the Master of the Hall.

The evening had already closed in around the great house when Philomena awoke. For a moment, she lay in the darkness, disoriented and confused. Everything was different. She sniffed the air and caught a hint of baking, redolent of cloves and ginger, with no trace of the dank, cabbage smell she was accustomed to in London. She listened to the subdued bustle of the house: the click of housemaids' shoes on wooden floors and stairs, a quiet, low-key laugh and a murmur of modulated voices. All were new to her senses, and all spoke of change and excitement. Philomena forced herself, with the success borne of long practice, to overcome her fears.

This was the long awaited adventure, after all. The train, the wreck, her short-lived deception and the loss of her hair, all in vain, flashed through her mind in a kaleidoscope. The spinning whirl of images halted abruptly at the memory of Lord Thatcham.

She had met him just three times in the past few hours, but he blazed in her memory. She recalled his face at the site of the accident, his stern profile softened by blond hair tumbling over deep, expressive eyes. Her pulses raced at the recollection and for a moment, despite every attempt to forget the man's face, her imagination ran wild. She longed to feel his hand on her shoulder, just once more. She wanted to bring that tiny smile to his lips and see the grey of his eyes soften.

What was this she felt? No man before had set her heart beating so fast or stopped the breath so painfully in her throat. Arrogant, stern, and self-righteous the man might be, but a light in his eye, a sudden gleam of amusement, came and went so fast it could have been nothing more than imagination. The sudden smile intrigued and touched her. She must see it again.

Hot tears filled her eyes. She would not be so foolish. She wiped them away, angry at such nonsense. She should be thankful to be safe both from Joseph and from the man with the green eyes, comfortable for a short time in this wonderful old Hall where there was plenty of warmth and good food.

With an effort of will, Philomena wrenched her thoughts away. Why had no mistress been in evidence at the Hall today, and why had Mrs. Rivers referred to "Poor Lady Thatcham?" She must be some sort of an invalid. Lord Thatcham's wife had not appeared in the kitchen, nor taken charge of John. Philomena sensed a mystery, but she disliked the idea of Lady Thatcham. She would not think about her. She rose, washed, and dressed in the plain costume and apron hanging on the rail at the foot of the bed. Mrs. Rivers must have put them there while she slept.

Fixing the cap took some time. She struggled to force her hair into something that did not resemble a bird's nest. At last, she had to spit on a finger to tame the curls into acceptable neatness. The locks of hair were far too short to tie back. *Bless me, will they never stay in place?* She could have saved her hair if she had been more careful. Fastidious pinning would surely have kept it in place. After years of planning, she had rushed into her escape. Philomena sighed. Impatience was often her downfall.

There was an oval mirror over the mantel, old and silvered, but good enough to show a face. Philomena grimaced at it. Whatever would poor Samuel say? He was always so pleased with her "ladylike appearance." She looked quite different from the old Philomena. She was an independent woman, now, and beauty was of no consequence.

Chapter Seven

Philomena slipped down the back stairs to the kitchen, treading self-consciously back into the warm heart of the Hall. The footman burst into uncouth laughter at her appearance. Mrs. Rivers rebuked him. "Be quiet, now, James. What did I tell you? Philomena is one of the household for a while, and you will treat her with respect. Now be off about your business." James fell silent and stalked from the kitchen. As he passed Philomena, she heard a barely muffled snort.

"Now then," Mrs. Rivers went on. "You follow me up to the nursery. Bring the tray for Master John's tea." The tray weighed heavy, stacked with teapot, plate of thinly sliced bread and butter, scones, jam and a small rice pudding. Philomena concentrated hard. She must not splash milk from the jug. She smiled. This light meal, full of delicate bites, was nothing like the heavy high tea of bread, dripping and oatmeal eaten in the poor streets of London.

The main meal of the day for John was luncheon in the middle of the day, with this insubstantial tea eaten at 6 o'clock. The adults in the family would enjoy a larger, more elaborate dinner of several courses later in the evening. It seemed very strange. No wonder the cook wore an air of permanent exhaustion.

"Excuse me." Philomena puffed with effort as they ascended the servants' stairs at the back of the house.

"Does Lady Thatcham wish to see me?" Mrs. Rivers stopped in her tracks.

"Bless my soul," she said. "Don't you go mentioning Lady Thatcham, now. Dear, oh dear, I suppose no one told you, did they? She died, you know. Just a year ago tomorrow, in fact. So it's to be a quiet time this Christmas with just Lord Thatcham's mother, the Dowager, and his sister. There will be no other guests this year."

The housekeeper folded her arms and leaned on the wall, ready for gossip. "Now, don't you go upsetting Master John by mentioning his mother, will you? It's hard enough for the boy, what with Lord Thatcham being so—eh—now, how can I put it? So distracted? Yes, that's it. He's been distracted, always working, never has time for the boy any more, though he used to spend more time with John than Lady Thatcham herself did." She shook her head. "It's all because of the accident."

"Accident?"

"Oh, dear me, you really don't know, do you? It was the horse, you see. Lady Thatcham's mare took a fall that killed the poor soul. She never was much on a horse, not like his lordship. He gave Lady Beatrice the gentlest of mares to ride, but even so, something must have frightened the horse that day, and her ladyship fell."

The housekeeper set off again up the stairs. "There's not much more to tell. You need know no more about it than that, anyway, and be sure not to mention it in the nursery. Or to Lord Thatcham himself." She lowered her voice. "Especially not to him," she murmured, "though he spends little enough time with John, of course." She stopped and closed her lips, as though determined not to say more.

Philomena waited. There must be more to the story. The poor little boy had lost his mother, and his father seemed to go near him only to punish him. No wonder he was a difficult child. Perhaps the housekeeper would say more in a moment.

Mrs. Rivers proved her right. "I don't know what will become of us all." She sighed. "Nothing but bad luck's come to the Hall lately. It was never like this, when I first came here as a scullery maid. Lord Thatcham was but a boy, then, and what a child he was. Always a wild one, scared of nothing and no one. Oh, the scrapes he was in when he was a boy. No matter how often Lord Thatcham beat him—that's the old Lord Thatcham, the present master's father, I mean."

She scratched her head, as though finding her thread again. "Yes, no matter what the punishment, he just gave a great laugh. When Master Hugh laughed like that, even the governess found it hard to be angry."

Philomena, fascinated, said nothing. It was difficult to imagine the stern, unforgiving Lord Thatcham as a wild boy.

Mrs. Rivers' tongue ran even further away from her. "I remember the day he took his father's favourite horse. It was a great, grey hunter, and Master Hugh was naught but a lad at the time, hardly tall enough to climb on the horse's back. The horse took him to London and back in the day. Can you imagine? All those miles in one day? Only young Master Hugh would try that." Mrs. Rivers chuckled. "By the time he returned, half the Hall was out looking for him, and his father's face was purple. Ooh, the master was so furious. Master Hugh went without his supper for days, shut up in his room."

She laughed harder and Philomena giggled too. Would anyone dare refuse to serve Lord Thatcham now? "Then he escaped. He climbed down the ivy. His mother kept that from the old Lord Thatcham. She had such a soft spot for the boy."

The housekeeper stopped laughing and shook her head. "Our Lord Thatcham was still hardly grown when the old Lord Thatcham died, and some say it was his wildness that hurried his father off."

Philomena's smile died away. Could anyone truly blame Lord Thatcham for his father's death? Why, the idea was ridiculous. No one held Joseph responsible for driving poor Samuel to his grave, though his drunkenness and dishonesty gave the poor tailor many a sleepless night. Unless…unless there was something else to the story? Could Joseph possibly have done something to hasten Samuel's death? Some poisonous herbs in the tea, maybe? No. She should not let her imagination run away.

Mrs. Rivers was still talking. "We did all think that the marriage to Miss Beatrice would settle things: that the master would calm down, lose that temper, and get along quieter. But then, poor Lady Beatrice was never right for him, and it all ended in disaster. He's not been the same since. All the fun gone, you might say."

Mrs. Rivers stopped and blinked hard at Philomena. "Now, just you keep everything I say to yourself, young lady. If you stay here at the Hall, you need to know about Lord Thatcham's ways. Just make sure you don't cross him, that's my advice." Closing her mouth firmly against further indiscretions, Mrs. Rivers finished the journey upstairs in silence and left

Philomena in the nursery.

Daisy, an under-housemaid, hissed at Philomena, relief written on her face. "Keep your eyes open," she said, making for the door. "Master John will be off given half a chance and up to mischief."

The child sat, bored, at a table, carelessly tearing up strips of gold paper and, so far as Philomena could see, gluing them indiscriminately to the table and to each other. His legs drummed against the table legs.

"What are you making?" She knew very few children—just a few ragged urchins who clustered around the doors and passages in London, begging for scraps and stealing what they could from the street-sellers. She'd certainly never known such a beautifully dressed, clean child as Master John.

He glared. "A boat."

"Oh." There was a pause. Philomena and Master John assessed each other. The child's feet kicked the table legs harder, but Philomena bit her lip and ignored it.

The child gave in first. "Mrs. River says you are to look after me." She nodded. "Then please finish this boat for me. I want to go outside." Hoping to wheedle her into giving him his own way, John smiled sweetly.

Philomena would not be tricked. She shook her head. "I think it a little late for exercise out of doors, so perhaps we can find something better to do here. But first, eat your bread and butter and drink your tea."

The boy's eyes lit up, and he tucked in with enthusiasm. Once eating, he forgot to tease, but munched in silence. From time to time, his eyes, half-closed, slid sideways, following Philomena. "Why did you wear boy's clothes today?"

"Well, I had to look like a boy so I could travel safely."

"Why?"

How could she explain? "Women must protect themselves when they are alone, because men are stronger than women."

"Why were you alone?"

"I had no one to be with me."

The child nodded, satisfied with the answer. "I have no one to be with me, most of the time. At least, I had Abigail and the others before she came. But they just tell me what to do. I would like a friend."

"Are there no children like you nearby?"

He shook his head. Philomena frowned. Why had Lord Thatcham left his son in such a predicament? What a lonely life for a child, in this huge Hall with no one to play with but a rapid succession of hopeless nurses. How could the boy's father be so thoughtless?

Philomena wracked her brains. There must be something the child would enjoy. What did a wealthy child of four do apart from ask disconcertingly direct questions? On the streets of London, boys of this age helped with the family finances by sorting scraps or selling clothes or spent the twilight hours tracking down a missing father, to bring him home from the public house. They had little time to spare for play.

Thinking like that would not help. It was no use blaming the child for his wealth and comfort. Clearly, John found tabletop work boring. Philomena, determined to behave as a nursemaid should, could not allow him to embark on energetic games. Once over-excited, the child would never sleep. She searched the room for inspiration.

She caught sight of a row of lavishly illustrated books stacked neatly on a shelf nearby. Relieved, she pulled out a book of brightly coloured nursery rhymes. "Do you like stories?"

The child glanced at the books and glowered. "I only like new stories. Abigail told me the same ones over and over, all about mices and flowers and good little children."

Philomena laughed aloud and put the book back on the shelf.

"Papa sometimes tells stories," John went on, "about soldiers and knights and battles. I like those stories. But when I'm bad, he won't tell me any."

"Are you often bad?"

"Oh yes, very often."

Philomena repressed a chuckle. She fixed the boy with a stare. "Well, if you wash and put your nightclothes on, I'll find a new story for you. How would that be?"

"Very well."

Philomena glanced through a window into the darkness. The wind had gathered strength again during the day and blew fiercely around the Hall. The view from the window was wild, of tree branches tossing in the gale and sheep huddled together in the fields. Tomorrow was Christmas Day. A wealthy child like this should be excited, looking forward to presents and a day of feasting and merriment. However, this was the house where John's mother, Lord Thatcham's wife, had died last Christmas. There was little merriment to be found here.

John, lured by the promise of the story, snuggled willingly into bed. Philomena turned out lamps and blew on candles until only one single light remained, flickering in the darkness. The candlelight seemed friendly. She was tempted to gather the little boy in her arms for a hug but decided against it. She would wait until she knew him better. Instead, she started on an old story. "A kind king," she began, her voice hushed, "lived many years ago, in an old castle in the forest."

The little boy shivered and snuggled deeper under the bedclothes. "Was it a deep, dark forest?"

"Oh yes, it was very deep indeed and extremely scary. And in the forest lived an old, old man who had no money and no wood to put on the fire to keep him warm."

John smiled sleepily as the new nurse's voice grew softer and slower, until his eyes flickered and closed. Finally, he slept.

A deep voice echoed through the room. "A good story for Christmas."

Chapter Eight

Hugh leaned his shoulder against the lintel outside the pool of light cast by the candle. He'd stood at the nursery door for several minutes, listening. Philomena seemed not to have noticed him. She looked so small and vulnerable, and was very obviously female, despite her shorn hair. How could he ever have mistaken her for a boy?

At the sound of his voice, she leapt up to face him, startled, eyes wide, one hand at her breast.

Hugh stepped forward into the flicker of the candlelight and the young woman took a corresponding pace backwards. He stopped short, irritated. Why was she so nervous? He was no ogre. "You need not fear me. I came to bid John goodnight. Mrs. Rivers suggested he might like this stocking to hang by the fire."

She made no reply.

"I see the boy is asleep already," Hugh went on. Why did he feel he must explain himself to this female? It was unwise. He had no need to justify himself. He was, after all, Master of the Hall. Still, conscience pricked. He cleared his throat. "Perhaps John may forget how harsh his father has been today." He scowled. What had prompted him to say such a thing?

The young woman smiled, tantalising dimples appearing and, just as suddenly, vanishing.

"You agree then, that my behaviour was unkind?" Hugh taunted.

The woman closed a hand on the chair back, as though for safety. "I am sorry I let your son fall asleep. I should have kept him awake for the visit."

Her face glowed in the light from the candle and a pair of blue eyes sparkled. Her tall, slim frame, dark lashes and wide mouth were as unlike Beatrice's petite, fair beauty as Hugh could imagine. Such an open face surprised him, like a gust of fresh air through a stuffy room. His breath caught.

"How could you know I would visit? Have you not been told that I avoid the boy?" Some demon inside tempted him to mock. Would she fight back, showing the spirit of the railway cutting?

"I am sorry John has no playfellows." Although the words were demure, her lips snapped shut in a straight line. A twinge of guilt struck Hugh. She thought John lonely. It was true; the child was isolated at the Hall, with no other boys nearby. "We are just coming out of mourning," he said, provoked into an excuse.

The young woman's hand dropped from the chair and her brow furrowed. She looked concerned. "I know that this is a sad time, my lord, and especially so for your son. I am sorry my arrival has caused further trouble."

Uncomfortable, Hugh swallowed hard. "Nonsense. I would not have missed today's events for the world. Breeches, my dear, become you more than you can imagine." The mockery was unfair. He should have held his tongue, for the young woman's cheeks flamed bright red. He must make those blue eyes sparkle once more. "Come with me."

Obediently, she followed him out of the child's bedroom, through the nursery into a smaller room. A bed in one corner lay snug beneath a bright coverlet and a pair of comfortable chairs stood together. A patterned china jug and ewer occupied a washstand under a tiny window. To the left of the window was a neat wooden wardrobe.

"This will be your room while you stay with us." Hugh watched.

The young woman's face broke into the broadest of grins. "Oh! It's lovely." She clasped her hands together and beamed at him. "It's the prettiest room I've ever known." Her cheeks glowed.

She looked delightful, her face so open and trusting. Hugh felt a pang of desire. If only she would be honest. Why would she not explain the reasons for her flight from London? Surely, such a wide smile could not hide a devious, false nature. "Tell me who you are and what you were doing, travelling through the length of the country alone." He spoke without heat. Would she set his mind at rest?

She bit her lip. "Who I am?" She gave a little laugh that rang false. "Why, I'm no one." Her eyes flickered from side to side.

Hugh's heart sank. She was searching for a lie, for some story. He must extract the truth. "Mrs. Rivers has suggested that since Abigail has left the Hall you should undertake the duties of nursemaid."

She nodded.

Hugh hardened his heart. "Tell me what qualifications you have."

"Why, none at all." Her head was high but her fingers twisted together. "I used to supervise children sometimes in London." Hugh heard a catch in the voice. "I taught them their letters and how to count."

"Indeed." Hugh folded his arms and leaned against the wall, tapping one boot on the floor, as irritation flooded back. "As you will have charge of my son, I need to know something about you." Impatient, willing to offer the woman a last chance, he fired rapid questions. "Where are you from? What possessed you to travel at night? I gather you wished to visit the West Country. Bath, perhaps, would be a suitable destination. Did you have no travelling companions?" *Tell me. Convince me that all is well.*

The young woman took a deep breath, unclasped her hands and hid them behind her back. "I am an orphan," she began in a voice that wavered. She coughed and continued with more confidence. "My mother died many years ago and I was brought up by-by my Uncle Samuel, a tailor."

"Uncle Samuel?" Why was she stammering, so? Was she telling the truth?

"Not a real uncle." The voice faltered again. "I believe he was an old friend of my mother."

"Hmm." Hugh considered. "No father, I gather?" An orphan, then. Some excuse for her conduct, perhaps.

She shook her head, so lost and sad. If only he could believe every word. "He cared for me most carefully and kindly." She spoke faster, words tumbling over one another. "Last month, he passed away. I always wondered where my mother's parents lived and from some hints Samuel dropped, I learned there is another uncle, living in Bristol, in a small way of business. I decided to visit the West Country." Her voice trailed away.

Hugh frowned. Could this really be the truth? Could he believe the story? It sounded unconvincing, but still, stranger things happened. It could all be sincere. His spirits rose. He must find out more. "Do you read and write?"

"Oh, yes, Samuel made sure I learned." A louder voice. This must be safer ground: surely, there was truth here. "I can sew, for I used to assist him. I can cook and keep house."

Hugh tore his eyes away and stared out through the window across the pleasure grounds and fields of the Hall. "You did not wait long before leaving London after the death of your uncle." He kept his gaze fixed on the fields he loved and must protect. The Hall must come first.

"I hoped to arrive at my uncle's house for Christmas."

"So your relative is expecting you?"

"His invitation arrived the day after Uncle Samuel died. I did not reply but planned to surprise him." The woman hesitated. "And his wife," she added.

He did not believe her. She was adding to the story as she spoke. Hugh swung round in time to disturb a telltale blush and his heart sank. He knew now. This was all nonsense: a story designed to gain sympathy. He tried in vain to hold the woman's gaze.

She spoke fast, now, as though hurrying to finish. "I was to travel with a maid, but she was unwell so I-I came alone." Her voice faded to nothing.

It was all lies. Hugh's jaw ached with tension as a long silence fell between them. He waited. Perhaps, even now, she would tell the truth. It was not too late.

With a sudden movement, the young woman

straightened. Lifting her chin, she met Hugh's eyes. "I am an honest woman," she declared in a firm voice, confident at last. "I will continue on to Bristol as soon as possible. I am most grateful for such kindness—for letting me stay here for a while." She curtsied. "I hope I can repay this consideration by helping to look after Master John, since the nursemaid has unfortunately been called away."

At last, some words rang true. Perhaps there was hope. "I am willing to allow you to continue here during the holiday and until your uncle sends for you. Please write a letter at once and request a companion for the next stage of the journey to Bristol. Mrs. Rivers will supply writing materials and ensure that James, the footman, puts the letter into the post."

Hugh watched the young woman closely. "I will not have it said that Thatcham Hall ever turned away anyone visited by misfortune."

Her eyes were enormous.

"Abigail's desertion of her post leaves me no alternative but to ask you to look after John for a day or two," Hugh kept his tone casual. "I am sure you will wish to be on your way as soon as may be after that."

The young woman's gaze fell to the floor, but she said nothing.

Hugh turned back to the window. "In the meantime." He gazed unseeing into the darkness, where the wind whined through the trees. "While you remain at the Hall, I expect you to obey the rules of the house."

"Of course," she whispered.

He tapped the whip on the glass of the windowpane, but spoke softly. "I am sure you will want to explore the Hall." He turned. "Resist the temptation.

The house is old. It is undergoing restoration, but the work takes time. Some parts are dangerous. Keep well away from the East Wing."

He pointed towards the gothic tower that loomed darkly through the trees. "Make sure John does not go there. You must keep a close eye on him." She said nothing. "Do you understand?" The woman nodded.

"Then, I will leave you." Tiredness hit Hugh with a sudden, overwhelming desire to sleep. "Please make yourself as comfortable as possible here during your short stay." Without another word, he stalked from the room.

His head whirled. He could not tell whether the woman told the truth or not. Why had fate brought her here to disturb the peace of the Hall? Hugh wanted no more complications. He desired her, but he would not let such feelings corrupt him.

He would let no one, not even such a pretty young woman as this, distract him from his duty to the Hall and to John. There would be no repetition of the foolish marriage to Beatrice. Lured into a web of beauty and charm, he had believed every lie. No woman would make such a fool of him again. He was no longer a callow youth, to be bowled over by bright eyes and dimples.

He yawned. He needed sleep. By morning, he would not give a fig for the woman.

Chapter Nine

Philomena sat upright on a chair, her mind in turmoil. She had slept through much of the previous afternoon. She hardly needed more slumber. The room was dark. By degrees, the wind died until silence lay all around the Hall, except for an occasional creaking branch and, once, a sudden terrifying shriek that brought Philomena scrambling to the window. She peered fearfully out into the dark. Used to the relentless bustle and noise of London, the quiet unnerved her.

What could have shrieked like that? A rabbit perhaps, caught by a weasel. Or, could it be an owl, speeding on silent wings to pounce on an unsuspecting mouse? She shivered. Was she the mouse and Lord Thatcham the owl? Had he believed her? She had tried so hard to convince him, but that grim expression spoke of doubt and disbelief. If only she could tell the truth.

Yet, how could anyone believe her story? Only Philomena knew the depths of Joseph's depravity, the horror of his touch and her fear of the future. She alone knew of the man with cold green eyes. Lord Thatcham, surrounded by luxury, could never understand the ways of the poor in London. The Hall was a world away. She squirmed, remembering the look on Lord Thatcham's face as he listened to the false story.

She stood up and paced around the room, hot with embarrassment. She must not think about the master of the Hall. She would think of other things. There were hints of secrets here at the Hall. Why had Lord Thatcham forbidden her from visiting the East Wing? Was something hidden there? Something wicked?

It was possible. The Hall was a place of contrasts. Elegant luxury enveloped the occupants in its silken embrace, but there were undercurrents Philomena did not understand. Sorrow affected everyone in the house. The servants grew quiet and watchful when their master was with them. John seemed over-full of mischief, as though fighting for attention. She wondered why Lord Thatcham was so stern.

Despite her intentions, Philomena's thoughts slid back to the owner of the Hall. She could not block the man out. She felt his presence everywhere, and he scared her. The expression in his eyes changed so fast. One moment warm with sardonic amusement, the next, cold as ice, they sent shivers through her body. Such a man, powerful and arrogant, full of the knowledge of his importance, could be capable of wickedness. What was it that the housekeeper had said? *Don't cross him.* Philomena shuddered.

Yet, the Lord Thatcham at the scene of the accident was a very different matter. Muddy and scratched, he had dispelled Philomena's fear and filled her with confidence. Their eyes had met, and a brief spark had flashed from one to the other. Raw with horror, in the midst of chaos, two souls had reached out to each other. Philomena had not imagined it. Whatever had happened at the Hall, whatever secrets its master hid behind his cold exterior, she could not ignore the feelings he aroused. She wanted to know more about him.

Philomena sighed. Since the night of the accident,

Lord Thatcham had gone out of his way to sneer at her. He clearly regretted that moment of shared feeling. There was nothing here for Philomena. She must leave, soon, and forget Thatcham Hall and everyone within. Her plan for independence was delayed, not destroyed. She had not even travelled half way to Bristol.

She shuddered as a new fear struck. She was only forty miles or so from London. Could Joseph even now be on her trail? Could he arrive at the Hall while everyone slept? No. This was nonsense. Joseph had no idea of her whereabouts and no way of following her.

Philomena could not rest. Stomach churning, she moved from window to bed and back. If Joseph arrived, any dream of an independent life would be over. She would be trapped.

It was not only the thought of Joseph's person that terrified her. He was a link to the dreadful secret. She did not know how much he knew about the secret marriage: there was no sign of his presence at the Church and he never spoke of it, but surely, he knew the secret. Otherwise, why had the man not attacked as soon as Samuel died?

Questions tumbled over each other in Philomena's head. Why did Joseph wait? What power did the man with the cold green eyes hold over him? What were they planning?

Thatcham Hall grew still. Footsteps sounded on the main staircase, as the Dowager and Selena went to bed. Philomena made a decision. She would not wait. She would leave, now, before Joseph made the journey from London. If she left tonight, there would be no need for Lord Thatcham to hear the truth. She could not bear to watch disgust creep across his face, if he heard the true story of her flight. He would despise such a tale.

The servants had left Joseph's clothes, clean and dry, in a neat pile on one of the chairs. Philomena shook them out and sniffed. They no longer stank of Joseph, but still, they disgusted her. No matter. She would leave the Hall as she had arrived, taking nothing that did not belong to her. Philomena hung the nursemaid's uniform in the closet, removed her mother's brooch, wrapped it carefully in a handkerchief and put the bundle in the jacket pocket.

She looked around the nursery for one last time. She saw the table where John took his meals, and the bookcase holding his books. Nothing here could keep her. It was time to go. She opened the door. It creaked a little. She stopped. The passage was silent, but John turned over in bed and murmured.

Philomena pulled at the door. It squeaked.

John cried out from his room. "No. No! Leave me alone!"

Philomena stood, uncertain. John shouted again. It must be a nightmare. What should she do? She waited. It would be over in a moment. When he was quiet, she would go.

John cried out again and burst into noisy sobbing. Philomena could not leave like this. She ran next door. The child sat up in bed, eyes wide and staring. "Don't let them take me!" he shouted, close to hysteria.

Philomena took him in her arms. She stroked damp hair away from wide eyes. "All is well, John. Go to sleep."

Slowly, the sobbing faded. John's eyes closed. Philomena snuggled him down into bed and smoothed the sheets. The child turned over, heaved a great sigh and fell back to sleep. Philomena watched as John slept. *The poor child needs me.*

She smiled. The feeling was new. John had seen so many others leave the Hall: first his mother, then one nursemaid after the other. How close Philomena had come to letting John down, just like the rest. For all the small boy chatter and bravado, this was a sad little boy with no mother and a distant father.

Philomena would not desert John, as everyone else had.

Slowly, she peeled off Joseph's clothes. She folded the trousers and laid the shirt on top. Soon, perhaps, Joseph would find her. Her only safety lay in flight, but she could not take it. She must remain here for John's sake.

As she lay in bed, she heard the distant clunk of the large clock in the corridor outside the nursery. She found comfort in its regularity. Her taut muscles relaxed, and her heart slowed to beat in time with the clock. She may be safe for a few days. After Christmas, when Lord Thatcham found a new nursemaid, she would run to Bristol.

She turned over again, her feet tangling in the nightdress. It was long and made of heavy cotton. She supposed Abigail left it behind as she shook the dust of Thatcham Hall from her feet.

How many nursemaids had left the Hall? Philomena tried to remember what Mrs. Rivers had said. Surely, that dear little boy could not be the only cause of their departure. Had they left because of Lord Thatcham? All her thoughts led back to him.

As sleep still refused to come, Philomena wondered about the death of his wife. How strange, for a lady of quality to be alone on horseback in the mid-winter cold when there were grooms, coachmen and stable-hands at her disposal: servants to spare in this grand establishment. A shiver ran round the back of Philomena's neck. Something was wrong at Thatcham Hall.

Think of something else, or sleep will never come.

She pulled out the brooch. The face in the portrait was lovely. Golden curls cascaded in ringlets around a heart-shaped face. A secret smile curved the corners of the lips. Could that beauty really be her mother? Philomena's own hair was dark, her chin determined and her mouth all too ready to break into a wide grin.

There was something about the eyes, though. Clear, sapphire blue, they were shaped like almonds and rimmed with luxuriant dark lashes. Philomena saw eyes like those every day, in the mirror. They were her only claim to beauty. Perhaps Samuel had told the truth, and the woman in the portrait truly was her mother.

At last, Philomena slept, restless, in a slumber filled with dark, gothic towers, hooded faces and cold, green eyes.

Chapter Ten

Christmas morning broke. It was a full year since Beatrice died. Hugh would never forget that day: John, weeping, kept away from the sickroom by white-faced servants; Beatrice's mother arriving just too late to bid farewell to her daughter; urgent messages of enquiry and then of condolence from surrounding families.

Hugh threw open the window and gazed out across the estate, hoping the ancient, familiar fields and trees may work their magic. He leaned his forehead on the glass, icy cold soothing hot skin. A watery sun struggled to peep out from the dark clouds of the night. Sure enough, Hugh's spirits lifted. Something stirred in him, like a spark in darkness.

Today was Christmas Day. It should be a day of new beginnings. This day, a full year since Beatrice's death, would mark the end of deep mourning. Today, Selena and the Dowager would sit around the table, eating and drinking, putting off their black drab, wearing a lighter style of mourning clothes. Beatrice's shade might leave him in peace at last.

The Hall was alive. Servants, up early, hastened to set fires, provide a hearty breakfast in the morning room, and ensure the day's feast was ready, before wearing their own Sunday best and walking in single file behind the family, to Church.

Hugh washed in hot water brought by Martin, the

valet. He drank a cup of chocolate while the man wielded the razor. He grimaced. A drink fit only for women and children. He would insist on coffee in future.

Hugh waved Martin away. "That's enough for now. Get yourself down to the kitchen. If I'm not mistaken, there'll be better cheer down there." Martin hesitated. Hugh's personal servant since his master had grown out of nursemaids and governesses, Hugh allowed him to criticise when others feared to speak.

"Begging your pardon, my lord." Martin watched his master out of the corner of his eye. Hugh said nothing. He waited. Martin took a breath and continued. "If your lordship will forgive me, it's my opinion, if you don't mind my saying so…"

"Oh, for God's sake, get on with it, man," said Hugh. "When has minding ever stopped you saying anything—strictly for my own good, of course?"

"Exactly, my lord. I was just about to remark that Master John has been down in the kitchen for some time already this morning, showing the staff some items which were apparently left in a stocking in his room by Good King Wenceslas."

Hugh blinked. "Good King Wenceslas?"

"Yes, my lord. I believe he enjoyed the story."

"So he did. I presume the nursemaid accompanied him to the kitchen?"

"Oh, yes, my lord, no problem with *that*."

"So what is the problem?" Hugh grinned. "Come on, you know you'll tell me in the end."

The valet sighed and shook his head. "One never wishes to cause trouble."

Hugh grunted. Doggedly, Martin continued. "No,

my lord, one does not. However, Master John appears to be dressed as a knight and waving his wooden sword. Very charming, of course, but with her Ladyship arriving this morning, you may wish his new nurse to ensure a certain increased level of decorum."

Hugh's lips twitched, even as he frowned. Martin hastened to deliver the rest of the message he carried. "I should perhaps add, my lord, that Master John has broken three pudding basins and severely damaged a silver sugar bowl by swinging the sword in a dangerous manner." He coughed. "In addition, Mrs. Bramble has hinted that today's feast may be at risk if Master John causes any more damage, especially to the remaining pudding basins which contain, the cook tells me, the figgy pudding."

Hugh chuckled. It was an intriguing picture. "Do you know, Martin, I do believe I shall take no action at all. I will leave the new nursemaid to deal appropriately with Master John."

He lingered a while after the valet left, smiling. How would the woman handle John? Hugh did not believe a word of her ridiculous stories, but this morning, such reservations hardly mattered. After all, she would only be here a short while. The prospect of watching a struggle was tempting. John had an infinite collection of ways to enrage an adult. Could such a young woman manage a child who seemed to respond only to punishment?

Hugh's smile died. The responsibility for John's bad behaviour lay at his father's feet. Beatrice had spoiled the boy, of course, meeting for an hour every day to feed him sweetmeats until his childish chatter bored her, leaving all childcare to the succession of nursemaids who appeared and disappeared with troublesome frequency.

Since Beatrice's death, John's behaviour had hardly improved. Hugh should have spent more time overseeing the child. It was obvious that a boy without a mother needed help. Last night was a surprise. John sat peacefully with Philomena, washed and ready for bed, with a stunning lack of kicking, screaming, or nightgown refusal.

Hugh's encounters with the boy were limited to occasional visits to the nursery and rare rides together, while John trotted next to an impatient Thunder on the trusty pony called Bear. There was always something on the estate to keep Hugh from his son. John, like his mother, knew exactly how to infuriate. Hugh could tolerate drawing on walls, tearing picture books, or shrieking loudly along the corridors of the Hall but would not endure lies. Unfortunately, John happily indulged in the most improbable falsehoods, if they might help avoid punishment.

"I did not break the statue, Papa," he insisted, when Hugh found a piece of Meissen shattered in the drawing room. "It must have been the maid." Hugh was furious. It was bad enough that John would tell such an obvious lie, but accusing one of the servants at the Hall was unforgiveable.

He had less awareness of how to raise a child than he had of dealing with his horses and dogs, that was the problem. Was lying normal for a four-year-old? Was John's behaviour just due to high spirits, or, worse, did he have bad blood?

Hugh envied the new young woman's skills with John. She had brought calm and happiness to the boy within a few hours of her arrival at the Hall. How did she do it? What made John so obedient when she spoke so quietly and gently to him?

He paced round the room. Yesterday's determination to channel his energies into duty had not supplied the hoped for peace of mind. That woman had held up a mirror to Hugh's behaviour, and he was ashamed.

Restless, he paced faster. He would think about John another time. Perhaps the young woman would keep him out of mischief for a while, at least until resuming the journey to Bristol.

Strange female. Why would she not account for herself? She was fearless at the site of the accident, tireless in her efforts to release the passengers from the overturned wagon before trudging without complaint back to the Hall. She must have felt sick with weariness. That blow to the head must have ached, but she had not whimpered. Not once had she relied on the feminine weakness that Beatrice so often employed.

Hugh admired her bravery. Why, then, did she offer such unlikely reasons for travelling to Bristol? And why was a young woman wearing men's clothes? All Hugh had asked for was honesty.

Despite his disquiet, Philomena intrigued him. He wished to know more. A sudden thought struck. His neck prickled. He had been cruel, yesterday, and, what's more, in front of the servants. The young woman was dressed as a boy at the time, that was true, but Hugh was ashamed to be the cause of her distress.

"We prefer people to be honest," he had said, unkindly, making his mistrust clear. He was too harsh. Such conduct was not worthy of a peer of the realm, one with power over so many fellow creatures. A hatred of lies was no excuse: the master of Thatcham Hall had behaved like a bully.

Hugh must make amends. It was no more than duty to ensure the woman had everything needed for reasonable comfort. He would call in to the kitchen on the way to the stables. He would surprise the butler and the rest of the household in the middle of the Christmas preparations. That would be an opportunity to witness the new nurse's conduct with John. It was not that Hugh wished to see more smiles, or watch her dimples. No, he simply wished to behave with kindness.

Lord Thatcham threw open the kitchen door, unannounced, to find John hopping on one leg, the new nursemaid smiling behind. Suitably attired in neatly pressed velvet, ready for a morning visit from a grandmother, the boy was happily presenting a small present, wrapped in gold paper, to Mrs. Bramble. Torn paper and an excess of glue hinted that John had wrapped the present himself. The offending wooden sword was nowhere in sight.

"Merry Christmas," John piped. The nursemaid leaned forward and touched the boy on the shoulder. He sighed and continued, each word running into the next in a rehearsed speech. "I hope you will forgive me for breaking the bowls. I will try to be a little quieter in future."

Love for his son welled up in Hugh's heart. John beamed so proudly, his eyes so full of mischief: such a small, happy child. Raising the boy should be a pleasure. Why had Hugh never seen it like that before?

He laughed aloud. The cook started, dropping pans on the hearth, and Philomena looked round. To Hugh's delight, she blushed. He lingered a moment on the faint pink glow of her cheeks. How could he ever have mistaken such a lovely young woman for a boy?

Her blush deepened. Hugh waited, delighted, until suddenly aware that the servants were watching with interest. He coughed. "That was well done, John."

The boy turned to smile, a wide grin splitting his face in half. A lump constricted Hugh's throat. He coughed again, tried and failed to think of something else to say, turned without another word and left by the outside door.

"Papa," John called, running. "May I ride with you?" Hugh, remembering the long list of tasks waiting, shook his head. Philomena, close behind, cleared her throat. Hugh raised an eyebrow. The woman frowned.

"What the devil's the matter with you?" Hugh asked, hurt. Had he not just praised John in front of the servants? Why was the woman displeased, this time?

"Nothing, my lord," she murmured. Lips pressed tightly together, she focused on John.

Hugh saw that the corners of John's mouth had turned down. The boy was a picture of comical disappointment. Hugh recognised this at once as John's usual expression when thwarted. Normally, patience exhausted, Hugh tapped one foot with impatience. Today, he pursed his lips to fight a smile. The glare could not fool John. The boy skipped with excitement.

"I have much to attend to this morning, as guests are due to arrive," Hugh said, "so I must leave you here a while. Later, however, we will take a walk together across the fields before greeting your grandmother and aunt."

The boy hopped from one leg to the other.

"That is if Miss Philomena allows, of course." Hugh narrowed his eyes at Philomena, daring her to disagree.

She nodded. "Of course." Her voice was demure. "Will you wish me to accompany you?"

"Oh." Hugh saw an opportunity to regain the upper hand. "I think your presence is essential to maintain order. Perhaps you would like to wear breeches again, in case there should be any chasing required?"

Two small vertical lines appeared between Philomena's brows, and Hugh bit his lip. He let out a puff of breath and offered an olive branch. "I trust there will be no disaster as unpleasant as the accident of the railway carriage." He smiled. "I hope you have fully recovered. I trust the exertion of looking after my son is not too tiring."

Two dimples appeared, one in either cheek. The young woman smiled, open and friendly. Her eyes sparkled. "Your son is delightful. We have enjoyed wrapping presents together today and can hardly wait to offer them to the guests."

"Is there a gift for me?" Hugh lifted an eyebrow.

"Ah, you must wait and see." She laughed. John chortled and jigged.

Hugh glanced from one to the other. Nurse and child, side by side, glowed with the excitement of Christmas Day present giving. Hugh could hardly tell which of the two was more animated. His breath caught. For a moment, he was at a loss. Abruptly, he nodded and walked away.

"Goodbye, Papa!" John scampered back to the kitchen in search of another adventure. Philomena set off in pursuit. Hugh could not reply. His head whirled.

It must be something about the day: Christmas had cast its transforming spell on John. Affection swelled Hugh's heart.

Philomena's presence was more disturbing. Neither demurely obedient like the maids, nor full of pomp like the senior servants, she disobeyed all the rules of behaviour. There was no flirting or simpering like the young ladies of quality who tittered and giggled. She did not try to catch her master's attention or strive to please. On the contrary, the girl made no secret of her disapproval at times. Such ways did not fit readily into any familiar patterns.

Hugh longed to know more. Fascination overcame good sense whenever he saw the woman. If only she would tell the truth.

Chapter Eleven

Winter held the countryside in thrall. It took Philomena half an hour to bundle John in layers of clothes. At last, the child was as round and plump as one of the exotic tangerine oranges imported at great expense from Africa that waited, piled high on platters in the kitchen, to grace the Christmas table. John and Philomena ran, laughing, down the path from the kitchens. Philomena's heart lurched as she caught sight of Hugh in the pleasure gardens.

"Look at me, Papa." John beamed. Hugh lifted the boy high into the air, tossed him even higher, and laughed into his son's face. Lord Thatcham was younger than Philomena had thought. She had taken him for an older man of nine and thirty or so. Now the Master of the Hall seemed hardly older than she. He tossed John ever higher, until Philomena gasped and darted forward, arms outstretched to catch the boy.

Lord Thatcham laughed. "We scared Miss Philomena, then." John's face glowed crimson with glee.

"You would not wish to drop the heir to the Hall," Philomena pointed out.

"With all these clothes, he'll bounce," Lord Thatcham said. "Though to tell the truth, young man, you weigh as much as one of Farmer Jones's cows. I will soon need a pitchfork to lift you off the ground."

He turned back to Philomena. She blushed.

"The Hall seems to suit you, Miss Philomena, despite the strains of the accident," Hugh said. "Take care you do not catch cold."

Was that concern in his face?

"It is not long since you were lying in the mud, a large bruise on your head. Are you well enough to walk through the fields?"

Philomena swallowed. She glanced away, unable to look Lord Thatcham full in the face, moved by such sudden kindness. His grey eyes gleamed. A lock of hair blew across the man's forehead and Philomena felt an urge to brush it back. Her neck grew hot.

She pointed to John's layers of clothes. "We are enjoying the walk and do not care how cold the air, is that not so, John?"

John was too busy making footprints on the frosty grass to listen.

"May I walk with you a little while John amuses himself?" Lord Thatcham asked.

"Of course." Philomena kept her eyes on the ground to hide a jolt of surprise. The master of the Hall had changed. Yesterday's sarcasm had turned to kindness and concern. Would it last, or would anger return?

He shortened his stride to keep pace as they strolled in silent harmony through the pleasure grounds, Philomena conscious every second of Lord Thatcham's presence. She kept both hands hidden in the woollen shawl, anxious to avoid any accidental touch. She searched for an appropriate topic of conversation, hoping to prevent him from asking further questions. She did not want to tell more lies.

"How fortunate you are to possess such a house and so much fertile land as this." She pulled one hand from the shawl and waved at the vista: a glory of well-regulated fields, then shuddered remembering how the children in London shivered in the cold, huddled beneath bridges and in doorways.

Forgetting for a moment where she was, Philomena murmured as though Lord Thatcham could not hear. "There is little justice in the world, when children huddle six to a bed."

His smile turned wintry. "I am perfectly aware of our good fortune in living here at Thatcham. I cannot cure all the ills of the world. How will it benefit the poor for more to join their number? Is it not better by far to make full use of such good fortune by growing food for the nation?"

Philomena went to speak, but he forestalled the words. "I am as aware as you, of the parable of the rich man and the camel, and the difficulty in passing through the eye of a needle. Perhaps you would have me throw John's inheritance away?"

He smiled, cold lips twisted. "Perhaps the boy should find some children to huddle with?"

"You think me naïve, my lord," she replied, angry now. "I did not mean to criticise. Pray, allow me to have some small understanding. You must be aware of the plight of the poor. Take Mrs. Cole, the woman you rescued from the train and the child, Betsy, as an example. What future can such a pair look forward to, do you suppose, in this world where some families have so much and others so little?"

"Your Mrs. Cole would manage better if she spent her money on food, rather than gin," Lord Thatcham snapped. "In any case, the woman is on the way to better things, if I understand correctly. Was not Mrs. Cole, along with others, on the way to visit wealthy relatives for Christmas?" He looked full into Philomena's face. She felt the blush of guilt flood her cheeks. This man saw straight through the stories she had told.

Guilt fuelled her irritation. "Not everyone has the benefit of education. How can Mrs. Cole know the best way to bring up a child? No one has taught her. She scrambles and scrapes to do the best possible, with no money and a dead husband. She does not deserve mockery."

Lord Thatcham stopped walking and stood still, brows knitted together. "You are right."

Philomena, surprised by this sudden suspension of hostilities, had nothing to say.

Lord Thatcham turned towards John, who lay happily on the ground, examining the frost on a spider's web. "You remind me to value what I have."

Philomena and Lord Thatcham stood side by side, close together, watching John. Philomena's rage dissolved into contentment. Lord Thatcham's words, full of acceptance and forgiveness, travelled straight to her heart. For a long moment, master and servant stood, almost as equals, watching over the child. Lord Thatcham stood close. Philomena breathed in the clean scent of soap and a faint masculine aroma of tobacco and wine.

"In any case," he said, "as we introduce better ways to produce food it becomes cheaper for Mrs. Cole and the rest. Bread on the table, milk in the jug, and the chance to learn the ABCs: that's what will change

Betsy's life. And there's so much more to be done. In the Americas, the farmers use machinery for the tasks still managed in England with horses and man power." Animated, Lord Thatcham's face lit up. The harsh lines fell away and his eyes gleamed with enthusiasm. He looked hard at Philomena. "You are laughing at me."

She shook her head. "No. I am excited to think the world can change for the better."

Philomena would not allow herself to think ahead. She was content, for now, that Lord Thatcham should walk by her side. She must hide any more dangerous feelings. No one must ever discover how high her spirits soared or how fast her heart beat when the Master of the Hall spoke. There was no future for such emotions.

She could not admit that she had felt the touch of love. Lord Thatcham remained as distant as the sun from the earth. These tender feelings, so unexpected, could not last.

Chapter Twelve

All too soon, Philomena and John returned to the nursery while Hugh prepared to dress for the arrival of his mother and sister. The Dowager Lady Thatcham's treasured barouche would bring them to the Hall at any moment.

Martin, determined not to allow his master to appear sloppily dressed on such on occasion, fussed endlessly about Hugh's cravat. As today was Christmas day, Hugh curbed his habitual impatience and allowed the valet to fiddle interminably.

He was astonished at the calming effect of this morning's short walk in the grounds. He had rarely so enjoyed a half hour's conversation. No other woman debated such matters with Philomena's unique style. Conversation with Beatrice had been limited, during the early years of their acquaintance, to flirtation at balls and compliments on her appearance. Later, as differences in character and opinion between the married couple grew exasperating, they avoided quarrels by barely conversing on any subject beyond the weather. Soon, the pair indulged in only the most trivial of polite dinner conversation.

This morning, Philomena had surprised Hugh with such unexpected thoughtfulness and strong opinions. He longed to know more about her. Something had forced such a young woman to undertake lengthy travel, alone and in disguise. She refused to tell the truth. Could Hugh trust that she had committed no crime? The thought surprised him. He had fallen out of the habit of trusting people. It was safer to think ill of others than risk betrayal.

Hugh waved Martin away and started down the stairs. Could Philomena be trusted, despite such a refusal to explain? Would he be a fool to have faith in an unknown waif?

The clatter of wheels on gravel signalled the approach of a carriage along the avenue. Well-shod hooves scattered stones, disturbing the newly raked gravel as the horses slowed to a walk, swirled round the drive and finally drew to a halt at the front entrance. As the carriage stopped, the servants of the Hall lined up dutifully by the door, ranged in order of importance, to greet the newcomers. Most remembered the Dowager Lady Thatcham from the days of her marriage to Lord Thatcham's father. Familiar with her standards, they knew better than to appear late, grubby or slipshod at her arrival.

Hugh strode forward, kissed his mother's outstretched hand and assisted her from the carriage. As light as a bird, the Dowager leaned on her son's arm for the few yards to the door. She greeted the servants with a general nod. "Good morning to you all and a Merry Christmas."

She received their bows and curtsies with a formal smile. "I look forward to one of your most accomplished dinners," she told Mrs. Bramble. Taken by surprise in mid curtsey, the cook wobbled and blushed.

Hugh, meanwhile, returned to the carriage to aid

Selena in the usual scramble to locate the boxes, shawls, handkerchiefs, and baskets that accompanied every journey. Why women surrounded themselves with so much baggage, Hugh could never understand. Unbidden, realisation struck that Philomena had travelled with next to nothing and seemed perfectly content. Hugh had no time to consider that thought further, for Selena, already chattering, jumped down unaided from the carriage.

"Oh, Hugh, we've had the most exciting journey," she cried. "We were almost set upon by hoards of vagabonds. I declare I thought they were Luddites, but Mama insists the law hanged the last of those fellows long ago. Nevertheless, there was the most dreadful crush of boys, all wearing caps and scarves and rushing about through the village in the most terrifying way."

"Enjoying the frosty Christmas morning, I have no doubt," said Hugh.

"Well, maybe so…" Selena was not to be quieted. "Then one of those dreadful iron horses came past making a terrible noise, and the horses became so skittish I was sure we were about to be thrown from the carriage." Her face glowed with excitement. "I do declare, Hugh, I thought we should never arrive alive at all!"

Her chatter displeased him, today. Did she not know of last night's dreadful disaster and the death in the mud and rain of a handful of unfortunate travellers?

"Selena, my dear," her mother spoke calmly. "Do show a little dignity. Hugh will think you have become a hoyden since last you met."

Such calm unconcern for anything other than appearance infuriated Hugh. His mother and sister seemed quite unaware of any events outside their circle. The Dowager's dignity had enabled her to sail calmly through the horror of Beatrice's death, all energies focused on ensuring no breath of scandal should touch the family.

Selena, bewildered, had followed her mother's example and behaved ever since as though nothing had happened, although Hugh had sometimes observed his sister watching closely, eyes narrowed, as though about to say something indiscreet. Hugh avoided such moments, cultivating a convenient reputation for ill humour, unable to begin to explain the horror that filled his heart at the thought of Beatrice's betrayal and premature death.

"I have always admired my sister's enthusiasm and high spirits." Hugh's voice was sharp with sarcasm. "I am delighted you have arrived safely through all the dangers of a trip of fewer than ten miles through England's mildest countryside."

He took the Dowager's arm. "Perhaps you have not heard that a real accident on the railway yesterday resulted in the death of several passengers?"

"Oh, how dreadful." Selena's hand flew to her mouth. "The poor things. I would never have made such a foolish joke, Hugh, had I but known. We must visit the families later today." Hugh saw real tears in his sister's eyes and instantly regretted his harshness. Selena was still a child, only just out of the schoolroom.

"I will tell you the details later," he said, more kindly.

He changed the subject. "What do you think of John's growth? Is he not a few inches taller?"

John, bursting with good behaviour, stood sturdily

at the door with Philomena close behind. As the Dowager approached, the small boy managed a highly creditable bow and received a grandmother's kiss with a brave show of nonchalance. Ignoring Philomena's previous instructions, he threw his arms cheerfully around Selena. His aunt bent low, and John kissed her wetly on the cheek. Selena dropped a favourite shawl in the crush. By the time Philomena retrieved and returned it, Hugh's sister had completely forgotten the unwelcome news of the accident.

The Dowager, possessed of a tiny stature that concealed a mighty personality, wore the Regency fashions of a bygone era. She stood straight as a ramrod under a green turban, decorated with a coquelicot feather. Her heavy travelling pelisse of merina cloth stretched almost to the floor.

She pulled it more comfortably around her shoulders and frowned at Philomena. "You," she boomed, "are not Abigail." She paused. "Why is that?"

Philomena curtsied but struggled to reply.

"Abigail had to return home unexpectedly." Smoothly, Hugh removed the need to explain.

"In-deed." The Dowager endowed the single word with a depth of meaning and an audible hyphen. Hugh turned away to hide his annoyance. He knew his mother disapproved of the way he ran his household in the absence of a wife. With a curt nod, he led on to the parlour where James, the footman, was laying out a tray of refreshments.

"Oh, how lovely," said Selena. "A glass of lemonade is exactly the thing one most needs after such a tiresome journey." Hugh, tempted to point out the great good fortune of a household able to afford such treats at Christmas, subsided. He would not vent his anger on his sister. The plight of the poor working men killed by the wreck in Sonning Cutting was not her fault.

In any case, she had clearly forgotten his reprimand. John, dismissed with a cool peck on the cheek from his grandmother, returned to the nursery with Philomena.

Hugh entertained his mother and sister with the story of Philomena's arrival, touching only lightly on the horrors of the crash, out of deference for his mother's sensibilities.

"How very fascinating." The Dowager took another sip of lemonade.

Chapter Thirteen

Philomena supervised John's luncheon, taken in the nursery. A sudden bustling on the stairs and the hum of voices gave warning that the visitors approached. Philomena had just time enough to straighten her dress and make sure the brooch was hidden from view before a footman threw open the door. Selena entered. Philomena breathed a sigh of relief.

Selena smiled. "Shall we take John outside, once more, while the weather remains clear? The child tells me he has already ventured out with Hugh, which is most unusual and a very good thing, I must say." Selena's hand flew to her mouth. "I meant, of course, to say that perhaps you would like to come out again? The sun seems set to shine, and there is time before I must dress for dinner."

Philomena enjoyed Selena's company. Younger than herself, Hugh's sister showed little sign of caring for any difference in rank and was not afraid of the exertion of running after John in the chill, fresh air. For Philomena, used to the fogs and smells of a city, the countryside held enchantment even in the starkness of winter. There was no need in this wide vista, to hold a handkerchief to her face to guard against the yellow fog that insinuated itself into every corner of London.

Selena kept up a steady stream of chatter, as

though Philomena was one of her usual companions. She gossiped about the new Queen and the dashing Prince Albert, and described the balls she planned to attend in London in the Season. "That is, if Hugh does not change his mind and decide he cannot afford for me to come out, this year." Philomena said nothing.

"He works so hard to maintain the Hall, and is always worrying." Selena continued. "He plans many alterations, designed for efficiency. Mama, of course, prefers to keep everything as it was when Papa was alive. She does not understand how the world is changing. She believes that all things can remain the same as they ever were."

Selena stopped to think, appearing to forget she was addressing the nursemaid. "Why, Mama hardly bows at all with many of our acquaintance. She becomes quite glacial when she meets Hugh's neighbour, even though Mr. Muldrow owns Fairford Manor. She does not think Mr. Muldrow is quite the thing." She leant closer to Philomena and giggled. "His father made money in trade, you know. Something to do with the cotton mills he used to own, up in the North." She whispered the last few words, as though it was impolite to name, "The North," in polite society.

She stopped talking abruptly to join her nephew in a scramble. The pair of them chased after something that rustled in the undergrowth, hoping for a glimpse of a rabbit. Unsuccessful, Selena returned to Philomena's side, dress muddied and face flushed. "In any case," she continued as though she had not broken off. "Mama thinks we should uphold the honour of Thatcham Hall and only receive those whose names are to be found in Burke's Peerage. I do declare, however, that if we were to insist on that, we would have very few companions, for many of the old houses are going to the new merchants nowadays. Mr. Muldrow—I mean the son, of course, not old Mr. Muldrow—used to visit often when Beatrice was alive, though I do not think Hugh liked him over much."

She glanced at Philomena's expression and added, hastily. "Oh, I do not mean that Hugh disliked him for being a merchant's son. Hugh cares nothing for such things. Indeed, he cares for little except hunting in the winter and building his ridiculous mechanical farming machines, and reading. And worrying about the tenants, of course. Hugh hardly even visits London in the summer, although he used to take his seat in the House regularly. Before his marriage, I mean."

Selena waved her muff in the air. "He talks of going overseas, you know, to the Americas, to observe farming methods, or some such, but says he cannot, for there is far too much to be done at Thatcham Hall, to prevent it all falling into disrepair. Papa," the girl confided in another loud whisper, "was not a good manager." She blushed crimson, and covered her mouth with one hand. "Oh, Philomena, I do not know what I can be thinking. I should not be telling you all this. Pray, do not tell Mama or Hugh. Please, you must promise."

"Of course I shall repeat nothing you say," Philomena said, "but perhaps we should restrict our conversation to other topics. Do you not enjoy this crisp weather?"

Selena giggled. "How sensible you are. No wonder Hugh wants so much for you to look after John."

The girl's hand flew to her face again, but

Philomena pretended not to have heard.

"Look," Selena cried, as they passed through a gateway into a prettily wooded area, where the bare branches of the trees pointed up towards the watery sun. "There's my favourite tree. I used to climb it when we were children. I'm sure I can still reach the top. "

Before Philomena could restrain her, she leapt onto a low-hanging branch and shinned up, clinging on by hands and feet, scrambling and giggling like a child, from branch to branch. At last, she stopped and hung suspended from a high branch.

Philomena laughed. "Now, please come down. Whatever would your mama think if she saw you?" Selena hooted, a most unladylike guffaw, and swung herself down. Just as she reached the base of the tree, a petticoat caught on a sharp twig. Undeterred, the girl leaped nimbly to the ground accompanied by an ominous sound of tearing muslin.

"Oh, dear me!" She glowed with excitement at her own daring. "My dress is ruined. I shall have to get back into the house without Mama seeing me. What a good thing..." Her voice trailed away, and her gaze grew fixed as Lord Thatcham appeared through the nearby gate.

The sun shone from behind, masking the stern face in shadow but haloing locks of fair hair in bright light. Philomena caught her breath. Her stomach lurched most inappropriately.

"I see you have not lost your tomboy habits," Hugh said sternly. "Perhaps our new nursemaid has been encouraging you to forget yourself."

Selena's ringlets quivered. "Nonsense," she laughed, "no one saw me except John, and he's far too young to mind."

"Ha," said Hugh. "Your nephew may be young, but he chatters like a ten-year-old. You may wish to keep away from Mama for a while if you prefer her not to know of such wild behaviour. And I suggest a change of dress and a comb for your hair."

Selena shook her head at him. "Now, don't be so cross. Philomena and I have been enjoying such a happy time. I never expect to enjoy myself here these days so don't begrudge me a little fun. Come Philomena, we will leave my brother to the grumps."

She called to John, who was running circles around the trunk of the largest oak tree in the wood. His aunt grasped his hand and set off at a run to the house.

Philomena took a step forward, meaning to follow the pair back to the Hall, but Lord Thatcham stood in her path, looking down with an unreadable expression. "My mother agrees that you are quite unsuitable. She has advised me to limit your time here with John to a few days."

Lord Thatcham's voice was formal, but there was a suspicious twinkle in his eye. Philomena stood as tall as possible. This, though her height was well above the average, brought her head only as high as Lord Thatcham's shoulder. "I can assure you," she snapped, "that I will remain here not a moment longer than I need to. I am sorry I am such a trouble. Your sister has been most kind."

"Meaning that I am not?" he asked.

"No, you are not," she exclaimed, temper getting the better of her. "You are full of your own importance—" Philomena stopped. "Oh, I am sorry, my lord, I forgot myself." Hot crimson flooded her cheeks.

If only she could learn to hold her tongue. The corners of Lord Thatcham's mouth twitched. It was infuriating.

Philomena stamped a stoutly clad foot on the hard ground. "There is no need for you to laugh."

Lord Thatcham's smile widened, spreading to his eyes. "You are a young woman with spirit." He took a step forward. "I value your opinions."

Philomena fought a panicky urge to run away. She must stand her ground. Lord Thatcham must not guess at her sudden longing to touch the furrowed brow and rest her head on that broad shoulder.

The stern face was close, now, one eyebrow raised, grey eyes sparkling. "Of course, only a brave soul would travel alone on the train. Even though you sought safety by dressing," the deep voice shook with mirth, "dressing as a boy."

Philomena felt a bubble of laughter. She fought to keep some semblance of dignity, but it was too late. Even biting her lips failed to prevent an answering smile. She knew her mouth was too wide and a row of white teeth must be visible, showing in a most unladylike way, but there was no stopping her laughter.

Lord Thatcham's mirth died away. He regarded Philomena steadily, grey eyes dark as the infectious smile melted. The short hairs on the back of Philomena's neck prickled. She gasped. Their eyes met and held.

Hugh took a step forward and took Philomena's hand. "I beg your pardon. I also forget myself. Please forgive this unsuitable conduct. Very little time has passed since that sad accident. You must still, I have no doubt, suffer from its effects. Instead of allowing time for healing, I have behaved shamefully on several occasions, both yesterday and today. I am an unfeeling wretch and far too inclined to forget compassion and remember rank and fortune."

As he bent towards Philomena, a sudden gust of wind blew a strand of fair hair across dark eyes. With a careless movement, Lord Thatcham swept it aside. Would that lock of hair feel as soft and silken to the touch as it appeared? Philomena's hand moved. She clenched it against her breast. She could not speak.

"The evening approaches early at this time of year," Lord Thatcham spoke as softly as a summer breeze. "We should follow Selena and John into the house to avoid the chill."

Neither moved. They stood immobile, barely inches apart. Philomena's breathing quickened. Her heart pounded. She was alone with this man. Lord Thatcham's face, so close, made her pulses race. She had never known such desire. Her eyes travelled across every feature, as if she would learn it by heart. Strong, sharp planes angled below deep grey eyes. Lines ran from nose to mouth. Forbidding and frightening, Lord Thatcham fascinated her. Something seemed to melt inside. Philomena felt weak and her head swam.

A new light shone in the grey eyes as Lord Thatcham bent his head ever closer. She must move away. She begged her body to obey her. Instead, it leaned closer as though a magnet pulled the two together. She could not resist.

"Philomena," Lord Thatcham murmured. "Is that name real? Who are you? What brought you here to make me—" He stopped abruptly and straightened a little, searching Philomena's face. He lingered on the black curls, the blue eyes, and then his gaze slid down to rest on her mouth. His lips parted. "You are very beautiful."

Philomena could not speak. Her body, responding to the hitherto unknown power of male magnetism, yearned for the first touch. Lord Thatcham's breath escaped in a rough gasp. He surrounded her, his arms gentle, and eased her body forward until Philomena felt his heart beat in time with her own.

Her eyes were half closed. His lips brushed gently, soft and warm, over her mouth. For an endless moment, she stayed quite still, beguiled by the spicy sharp taste of his lips. A charge electrified her body.

Then her head cleared. She gasped. Was she mad? This was Lord Thatcham and she was nothing but a penniless waif in his power. He meant to have his way with her, just as Joseph had tried to do.

She tore herself away from the embrace. "How dare you." Her voice shook with fury. "How dare you treat me so?"

Lord Thatcham's arms fell away. Blood drained from his countenance, leaving the dark eyes aglow in a white face. He said not a word.

Philomena wanted to run but at the same time longed to stay. She craved the warmth of his arms but dreaded what would happen next. An intoxicating male scent choked the breath in her throat and her legs trembled. Delight turned to horror. She yearned to hold him close, to touch her lips to that pale, shocked face and brush away those wilful strands of hair. She stepped back, sick with despair.

"You care nothing for me." Philomena threw the angry, bitter words into the cold air. Her voice shook. "My Lord Thatcham, you may be used to take your pleasure wherever you choose but believe me, sir, you may not take me."

She stood a moment, hesitating and shaking, then stumbled away and ran on trembling legs, eyes blinded by unshed tears. She did not see the gate that rose up at the end of the path and ran hard into the gatepost. She gasped, winded by the impact.

Lord Thatcham grasped her shoulder. "You need not fear." The words rang with contempt. "Rest assured, you will come to no harm here, despite your lies. What sort of woman can you be? I cannot read your mind, but no master of Thatcham Hall has forced himself upon any woman who does not wish it. You are quite safe."

Philomena ran, tears streaking her face, back towards the safety of the Hall and John's nursery.

Chapter Fourteen

As Philomena disappeared into the distance, Hugh felt sick. He shook his head, trying to clear it. What had happened? Had he been bewitched? The light, fading from the sky while the last crystals of ice in the shadow under the trees sparkled, diamond-bright, had charmed him. He had reached out to touch the strange creature who had invaded the tranquillity of Thatcham Hall. She had cast a spell on him with an air of mystery and secrecy. His desire had engulfed him, unexpected and confusing. He had forgotten his vow to put responsibility and duty before pleasure. He had made himself ridiculous.

It was the woman's fault. She had deliberately enticed him to her, only to draw back. Nothing but a street urchin, she had somehow entrapped the master of Thatcham Hall. He would have no more to do with her.

He kicked with passion at the trunk of a tree and slashed at the hedge with a cane. Let the wench spend this day and the next at the Hall, as promised. Then she would be on her way. It mattered not at all, whether this so-called uncle existed. Hugh did not care what became of her. He stalked from the wood. It would be easy to overcome the flood of wasted emotion that had led to his foolish conduct. He would forget Miss Philomena within days. He strode towards the Hall, but with every step, the rage that had engulfed his heart subsided.

Before he had covered a hundred paces, his fury had ebbed, leaving nothing but sorrow and loss.

He did not want Philomena to leave. In truth, he longed to see the broad, unselfconscious smile that lit her eyes. He wanted to hear again that clear voice, by turns gentle and fierce, and smell the faint hint of jasmine that hung in the air wherever Philomena had been.

At dinner, the table groaned. Mrs. Bramble had spared no effort to provide an irresistible feast. Three complicated courses followed each other to the table, but Hugh could eat none of them. The soup seemed insipid, the fish dry. Turkey and beef accompanied by lark pudding was enough to make anyone ill. Plum pudding tempted for a moment, rich and crumbling, scented with spice and fruit, but every mouthful tasted of dust.

A fire raged in the grate, burning the massive log that would smoulder throughout the holiday. The Dowager's conversation centred on the Queen, Prince Albert and the German features her new husband was introducing to his adoring wife. "Why anyone should wish to emulate that nation," said the Dowager, "I have no idea. Do you know, I heard that Prince Albert insisted on bringing a tree into the house and putting candles all around it? Imagine. How very odd he must be. Our poor Queen surely suffers a great deal from such nonsense."

"Why, no, Mama. Everyone says the Queen simply adores Prince Albert, and that anything he suggests is immediately to be undertaken." Selena spoke to Hugh, looking for agreement. Pushing a morsel of fig around an almost-empty plate, he did not reply.

She turned back to her Mama. "I think it must be fun to have a tree for Christmas, much more fun than our boring old Yule log. All that does is burn away and make a great deal of smoke in the process. What do you think, Hugh?" Selena raised her voice.

Hugh looked up, refocusing his eyes. His thoughts had drifted back to the wood, recalling the scent of the old trees and the magic of the fading light. He imagined Philomena was there, enticing him into taking leave of every vestige of good sense.

Called upon by automatic good manners to answer, Hugh nevertheless found himself unable to offer an opinion on the unknown merits of the Christmas celebrations at Windsor.

He said so, causing Selena to sigh and the Dowager to glare. His mother asked, in an icy voice, whether he had taken cold during such a long sojourn outside this afternoon, undertaken for no reason that could be fathomed.

The Dowager talked on. Hardly listening, Hugh let his thoughts stray again, this time to the nursery. He watched the hands click round on the grandfather clock. They edged in interminably small measures towards the hour when Philomena would bring John down to talk to the Christmas visitors. Did he long for or dread the event?

At last, the meal ended. Since Hugh was the only man dining, the ladies retired for only a few moments, to take tea. Hugh, relieved to be alone, tossed back two large glasses of port, feeling the effect as a briefly pleasing shock of warmth. It failed, though, to overcome his angry mood. He drank one more glass. Two bottles of his most prized claret had accompanied the meal, but Hugh had hardly tasted the wine. His legs, though, shook a little as he joined Selena and the Dowager.

John, when Philomena brought him to see his grandmother, seemed subdued. Selena chuckled. "I do believe we tired him out," she said to Philomena, who smiled through tight lips. Hugh avoided her eye. After a few moments of lack-lustre question and answer, the Dowager gave up the unequal struggle and allowed John to return to the nursery.

Selena seized the opportunity to take Hugh's arm and walk him around the room. "We had such fun, you know. You need not have been cross, because Philomena mended my dress perfectly, so that no one would ever know it was torn at all. She even curled my hair herself so that Alice, my maid, would not scold."

Hugh, despite his mood, smiled a little at his sister's fear of a scolding from her own maid.

"Now, that's better." She gave his arm a little squeeze. "You are so bad-tempered these days. I'm sure you were never so before you married Beatrice—" She stopped, face red, but it was too late.

Hugh shook his arm free and glared. Selena's eyes grew large with horror. Recollecting the need for good manners, Hugh forced himself to smile and pat her hand. How much had she understood of his marriage? Had she seen the depths of unhappiness and discontent at the Hall?

As soon as was polite, he excused himself, leaving the two ladies to amuse themselves as best they could with cards and parlour games. He knew he was behaving badly. Perhaps Beatrice had been right to fling those insults at him, during the last of the seemingly endless string of quarrels. He could remember every angry word they had exchanged.

"I wish I had never allowed Papa to persuade me to marry at all," she had cried, wiping her eyes on a scrap of lace and peeping through lowered lashes. "Indeed, you are quite unfit for polite society. My friends are all so sad on my account, cooped up here so far from London, with hardly any society at all."

"Am I not enough society?" Hugh asked. How far he must be from the dashing husband she had expected.

"All you care about are those ridiculous tenants, who are all so muddy and smelly that it makes me quite unwell when I have to visit their dirty homes. You care nothing for me. Why, any other man would allow balls and parties, and invite all the neighbours."

"You mean, invite that jackass, Muldrow?" Hugh, enraged, took a step towards his wife. "If you think I will encourage that snivelling creature to my house, you are greatly mistaken, Madam. I saw more than enough of the wretch when at Oxford. I have no wish to continue the acquaintance beyond what is necessary."

Beatrice's eyes glinted green. "I do believe you are jealous." She spoke deliberately. Hugh laughed, his voice rough. "I would as likely feel jealousy towards the rats that steal corn from the barns as towards such a deceitful poltroon as Muldrow. If you had seen the man's cruelty towards others, by heaven, you would want nothing of him and be less inclined to spend so much time in his company, I assure you.

"Why, he accused poor Jessop of holding a horse back in races and tried to have the poor lad—" Hugh broke off, biting his lip to keep from setting more of Muldrow's faults before Beatrice. He did not even tell of the suspicion that Muldrow deliberately lamed young Jessop's favourite chestnut the night before the race, so that poor Jessop failed to win the badly needed prize money. The poor boy had to leave the University at the end of the year.

Such reticence mattered little to Beatrice. Hugh saw his exasperation reflected in his wife's face. "I will try to make your life more pleasant," he said, at last, keeping his feelings under control. "Say what you would like."

"I would like to leave this dark and dingy old house and go back to London," Beatrice snapped. "I hate it here. I hate you, this horrid house and everyone in it." She stamped her neat little foot and flounced away to her room, leaving Hugh seething with an impotent fury.

Next morning, Beatrice rode out for the last time.

Hugh's head ached. These memories were no more conducive to happiness than the recollection of his behaviour with Philomena. Too distraught to remain in the house for a moment longer, he made his way to the stables and, in the familiar rhythm of so many evenings, soothed his spirits by settling the horses quietly in the boxes. Thunder's uncomplicated pleasure in his master's presence quietened Hugh's agitation. He gave every horse additional rations, for this was, after all, a holiday, stroked Thunder's nose and leaned awhile on the black stallion's neck.

At last, away from the responsibilities of the Hall, the demands of the family, and the unsettling presence of Philomena, Hugh's head cleared. He must control himself better. His conduct today had been unforgivable. His mother and sister would forgive him.

They always did. Even poor John was used to his angry humours.

But what of Philomena? Hugh groaned. How could that child ever forgive him for forcing such unwanted attentions upon her? He should not have indulged his longings by spending time in the woman's company. As they walked through the fields this morning, Philomena had enchanted him. He had overlooked every lie, needing to trust her. Why had he allowed this ridiculous attachment to an unknown female?

Hugh scrubbed his face with his hands. He would salve his conscience with a kind gesture. He made his way to the kitchen where Mrs. Bramble was busying herself in the larder. "Tonight's meal was delicious. Thank you."

"I am glad your lordship enjoyed it," she said. "I hope the beef was to your lordship's liking. I have asked Mr. Jones to undertake the hanging of the meat, rather than Addison."

The two farmers carried on a long-term rivalry over competing butchery skills. Hugh hardly cared which one currently had the honour of slaughtering cattle from the herd for the dining table, but the welfare of every tenant was important.

"Has Mr. Addison been ill?" he asked.

"No, sir." The cook's lips shut tight.

"Come now, Mrs. Bramble," Hugh said, intrigued. "You must tell me more." He helped himself to a mouthful of one of her famous apple pies.

"Well, now, it's just that Addison's wife has a loose tongue, and I don't like gossip." She shook her head. "That's all I can say."

Hugh said no more, but later, curiosity piqued, he

raised the matter with Martin. "I hear Addison has fallen out of favour with Mrs. Bramble, due, I gather, to a quarrel over some of Mrs. Addison's gossip and nonsense."

"Well, my lord, if you already know all about it, I can see no harm in telling you that those of us here at the Hall told Addison in no uncertain terms that if his wife spread any more tales, he would suffer for it, and that's a fact. There's none of us willing to hear such lies about the family."

Hugh stiffened. "About the family?"

His valet's face turned brick red. "But...but you said you knew, my lord."

"Come on, man, tell me the tale."

Martin's eyes flickered everywhere but towards the master. A clock ticked loudly in the room, and Hugh waited. At last, seeing there was no help for it, the valet swallowed hard. "It's about that terrible day, my lord. Lady Thatcham's death, I mean."

He glanced up at Hugh's face, saw the master's expression and looked down again. "Addison's wife told the post mistress that one of the kitchen maids from Fairview Manor told her she saw Lady Thatcham riding out that morning. She said someone else rode along behind her on a black horse: a black horse like Thunder."

Hugh's breath stopped in his throat. He closed his eyes for a moment. The valet twisted his hands together. "I'm sorry. I wouldn't have mentioned such nonsense, my lord. You know how these old wives talk. Addison won't let her tell any such tales after the drubbing Ince and some of the others gave him; you may be assured of that, my lord."

Hugh, seething, contained his fury in front of Martin, made as light as he could of the matter as no more than ludicrous village gossip and sent the man away. Thank God for the loyalty of his servants.

Chapter Fifteen

Philomena could not sit still next morning, nor control her restless agitation. She had set out on this adventure perfectly sure of her own ability to make a new start in life. She must be her own mistress. The last thing she expected was to find her determination undermined by outrageous feelings.

No man, she had long ago decided, was worth a moment's thought. Her circumstances prevented her from showing any interest in men. After all, the unpleasant fact was that she was already married to an unknown man with cold green eyes, who had remained comfortably out of sight since the wedding, eight years ago. With luck, she would never see him again and would remain entirely free to live a life of hard won independence. Philomena had no fear of hard work and no need of a man's protection. Had she ever felt the slightest wish to consider allowing a man into her life, Joseph's advances would have cured her of such foolishness.

She tucked wilful black curls into her cap, tugging them ruthlessly until her scalp ached. She smoothed down the starched apron. She refused to glance in the mirror. She would not look at the glow that spread over her cheeks whenever she chanced to remember yesterday's scene in the woods. It was anger alone that caused her heart to thunder so, pumping blood through every vein until each fingertip tingled. She would acknowledge no other feeling. It was simple anger she felt as her thoughts returned, despite her best efforts, to those moments in the woods. Lord Thatcham's arms around her had sent that unfamiliar rush of need through an untested body. That had led to a foolish but almost overwhelming yearning to caress the master's face.

Philomena kept her eyes firmly turned away from the scene through the nursery windows, for fear they should betray her by gazing out towards the trees. She did not want to remember. She would certainly not succumb to the kind of foolish weeping that overcame her yesterday. How foolish to cry such bitter tears simply because the rich, spoilt owner of Thatcham Hall had tried to dally with her. No doubt, he behaved so with any servant who took his fancy. Perhaps most would not dare to refuse the advances of such a powerful man.

"Very well, then," Philomena said.

She would forget all about Lord Thatcham. Today was Boxing Day, so both Lord Thatcham and Selena would be absent. They planned to ride out with the Hunt. The Dowager had expressed the intention of visiting neighbours, so would also be away for most of the day. Philomena and John would have no one but the servants for company. She was safe from any encounter with Lord Thatcham.

A new plan insinuated itself into Philomena's thoughts. Lord Thatcham had warned her to keep away from the East Wing. The warning had piqued her interest. What did the man have to hide? His presence was unsettling, even when she could not feel his breath on her face or the beat of his heart. It would be entertaining to find out more about Lord Thatcham.

Philomena shook her head. She must not allow herself to dwell on thoughts of the master. She forced herself, instead, to wonder about his wife. Lord Thatcham grew at times so angry that he might be capable of any wickedness. How mysterious Lady Thatcham's death was. No one would speak about it, even Mrs. Rivers who, no doubt regretting yesterday's loose tongue, had allowed no further gossip to pass her lips.

What if…

Philomena hardly dared to think it, it was such a dreadful notion, but she could not rid her mind of the idea. Could Lord Thatcham have done away with Lady Beatrice? Or, worse still, what if Lady Thatcham was still alive, shut away in a part of the Hall that her cruel husband forbade anyone to enter?

Philomena shook her head. She was being foolish. She had thoroughly enjoyed reading Northanger Abbey, Miss Austen's wonderfully satirical novel that poked fun at a silly young girl's absurd imaginings of terrible deeds. Surely, she had more sense than that untried fictional heroine, Catherine Morland?

Nevertheless, Philomena could not escape the fact that some mystery surrounded Lady Thatcham's death. The longer she thought about it, the more convinced she became that Beatrice's widowed husband, Lord Thatcham, had something to hide. If that was so, then clearly the East Wing of the Hall held the key to the mystery. He had made such a point of forbidding a visit there that the East Wing must surely contain something truly dreadful.

There was only one way to find out the truth. While Lord Thatcham and the other members of the family were away, Philomena would make an excuse and visit the East Wing. She would be quite safe while the master was out, riding across the fields. She would discover every guilty secret and make the man pay for his wickedness.

She giggled with excitement. She had said she wanted adventures: well, here was one right in front of her. Unravelling a mystery would be the perfect way to forget that unsettling encounter with the master of the house yesterday. The mystery of Beatrice, the missing wife, seemed to reach out and beg Philomena to solve it. Such a venture would clear away every trace of restlessness. Of course, she cared nothing for Lord Thatcham. She simply found him unbearable, arrogant and proud. She would discover his guilty secrets and humble him before her.

She supervised John over breakfast: a hearty spread of eggs, bacon and kidneys, washed down with plenty of milk and followed by warm muffins smothered with butter and jam. No wonder the boy was so sturdy and strong. Replenished by the food, the child's energy levels soared.

He would not concentrate on books, drawing or quiet filigree work. "Can we go out?"

Indoor activity was not likely to calm such energetic liveliness and so Philomena, feeling equally restless, agreed to take the boy walking into the village while she considered the plan of revenge on his father.

First, they descended to the Servants' Hall where the upper members of the indoor staff, the butler, housekeeper, cook and ladies' maids, were finishing their own morning repast. "Good morning, Master John," they chorused, and rose to their feet. John chuckled and trotted through into the kitchen, quickly homing in on Ivy, the kitchen maid, grinning at her and demanding cake. None of the kitchen staff was ever able to refuse him anything, so he seemed assured of success.

Philomena took his hand firmly. "I think not," she said with a smile. John looked up, his face turning red, prepared to demand his rights. Philomena raised her eyebrows and frowned. The fierce expression left him in no doubt that the nurse would confiscate anything he managed to extort from Ivy, so, reluctantly, he gave up.

"Master John and I will visit the village, this morning," Philomena told the cook, who nodded approvingly at the new nursemaid's command of the young master. "I wondered if there were any messages we could undertake for you."

Ivy sighed. "I wish I could come along with you," she said, her voice shrill with complaint. "It ain't fair. There are that many pots to wash I'm sure my hands will shrivel away, and I won't have a half day off to walk around the village for over a week."

"Now, be quiet, Ivy," said Mrs. Bramble. "You know what your job is, and it's no good aping your betters."

"She ain't my betters," muttered Ivy.

Mrs. Bramble pretended she had not heard and offered Philomena a list of items for purchase in the village.

"Maybe you'll see the Hunt," offered Ivy, regaining a degree of good humour in spite of Mrs. Bramble's set down. "They do say that the Master is gone out looking for that Mr. Muldrow, to teach him a lesson."

The cook gasped. "How dare you speak like that, Ivy? You don't know what you're talking about, and it's none of your business anyway."

She leaned forward to hiss at the girl. "Especially with Master John so close by." In a normal voice, Mrs. Bramble went on, "You get on with those pots and don't leave any rings around them, neither, or you'll be washing up all day."

"Yes, Mrs. Bramble." Ivy sighed and fell silent.

"Don't you take no notice of her," Mrs. Bramble advised Philomena, handing over a wicker basket for the shopping. "Young Ivy listens to a lot of gossip in the village from people who know no better. I'm sure I don't know what they've been a-saying."

The cook could not quite meet Philomena's eyes. She fumbled with cloths and pots as if something was amiss. Philomena frowned. The mystery deepened. What had Mr. Muldrow to do with Lord Thatcham?

Thoughtful, she set a brisk pace towards the village. John pulled away, thrusting his stout stick into the hedgerows, chasing after imaginary rabbits and weasels. Philomena was left free to follow some intriguing thoughts. Who were the Muldrows? What deed of Arthur Muldrow's had so displeased Lord Thatcham that he deserved a lesson? Mrs. Bramble's reaction left Philomena in no doubt that Ivy had been telling the truth. It added to the growing certainty that the master of the Hall was possessed of a guilty secret connected to the mysterious disappearance of Lady Thatcham.

Their walk took them first to the Post Office where

Philomena made an effort to establish the story of a fictional uncle in Bristol. "Has a letter been delivered for me?" she enquired, writing her name on a piece of paper.

Lord Thatcham had commanded that she provide a letter to this mythical uncle. In order to support the story of her flight to Bristol, she had felt compelled to comply. Despite a few moments hesitation and some scratching of the head, she had relished the challenge of writing to a non-existent relative, taking care to avoid any hint that the whole letter was a farrago of nonsense, in case it should fall into the wrong hands.

The direction of the note had given her cause to think hard, for she had no idea of the names of streets in Bristol. In the end, she had crossed her fingers and directed the letter to Number 6 Baker Street. Surely, every city must have a street where bakers sold bread. James, the footman, under instruction from Lord Thatcham, had taken the letter for franking and dispatch. Philomena maintained the pretence of eagerly awaited a reply and spent some time discussing the tardy arrival of the post with the postmistress.

This was a dumpy little woman with a bun of white hair tied tightly at the back of her neck. John decided to spend the morning "helping" her. The kind soul dealt patiently with an endless stream of childish questions.

"What's that for?" John pointed to the brass scales.

"I weigh the letters to see how much they cost to post," the postmistress replied.

"How does it work? Can I do it?" While John fiddled happily with the weights, he kept up a running stream of commentary. "This one is only little, this one is big. I can put this letter on and this one and this one and then it all falls down."

The postmistress was enchanted. She leaned comfortably against the wooden counter to relish in full the chance to talk to the newest occupant of the Hall. "I hear you were one of those poor souls that fell out of the train. It's all in this newspaper, here."

Philomena spread out a copy of The Times, wrinkled with use. *Frightful Accident*, it said, *on Great Western Railway*. Philomena shivered. She took the paper and scanned it. Several people had died. A knot of anxiety tied itself in her stomach. The accident in all its noise and terror haunted her, the memory returning several times a day, complete with flashes of light and the acrid smell of smoke whenever she closed her eyes.

Which of the labourers who had sat near to her in the wagon had died? She felt sick. She pressed sticky palms, damp with sweat, against the counter and willed her breathing to return to normal.

The postmistress, excited by the drama of the accident, noticed nothing amiss. "We've never known such a thing in these parts, not since…" She leaned close to Philomena and glanced round quickly to make sure John was too busy to hear. Lining up the brass weights like soldiers on the counter, he had no interest in the adult conversation. "Not since Lady Thatcham fell from that horse last year and killed herself," the postmistress went on. "And what Lord Thatcham's wife can have been about, riding alone in the early morning before anyone else was around, I will never know. And her, a lady of quality. They do say," she whispered even lower, her voice hardly audible. "They do say that Lady Beatrice was running away, and, what's more, someone was chasing her." Stepping back, the postmistress reverted to a more normal tone and finished happily. "And of course, that was only one dead body." The current disaster, comprising as it did the death of eight or nine unfortunate mortals, quite eclipsed the wonder of Lady Thatcham's demise.

The postmistress followed Philomena out the door, still talking about the poor dead people and the terrible danger posed by those new steam trains until Philomena, once more in control of her emotions, wondered if the woman planned to walk with her all the way back up the hill to the Hall.

The air was still cold, with a north wind returning after the calm of Christmas day. The wind cut sharply through Philomena's clothes and she hustled John along at a rapid pace. They must reach home before he became chilled. She did not wish to anger the Dowager by returning late. She did not want to endanger her plan for that evening, by attracting the Dowager's notice.

As she walked, Philomena put the final touches to the plan. Her heart beat fast with anticipation. She intended to explore the East Wing this very evening, as soon as John slept.

She must satisfy her curiosity. Lord Thatcham had told her not to take John there, and she would obey that command, but nothing would prevent Philomena from venturing to the East Wing alone. Perhaps she would find a hidden clue to the mysterious disappearance of Lady Thatcham. There were a host of possibilities, any one of which could be true. Philomena would not worry about the postmistress's version. The woman was obviously fond of gossip, the more unlikely the better. Lady Thatcham may not be dead at all. Perhaps the young bride lived tragically alone, locked away in the

East Wing in the care of an old retainer.

More possibilities sprang to Philomena's fertile mind. Perhaps Lord Thatcham used the wing for other purposes. She had heard whispers in London of shocking Hellfire Clubs. It seemed that bored members of the aristocracy had instigated these clubs many years ago solely for the purposes of drinking, carousing with women and worse.

Philomena had heard that their motto was "do what thou wilt" and that they took part in devilish practices. Lord Thatcham was just such a man as might belong to a Hellfire Club. When his eyebrows rose sardonically and his eyes gleamed dark, Philomena could believe the man capable of any devilishness.

She imagined the forbidding Lord Thatcham indulging in all kinds of wickedness in the darkness of the East Wing, where his sister and mother would never venture and where no lights shone from the windows. Philomena's hands flew to her burning cheeks. Horrified by her own thoughts, she shivered. She had to find out. Tonight, she must discover the secret of the East Wing.

Chapter Sixteen

The Boxing Day hunt promised a great run, with clear skies and a bite to the air. Excited horses tossed their heads and the stirrup cup circulated rapidly, in preparation for the horn that would signal the start of the day's ride.

As Hugh swallowed a tot of brandy, a narrow-shouldered grey, sloppily ridden by a red-faced farmer, barged carelessly into Thunder. Hugh's horse, in the peak of condition and excited by the prospect of a good run, backed nervously, and Hugh needed all his skill to control the animal without dropping the silver cup.

Turning to acknowledge loud apologies from the rider behind him, Hugh came face to face with Arthur Muldrow. Sick from the gossip Martin had passed on last night, and well aware that Muldrow was most likely to have started the rumours, Hugh felt his fingers itch. He would love to use his whip on the snivelling rogue. He held back, though, teeth clamped together with frustration. Any reaction to the gossip passed on to the village by Muldrow's household would only add to its power. Hugh had no alternative but to ignore what he had heard. One day, though, he would teach Muldrow a lesson.

Rigid in the saddle, he nodded slightly, and moved away. Muldrow grinned.

Hugh noticed Raincloud, Selena's gentle grey

mare, trotting quietly towards Muldrow. He hesitated. He could interrupt and forbid his sister to have anything to do with the man, but that would make a scene. The eyes of the hunt bored into his back. Had everyone present heard the tales?

Hugh held his tongue. He would offer up no more snippets of gossip to the neighbourhood. Selena would come to no harm from Muldrow on the hunting field today, surrounded on all sides by farmers and landowners and in clear view of the hunt followers. Hugh need not spoil his sister's day. He put his worries to one side in order to concentrate on guiding the excited horse.

The day's gallop left him refreshed. Returning home, ravenously hungry, he was pleased to see a mountain of food weighing down the dining table. "Ah. Mince pies." He chewed and swallowed with enthusiasm.

"Well," said the Dowager. "I am pleased to see you so cheerful, Hugh. Let us hope such good humour may continue."

Hugh bowed his head. He enquired politely about the Dowager's day. The railway accident and the forthcoming inquest had featured high on the list of topics for her morning visits, and she had taken care to read the full story in the newspaper. With great pleasure and, no doubt, to the irritation of her hostess, Hugh's mother had explained the event, in detail, to her acquaintance. The Hall, after all, had taken in one of the poor passengers from the disaster, raising the Dowager to the status of insider and unique source of information. Hugh was relieved, though not surprised, to find that no hint of gossip about Beatrice's death had spoiled his mother's day. No one would dare to raise such a matter with the formidable Dowager.

"You know," she said. "Perhaps we should invite that young woman to remain at the Hall a while. We would not want any harm to befall such an unfortunate soul through sending her away too soon."

The Dowager's attitude towards the new nursemaid appeared to have undergone something of a transformation. Was it due to Philomena's role in the accident? Perhaps it was simply John's improved conduct under her guidance. Hugh could not decide whether he was pleased or not.

While he considered how to reply, Selena broke in. "Oh, Hugh, do agree to ask Philomena to stay on. John does like her so, and Mama is right. It would be so unkind to send her away before she has had time to recover from the terrible shock of the train crash. After all, everyone knows the Hall is in the healthiest situation in the whole country."

Hugh, unwilling to argue, agreed. "As you wish."

"Well, brother. I have never before known you to give way so quickly to any request I might make."

"I have more important things on my mind than the nursemaid."

He paused. Selena's cheeks were pink. "My concerns involve you," he said, as mildly as possible.

Selena blushed. "Me?" She said it so innocently that Hugh suspected his sister had an idea of his intentions.

"I would prefer you to spend less time in conversation with Mr. Muldrow," said Hugh. Selena's face grew pale.

Before she could reply, however, the Dowager

roused herself to add her opinion, waving an admonishing finger at her daughter. "We are polite to the Muldrows, but no more than that. Remember that our house and title have been in the family since they were awarded at the Battle of Thatcham." She nodded for emphasis and the feathers in her turban trembled. "The Muldrows are upstarts, using money earned in the dust and unpleasantness of cotton mills to supplant their betters. So many old houses have fallen into the wrong hands of late. Do you not remember our friend, poor Elizabeth Woodbridge? She was so sad to leave Bushey House."

The Dowager's eyes twinkled as she recalled the distress of her dear friend, Lady Woodbridge, at the loss of her husband's fortune. "Your brother is right to warn you against such a low family, Selena."

Hugh sipped from his glass, his fingers rigid on the delicate stem. How could his mother set his motives down to snobbishness and pride? "No, Mama." He kept his tone carefully even. "I have no objection to Mr. Muldrow on account of his forbears. His father worked hard and deserves the place he earned in society and I, for one, am happy to receive the elder Mr. Muldrow at any time."

The Dowager sniffed.

"However," Hugh went on, pretending he had not heard. "I heartily dislike his son Arthur…" He hesitated. He would not speak Beatrice's name along with that of Muldrow. He must find another reason to forbid Selena's acquaintance with the man. "Since our days in Oxford," he finished.

"He behaved most unkindly towards a young friend. I mistrust the man and wish Selena to choose her acquaintances more carefully."

"Well…" Selena had sat for an unusually long period in silence, though three fingers tapped on the table impatiently. Her voice quivered passionately. "I will have you know, brother, that I will not submit to your every whim. Do you not recall that it was Beatrice who introduced Arthur Muldrow?" She ignored the Dowager's gasp of horror and narrowed her eyes at Hugh.

Her brother winced. Selena so rarely spoke of Beatrice. Although she had seen little of the marriage, Hugh was certain his sister had been aware, from the schoolroom, of his misery.

"Beatrice was quite content that I should make Mr. Muldrow's acquaintance," Selena continued, her face defiant, "and her family was at least the equal of ours, and moreover one with more extensive lands and—and properties." She stammered into silence at the expression on her brother's face.

Hugh rose to his feet. "Remember you are in my house," he growled through clenched teeth. He grasped the back of the chair, knuckles white against the polished mahogany. "I will not have that man in my house or near to members of this family. If you, sister, choose to speak further with Mr. Muldrow, I must insist you cut short this Christmas holiday. Perhaps you have a friend to whom you may wish to pay a visit."

Leaving his mother and sister open-mouthed, Hugh stalked from the room, turning at the door to remark, "Obey me, Selena, and you may remain here as long as you wish. I will leave you to decide. Good evening, Mama."

He glared so fiercely at James, who moved to close

the door that the footman stopped dead, allowing Hugh to pull the heavy oak together with a resounding and satisfactory thud.

There was no sign of any other servant nearby. Understanding that discretion was usually wise during moments of family dissent, both James and the butler found employment discreetly downstairs, behind the baize door. Hugh passed unmolested through the house. He needed to be alone. He strode up stairs and along corridors, desperate to relieve today's riot of feelings with a spell of solitary peace and quiet.

Chapter Seventeen

Once back at the Hall, Philomena fought to stay calm. *I won't think about him.* Instead, she planned the evening's trip to the East Wing. This was her chance. John was tired from a day in the fresh air and happy to play quietly with Alice. No one would notice Philomena's absence for half an hour. Alice, relieved of full responsibility in the nursery, assured Philomena she could easily manage the boy for an hour or two. She seemed happy to remain in the cosy nursery for a while longer and avoid other, harder duties downstairs.

Philomena took a lamp and checked the wick and the oil level. She had no wish to be plunged into sudden darkness in the east wing. All was well. Casting a final glance at John, playing happily, she slipped out of the nursery and set off along the corridor that traversed the length of the house.

Rows of closed doors, blank and intimidating, lined the passage. Determined to ignore foolish fears so early in the adventure, Philomena tried a handle, curious to see inside the room. The handle turned easily and opened without a sound. There was little to see but outlines of heavy oak furniture shrouded in dustsheets. The room lay silent, with a depressed air of desolation, as though lonely from a lack of visitors.

Impatient with such a fanciful idea, Philomena pasted a smile on her face. *As if a room could have thoughts*. She eased the door shut and continued, heading east, past door after door of deserted rooms. She shook her head. What a waste of space. So many families at home shared lodgings, five or six to a room. How comfortable they could all be in the Hall where there was space enough, it seemed, for half of London.

She met no one. The corridor ended at last. Yet another closed door barred her route. Suddenly nervous, Philomena ran her tongue over dry lips. What lay beyond? The only way to find out was to open the door, yet she hesitated.

The adventure seemed suddenly more serious. What if there really was something horrible in the East Wing? Perhaps her wild imaginings were right. Lord Thatcham's wife might exist, hidden, behind this door. Philomena's stomach fluttered. She paused a moment longer, bracing herself. She listened, one ear to the door, but heard nothing. The silence was more chilling than any amount of ghostly shrieks and groans.

She shivered. The hairs on the back of her neck rose. Someone, or something, was watching her from behind. She froze. *There's nothing there*. Still, Philomena's flesh crept. She fought against terror, one hand on her mouth, until she could bear it no longer. She must look round or she would scream.

Fearful, trying to move without a sound, she half-turned, eyes wide in the gloom. A point of light to her left moved. She knew it. There was someone there.

The lamp flickered as her hand shook. The beam moved. She held her wrist steady and the glimmer of light was still. She moved again and the light shifted. She released a gust of pent-up breath in a sigh.

How ridiculous. The beam was no more than a

reflection of her lamp. Its beam reflected in each of a row of huge mirrors that lined the passageway. Her own face glowed, wraith-like, above it. She blushed. Imagine being scared by a mirror.

Steadying herself, for her pounding heart threatened to jump straight out of her chest, Philomena took a firmer grip on the lamp, reached her hand out to the door and pushed, hard.

Nothing happened. The door yielded neither to her tentative push nor to a twist of the handle. She could not get through. *It's locked.* She rattled the handle, wincing at the noise. No. It would not open. She would have to return to the safety of the nursery.

Slowly, her heartbeat returned to normal. Resigned to defeat, she turned to retreat when a glint of metal shining on the lintel above the door caught her eye. She stretched high to feel along the ledge with the tips of shaking fingers.

Her fingers encountered something cold and hard. Philomena flicked at it, and a key clattered to the floor. The noise resounded like a thunderclap and she flinched. For a count of ten, she held her breath and rubbed her fingertips together. They were clean. The lintel was quite free from dust. Someone had been here recently.

She slid the key into the lock. It turned without resistance and the door swung open. Moving fast, she stepped inside and closed the door. Now, she could not go back. This was the forbidden East Wing. She held the lamp high to light the way. A flight of stairs spiralled upwards, narrowing as it turned. The light sputtered as her hand trembled. She tiptoed on the wood of the stairway, trying to make no sound, listening all the while for danger.

At a turn on the stairs was a small window. Philomena squinted through into the darkness. In the moonlight, she made out the shapes of the trees in the wood. Sensations flooded back. Over there, Lord Thatcham had clasped her to him. Her lip quivered. Why had he been so cruel? He had treated her like a toy designed for his selfish pleasure.

She grew hot with shame. She had not protested for long moments as she cherished each new sensation. Had he noticed? She brushed the thought aside. She had no time to waste. She was on the brink of discovering Lord Thatcham's guilty secret. The arrogant man deserved a lesson.

A few more steps took Philomena to a low doorway set in a turn of the stairs. She tried the handle. It turned with ease, and the heavy oak door creaked open. She grimaced.

This was the moment. It took a few seconds to gather her resolve. Inside this room, hidden from the rest of the Hall, was the evidence of Lord Thatcham's guilt. Philomena stood tall, lifted her chin and stepped boldly inside.

An eerie glow lit the sparsely furnished room. A line of tables marched along the centre of the room. In the strange light, Philomena saw a set of rough wooden shelves, an old, well-used armchair and a plain stool. Leather bound books lay in heaps on one of the tables, near to a small reading light. One was open, the pages covered in diagrams. A second table held a brown wooden box, about ten inches long and seven inches high, and a mirror covered the entire surface of a third. Rows of opaque glass jars in blue and red lined the shelves.

Philomena hardly registered the contents of the room, though, for the source of the strange light caught her attention. She tilted her head backwards and gazed, entranced, for the ceiling was perfectly round and constructed, as far as she could tell, completely of glass. Through the glass, the sky glowed with the light of a thousand stars like fireflies. They lit the winter night and illuminated the room with a ghostly glow that outshone the light from the lantern.

Transfixed, her purpose forgotten, Philomena drank in the beauty of the night sky. She had seen star configurations in Samuel's books, and she recognised one or two. There was the hunter, with three stars for a belt, and nearby, the plough, leading the way to the North Star. Philomena felt dizzy and a little faint. This was beyond anything she had expected.

Her legs gave way and she dropped onto a stool. What had she found? Was the room some strange chamber where secret societies carried out dreadful deeds? Indeed, there were levers and hooks against one of the walls; she could not imagine what use they could possibly have. She shuddered, her head full of fancies of capture and torment. For a few moments, imagination took over. Common sense, though, was not far behind.

This was foolish. There was nothing here to frighten anyone. Philomena stood up. The room was just another puzzle. The time had come to forget her fears and solve it. She picked up the wooden box from the table in the centre of the room and turned it around, peering at every surface. She spotted a wooden disc to one side. She twisted it and it unscrewed without resistance. A glass lens shimmered in the silvery light from the sky. So that was it: a camera.

How could she have been such a ninny? She was in no danger. The mystery solved and her confidence returned, Philomena stepped across the room to investigate a vast iron handle. It shifted at her touch. Levers whispered and a wooden ceiling glided across, inch by inch, hiding the night sky. Now, only her lantern penetrated the dark of the strange room. She waited for her eyes to adjust to the gloom.

"What do you mean by this?"

Philomena leaped in the air and turned, terrified. Lord Thatcham, tall and menacing, glowered at her from the doorway, his eyes ablaze with fury.

Chapter Eighteen

Hugh bit back an explosion of anger. Of all places, this woman had chosen to invade his precious sanctuary, the one place he expected to find tranquillity. Philomena gasped and stumbled, colliding with the nearest table. A pile of precious books teetered a moment and three heavy volumes crashed to the floor, spines splayed and pages creased.

"Oh," the woman squeaked. Trembling, she stooped to fumble with the largest of the books. "I hope it is not damaged. No, look, I am sure it is not." She held out the book. Her hands trembled.

Hugh grasped the volume and watched, eyes narrowed, as Philomena edged away, further and further, until her back rested against the wall. She raised her eyes. Enormous as dark pebbles, they glowed in the ghostly pallor of her face.

Angry words faded from Hugh's tongue, and his fury shrivelled at the child's look of fear. "You are afraid of me?"

She shook her head but the blue eyes widened further and her lip trembled. She caught it between white teeth.

Hugh's anger ebbed away. This child really was the most ridiculous person he had ever met. "Now, I wonder why you are so scared." He made an effort to speak quietly. "Perhaps you are frightened because I warned you not to come here?" He took a step forward. Her hands flew into the air, poised to fight. Hugh stopped. Her terror was real.

"I-I am not at all afraid," she stammered.

"Well, you should be. Did I not tell you to stay away from the East Wing?"

She nodded.

"Then, why did you disobey me?" How reasonable he sounded. "This is my house, is it not? I explained that there are rules you must obey while you are here." Still, she said nothing. He lost patience. "Well, it seems you have discovered my secret."

Her eyes flickered and with a start, Hugh understood.

"I do believe you have been listening to the talk in the village." He closed his eyes. Would his reputation never recover? Muldrow's cunning lies had spread like poison through the village, but Hugh could not explain the truth of Beatrice's deception. Only he knew of her desertion. She had run to Muldrow, in spite of her marriage vows.

She had been kind enough to leave a letter for Hugh. Her words haunted him. "I will show you that someone appreciates me, even though you do not." He'd torn the letter into a dozen pieces and threw them on the fire, but the words burned themselves forever into his brain. He had not harmed Beatrice, but his failure as a husband had driven her into the arms of a scoundrel. Her flight had ended in tragedy.

Hugh took Philomena's arm. She flinched and he dropped his hand. Regret weighed heavy on him. "I see you have heard that Lady Beatrice died at my hands." His voice was flat.

He waited for the child to cry or run or perhaps to plead. To his surprise, she did none of those things. She shook her head, once. She still trembled.

"It is no use to deny it, for I see that you have heard such rumours," Hugh went on, harsh with bitterness. He had no defence except the truth, but to explain would destroy Beatrice's reputation. He turned away and thrust the door wide. "Be off with you," he said. "You need not fear me." Philomena did not move. Her trembling ceased.

Slowly, she raised her eyes and looked Hugh full in the face, a puzzled frown playing between her eyes.

"Well? Will you not escape while you may?"

"I am sorry," she said at last.

"Sorry?" Hugh was puzzled. "Sorry you disobeyed me?"

She grinned. "Of course I should not have done so, my lord, but that is not why I am sorry. I am ashamed. I am afraid I listened to wicked and ridiculous gossip, which was quite stupid of me." A dimple appeared in each cheek. "Just because you are bad-tempered and proud and think everyone beneath you, and seem to have disliked your wife and take hardly any notice of your son, it does not mean you had anything to do with your wife's death. Of course, you did not. No one could think so."

Hugh's jaw dropped. No one ever dared to speak to him like that. He opened his mouth but had to clear his throat before any words would come. This was beyond anything. Yet, she did not think him guilty or wicked. The child was scared of him, but still, she smiled. Her smile was delightful.

"Do not be afraid that I will repeat my behaviour of

earlier today. I hope you will forgive me. I treated you extremely badly. I am sad to hear that, because of my ill-mannered conduct, you find me—er, what was it you said? Bad-tempered? Proud?" He tried and failed to hold back a smile. "By the way, I thank you for your kindness and I am pleased to assure you that I am not, in fact, a murderer."

"I think that the excitements of the past few days overcame us both today, when we were in the woods," she said. "We were very foolish and both to blame."

Hugh detected a trace of mischief in her dimples. "Ah, but I see in your face that you blame me the more, for I am the master of the house and should know better. Is that not so?"

She paused, thoughtful. "No. As the master of Thatcham Hall, you are accustomed to take anything you desire. I believe it is well accepted that wealthy persons such as you wield considerable power over lesser mortals such as I."

Hugh frowned. "You are clever with your tongue. You pretend to forgive me but berate me instead. I do not like this talk of 'such as you' and 'such as I'. The world is changing. Those you would call 'such as you'—I mean, myself and other members of the aristocracy who are wealthy in both name and land— must work as hard as any labourer to maintain our way of life."

He paused. "Will you not sit and talk a while?" he asked on impulse, settling into the armchair. Philomena perched on one of the stools, hands folded on her lap. Such an attitude reminded Hugh of a robin, hopping bravely near a gardener, poised to take flight at any moment. He sighed. "Now, I am become ungentlemanly for allowing you to sit on a stool while I, true to my custom of taking what I desire, sit in comfort. I will move." He put out a foot, pulled over a stool and sat on it, a few inches from Philomena. "Now we are equal and comfortable," he said, watching her relax. "Now you may say whatever you wish to me."

Despite the nonsensical talk of 'you' and 'I' and the child's insistence on their social differences, Hugh wanted to stay with her. She was neither a grand lady of the kind who moved in his familiar circles, nor a simple village girl looking for work in service in a great house. She differed, even, from the scores of well-to-do wives and daughters of merchants, doctors or lawyers. Her dignity intrigued him. He must understand her better.

Her beauty alone did not account for her charm. Who, watching those dimples play about her cheeks or seeing her white teeth peep between the rose of her lips as she smiled, could fail to feel a lift of the heart and a rush of sudden, naked desire?

Hugh felt that hunger for her now. His head swam. She spoke, but he hardly heard what she said. After a moment, she stopped talking and smiled at him, blinking a little as though shy. He shook his head. "I'm sorry," he said, softly. "I was distracted. What did you say?"

She hesitated. "I pray you, my lord, do not be angry if I ask you this, but I have been placed in charge of your son and so I must know. Do you dislike him?"

Hugh gaped. Startled, he rose and paced the floor, his highly polished boots jangling and clanking. "Dislike him?" he barked. "My own son? What can you mean?"

"Oh." Philomena sighed. "I knew you would

become angry again."

Hugh clenched his fists. "I am not angry." He struggled to keep control of himself, though he longing to throw a book at the woman's head. "No, I am surprised...shocked, in fact. How dare you speak to me like that?" He glared.

Philomena's face hardly changed. She remained calm and serious, as though discussing an important debating point.

Hugh's rage subsided. "In fact..." It was hot in the room. Hugh ran a finger around his collar. "I suppose you may be forgiven. Perhaps I gave you a wrong impression. I can assure you, however, that your charge is as dear to me as...as ..."

Words were insufficient to describe Hugh's feelings for John. How to explain the mix of guilt and love that threatened to choke him whenever he saw the boy, no matter what mischief the child had committed?

"I will be honest," Hugh said at last, speaking slowly and painfully, stretching his legs before him as he subsided on to his stool. "Since my wife died, I have found it difficult to—I have not been able to..." He paused, searching again for words.

How could he describe his feelings to Philomena, when he was hardly sure of them himself? He wanted to be with his son. He loved John, but when they were together an emotion Hugh could not name threatened to overwhelm him. So often, the sight of the boy's face made his heart sink, his chest contract and his palms sweat with something very like fear. It was easier to avoid the boy and leave him to nursemaids and servants. They did not see John's dead mother staring straight out of the boy's eyes, accusing Hugh of lacking the capacity for love.

"He reminds me of his mother," Hugh said at last, so softly that Philomena leaned forward to catch the words. Her face did not change. Hugh searched for signs of disgust and revulsion but her expression remained calm. He swallowed hard. A silence stretched between them that threatened never to end.

With nothing left to say, Hugh waited, until at last, Philomena spoke. "Perhaps you will come to the nursery now, to see John before he sleeps? I am sure he will be leading Alice a merry dance and may not even have changed into his night clothes." Philomena held Hugh's eyes. "And perhaps, tomorrow, you could show him something of your experiments in this room. It is called a camera obscura, I believe."

Hugh, shocked, looked around his sanctuary. Imagine John careering wildly around the room. On the brink of a vehement refusal, he caught a spark of amusement in Philomena's eyes. "If you think John will find it of interest. I will show you both how to take photographs with this new camera."

John was tidying his toys as Hugh followed Philomena in to the nursery. He looked sideways at Philomena. "Are you pleased with me, Miss 'Mena? Alice said you would be pleased if I made the room spick and span." He frowned. "Although, I do not know what spick and span means."

"It means neat and tidy," said Philomena, "and you have made this room very spick and span indeed. I am pleased with you and so is your father, no doubt."

John looked up at Hugh and beamed, pink with delight. "I am a good boy, today, Papa."

Hugh strode across and picked up his son. "Miss

Philomena thought you might like a special story tonight. I know a very scary tale, full of monsters and dragons."

John wriggled with pleasure. "Lots of dragons, Papa, please, and swords. I won't be frightened with you and Miss 'Mena here."

As Hugh wove the story, he watched Philomena from the corner of his eye. She busied herself with folding John's clothes. Perhaps she had forgiven him for his conduct in the wood, although his recollection made Hugh writhe. He would never make such a mistake again.

Philomena's arrival at the Hall with such big eyes, so sharp a tongue and a cheerful, ready laugh had shaken the foundations of Hugh's life, just when he had thought them secure. He had no idea who or what the strange female could be. She had arrived on a stormy night like a stray child of the wind and proceeded to entrance the master of Thatcham Hall. She had grasped his heart in her small, strong hands and would not let go.

Hugh had fought his own desires, taking refuge in rank and position, but the newcomer matched him, word for word. A spark of joy had found its way back into Hugh's soul.

Philomena was happy to stroll companionably beside the owner of the Hall, berate him for his wealth and disobey his express commands. Every time Hugh saw her, all control over his feelings slipped away.

Philomena's dimples were fascinating. Her mouth was too wide and wickedly inviting, and those unruly dark curls bobbed too jauntily. Her face had begun to haunt Hugh at the most inappropriate moments. This morning, his agent had had to speak three times before his master answered. At the man's puzzled frown, Hugh had pulled himself together, but he could not banish that dear face from his thoughts. He wanted Philomena to stay, despite the differences of fortune, position and breeding that lay between them. Could she possibly feel the same way?

Tonight, Hugh had felt almost sure she cared for him in return. Such warmth shone from her eyes. His heart soared when she smiled. Perhaps, it was not cold and dead, after all. Philomena had managed to break through the armour of icy steel that frustration and guilt had wrapped around him.

If only she would tell him the truth. Why would she not disclose the true reason for her flight from London? Hugh shivered as an icy trickle of something like fear ran down his back. Was there something truly terrible in Philomena's past? What could such a young person have done? Surely, in the light of their new understanding, she could tell him. If not, how could he dare to trust her?

She moved around John's room, smiling at the bedtime story with that irresistible, too-wide mouth, her face gentle and tender. Perhaps Hugh put too much emphasis on truth. After all, he had told no one the true story of Beatrice's betrayal. He had secrets. Why should Philomena not? She believed Hugh innocent of any crime, despite the rumours and gossip that swirled around the village. Whatever her secret might be, it could be no worse than those lies. If Philomena could show faith in Hugh, perhaps he should trust her in return.

Chapter Nineteen

Philomena and John clattered downstairs. John insisted on a daily visit to the kitchen in search of the company of the admiring servants and the possibility of getting greedy fingers on forbidden titbits of food. The kitchen, as always, was a-bustle with activity. To Philomena's eyes, new to life in a country house, it seemed that the staff undertook each day a carefully planned dance. It had no beginning and no end, but each person knew his or her steps and performed them neatly, weaving intricate patterns on the ground.

The dancers accompanied their own steps.

"Ivy, take care with that dish."

"Mrs. Bramble, her Ladyship would like an extra muffin this morning, if you please."

"Where do you think you might be going with that tray before you've laid it properly?"

The dance paused when John entered and the rhythm changed. The young master became the centre of attention. Once he had been offered a variety of treats, and had selected bread and honey, the relentless stream of daily tasks continued.

James strolled graciously across to speak to Philomena. A young man of above medium height and with a strong build, his dark good looks suited the position of footman in a great country house. His brains were not up to the standard of his appearance, but since he spent much of his day standing in the hall looking handsome, opening doors and handing letters on silver salvers, intellect did not matter. He sometimes unbent enough to chase John round the yard, an activity that usually ended with John in a puddle. At that moment, James would make himself scarce to avoid a scolding.

Today, however, a smug smile played across the footman's face. "You will be pleased with me, *Miss* Philomena." James always emphasised the "Miss." He liked to remind the newcomer of her undignified first appearance in the kitchen, dressed in man's clothes.

"Why, what have you done?" she asked.

"Ah." James coughed, summoning his wits in readiness to tell the story. "You gave me the letter and I took it for posting." Philomena waited, but the footman appeared to have come to a halt.

She saw he could not continue without encouragement. "That's right." Her voice was level, like the one she used with John.

"Ah," James said again.

Philomena wondered if he would ever get to the point. She nodded, helpfully.

"It had your uncle's address on it," James continued with a rush, beaming at the progress of the story.

Philomena nodded again, fearful of interrupting the sudden flow.

"I gave it to that old friend of yours who came yesterday while you were away." James delivered the blow with a smile, quite unaware of its devastating effect on Philomena.

"My friend?" she gasped. "Here?"

James nodded. "Short little fellow, said he was a

friend of yours. Can't recall the name. Jacob, was it? Joshua? Something of that nature?"

"Joseph?"

"That was it." James slapped the table with the palm of his hand, triumphant. "Joseph, that was the name, by Jove. Said he'd come to visit you."

James leaned towards Philomena and winked. "But I had his measure. You never mentioned no friend, and so when he asked if you was here, I thought to myself, James, I thought, don't you go giving Miss Philomena away. Maybe she don't like this chap. Weaselly kind of fellow, he was. Not good enough for our Miss Philomena. So I said as how you'd already gone west." James beamed.

Philomena reached up on tiptoe and threw her arms around him, weak with relief. "James, you are an absolute treasure. Tell me again."

Slowly, pausing now and then to make sure he got it right, James told the full story. Joseph had appeared at the kitchen door asking for Philomena by name and had given a good description. He asked James where she was and James, thinking astonishingly fast, pretended she had left the Hall. Philomena was astonished at the footman's display of quick wits. She was tempted to kiss his cheek. With one masterstroke, he had safeguarded her deception and sent Joseph off on a wild goose chase.

Philomena ran her hand affectionately along the old stone of the kitchen wall, as the pounding of her heart slowly died down. How ridiculous she had been to worry. All the danger of discovery had passed, thanks to James. She could stay here.

Today she had a rare afternoon to herself. The

Dowager and Selena wished to take John to visit some of their acquaintance. Daisy, the housemaid, had a sister in service with that family and had asked to accompany him.

Ivy, the scullery maid, brought the nursery tea up on a tray. Her cheeks were flushed with excitement and her hand shook, rattling the cups as she set down the tray. What could be the matter with the girl?

Ivy tugged at her hair until wispy clumps escaped from the confines of her cap. Philomena could bear the tension no longer. "What on earth is it? I can see you have something to ask me."

Ivy fidgeted even more until Philomena thought she would scream. "Excuse me, miss," the scullery maid began, unusually polite. "I heard you were planning to take the air this afternoon."

Philomena smiled. News travelled fast in the servants' hall. She had mentioned plans for a walk only a few moments past, enquiring of Mrs. Bramble whether she supposed the bright weather would last.

Ivy twisted grimy hands together, catching up her apron and wringing it until it was a mass of creases. "W-w-would you be able to take something across to Jones's farm?"

Philomena began to see where this was leading. Ivy took a keen interest in boys. There were few to be found in the village, but she had begun a flirtation with a certain Thomas. Thomas' father worked on one of Lord Thatcham's farms, and Thomas was planning to follow his father's example. Philomena had once or twice noticed him lingering in the kitchen, delivering fresh vegetables and whispering with Ivy. She had a suspicion that the pair had embarked upon a semi-secret romance.

"Mrs. Bramble won't let me have followers," confided Ivy. "It's not fair, because Daisy's always going about with James, and nobody ever minds that. I can only see Thomas when I go over to Farmer Jones's, which is hardly ever." Philomena sympathised a little. The rules on servant behaviour were strict. Still, Ivy was only just into her teens and as foolish as a kitten.

"Your mother would want to know that you are being looked after properly," Philomena pointed out.

Grudgingly, Ivy sighed. "We-ell, any road, it's the beef, you see."

Philomena frowned deeper. What did Ivy's flirtations have to do with beef?

"There's some beef left in the kitchen," the girl went on. "Mrs. Bramble says that Lady Thatcham, Lord Thatcham's mother that is, told her to send it over to the outdoor servants. I said, does that mean those that work over on Mr. Jones's farm and she said, 'Yes, it does.'" Ivy paused for breath.

"I suppose you would like me to take it across to the farm this afternoon? Is that it?" asked Philomena.

"Oh, miss, I'd be ever so grateful." Ivy clasped her fists to her cheeks. "Really I would. And can you tell Thomas, if you see him…" She had the grace to blush. "Tell him that I asked Mrs. Bramble special, like, so he knows it's from me?"

Solemnly, Philomena agreed to take her walk this afternoon across the fields to the farm. Joseph's defeat had left her so relieved that she would have agreed to any favour.

The weather had turned a little warmer and Philomena anticipated the afternoon exercise with pleasure. She still found the country air a delight. Melting ice had muddied the paths, so she wore a strong pair of boots. She eyed the sky with caution. Despite Mrs. Bramble's opinion that the day was "set fair," there was no doubt that dark clouds were gathering. Still, she did not want give up her walk. There was plenty of time to reach the farm and return without a soaking. In any case, she had made a promise to Ivy. It would be a shame to disappoint the girl who sang so happily, loudly and tunelessly around the kitchen all morning that Mrs. Bramble begged her to stop.

Philomena enjoyed a pleasant hour's walk through pastures where cattle grazed. She strode happily along the water meadow, beside a stream that threatened to burst its banks before too long, laughing at the wind as it blew her hair free of its pins and threatened to steal her hat and whisk it away. The weather held as she delivered her basket to Mrs. Jones along with Ivy's message.

Mrs. Jones smiled. "He's a fine catch for young Ivy, is Thomas. He's a good boy, and he works hard. Lord Thatcham himself spoke to him the other day, something about some new machine or other. Thomas'll take over the farm when his father's ready. Maybe Ivy's just the wife for him." Ivy would be ecstatic.

Philomena drank a glass of lemonade and set off on the return journey. Her legs ached. She wondered whether she had taken cold: several of the household had begun sniffling into kerchiefs lately.

Apprehensive, she squinted at the sky. Black clouds eddied and swirled, building fast into a heavy mass. The wind seemed to grow wilder by the moment. Philomena shivered and quickened her step. A drop of rain spotted her pelisse and another plinked on the tip of her nose. She walked faster, looking for some kind of shelter.

Chapter Twenty

In other circumstances, Philomena would have enjoyed the walk through one of the prettiest parts of the estate. Lord Thatcham's father had built a small gazebo on top of a lightly wooded hill, overlooking the stream. Today's change in the weather, though, hastened her step. There was no time to drink in the surroundings. She hurried towards the safety of the Hall.

Cold drops of rain, heavy now, fell faster. Philomena had misjudged both the distance and the weather. There was precious little hope of arriving back at the Hall without a soaking. She wrapped her shawl tighter around her head, turned off the path and set off up the hill towards the gazebo. Mud clung to her boots as she stumbled upwards through ground that quickly turned slippery. Philomena panted, muttering breathless curses on Ivy's head for persuading her to set out on such a walk at this uncertain time of the year.

Thunder clapped and she jumped. One foot slipped and Philomena fell, sliding several feet down the hill. Furious, she scrambled up, her clothes heavy with mud from the waist down. Grimly, she struggled upwards, heading for the gazebo until, over the whistle of the wind, she heard a shout. "Can you make it to the summer house?"

Lord Thatcham, astride Thunder, pulled alongside

her and bent to inspect the damage.

"No," Lord Thatcham went on, "I can see you will never get there." He laughed down from his seat on the black stallion, rain streaming down his face. Jumping to the ground, he held fast to Thunder's bridle, bent over and cupped a hand for Philomena's foot.

She drew back. Any horse terrified her, let alone such a thoroughbred as Thunder. "I cannot ride." Thunder rolled his eyes and snorted, fidgeting from one foot to another. She flinched further away.

"You've never ridden?" Lord Thatcham shouted, his voice battling with the noise of the rain and the rising wind, a grin beginning to twist the corners of his mouth.

"No, never."

He laughed aloud, eyes gleaming. Philomena could not tell which he found more amusing: the storm or the sight of the nursemaid's discomfiture. "No matter. Thunder will keep you safe."

Philomena sincerely doubted that. She disliked the way the horse looked at her out of the corner of its eye and snorted.

"Put your foot in my hand," Lord Thatcham cried again.

"It's covered in mud."

He laughed harder, strands of wet hair clinging to his face. "So are you. I can wash mud from my hand more easily than you can clean it from your clothes. Now, stop wasting time or carry on up the hill by yourself and watch me ride away."

His teasing was infectious. Philomena chuckled, put her foot in his hand, closed her eyes and jumped. Then she was in the saddle, clinging with white knuckles to the ridge at the front. She must be at least a mile in the air. The horse fidgeted restlessly. Surely, he would throw her to the ground. She gripped the saddle, wondering how anyone could wish to ride a horse for pleasure.

Lord Thatcham led Thunder up the hill, head down against the rain. Philomena shivered. The wind was icy and it cut through her clothes.

They arrived safely at the summerhouse. Lord Thatcham pushed the door open, reached to Philomena's waist and lifted her down. At last, her feet touched solid ground. Lord Thatcham steadied her as she slid in the mud. His hands surrounded her waist and they laughed aloud, wet faces only inches apart.

Philomena's stomach lurched. She would happily drown in his eyes. Lord Thatcham took a long breath. "Whatever were you doing out in weather like this?" He released her, his voice hoarse.

She breathed deeply, trembling. "I came from Jones's Farm. It was not raining when I set off."

"No, the storm came suddenly. How lucky it is that I saw you."

She winced. "Did you see me fall?"

"Oh, yes. Flat on your face in the mud. I would not have missed that for all the world." Lord Thatcham stepped back and slipped Thunder's reins around a post. "He'll be safe there until the storm ends. Now, let's get inside, out of this rain, and see what we can do about you."

Laughing, he pulled Philomena into the summerhouse. "You're drenched. Ah, there's the very thing." He strode to a trunk set against the wall and opened it. "We keep blankets here in case we wish to picnic." He sniffed one. "Not too musty, though it's been out here all winter. At least it will keep you warm."

Philomena took the blanket and wrapped it around her shoulders.

Lord Thatcham caught her hand. "No. You will take cold. You must take off those wet clothes."

Philomena gasped. How dare he?

She stepped back, shocked, and he laughed. "Are you still afraid of the wicked Lord Thatcham?" he chuckled. She hesitated. He turned around. "Do not be. See, I am not looking. Be quick. Hang the wet garments over this wicker chair and wrap yourself in the blanket."

She hurried to obey, a giggle rising in her throat. If only the Dowager could see her now.

"Are you finished?"

"Not yet." She gave a final wriggle, dropped her wet outer garments on the chair and clasped the blanket to her. It was soft and dry. The sudden warmth caressed her skin. She shivered. "Oh, that's better."

Lord Thatcham turned around, still smiling.

"You are as wet as I," Philomena commented.

"But nowhere near so muddy. In any case, I am used to the country. A drop of rain will not hurt me."

Philomena could hardly speak for a lump that had formed in her throat. Her head throbbed. She coughed. "I would not wish you to take cold," she murmured.

"Very well. Hand me that blanket and turn away, if you please."

She heard Lord Thatcham tussling with his clothes. "You miss your valet," she teased.

"Will you help, then?" he asked.

His voice held no laughter, now. A new, deep resonance stole Philomena's breath away. She stood quite still for a long moment, her pulse racing. Slowly, knowing she should not, not caring if this was a terrible mistake, she turned to face her master. She took a step forward.

Lord Thatcham met her halfway. "Philomena, my dear," he said, his voice gentle, a caress. He enveloped her hand with warm, strong fingers and drew her closer. His face was only inches away. Philomena felt warm breath tickle her cheek. She held her breath and waited. He did not move.

Philomena knew that this time she alone must decide what happened next.

Blue eyes met grey and held for a long moment. Then, Philomena's gaze swept over his face, encompassing the faint, ever-present frown lines, the strands of wet hair, a tiny mole at the corner of the firm mouth. Her eyes rested there, watching as his lips parted in a crooked smile.

"Am I still the wicked Lord Thatcham?" he asked softly. Gently, unable to prevent herself, Philomena reached out and softly touched his mouth with her fingertips. "You were never wicked," she breathed.

He bent his head, then, and his lips, soft, warm and dry, touched hers. Philomena tasted rain and fresh air. His lips moved, slowly, gently. Philomena's own mouth stirred in response. Lord Thatcham pulled back, looked deep into Philomena's eyes and smiled. She melted under his gaze. He kissed her again, harder. Now, his lips were no longer gentle but urgent, demanding. Philomena stroked his hair and the blanket fell away, unheeded, leaving her in a simple shift.

Lord Thatcham lifted his head. Philomena traced his crooked smile with one finger.

"Philomena," he whispered.

"Hugh." She spoke his name for the first time, releasing her breath in a long sigh.

Hugh pulled her to him and kissed her again, long and hard on the mouth. Philomena responded, tasting his breath. A soft whimper of delight escaped from her soul and she shuddered. If only this could last forever.

Hugh's heart thudded against her chest. His hands laced through her hair as he held her face close. Her lips opened as his tongue entered her mouth.

Long, long moments later, he pulled gently away. "No." He held her a little away and kissed her eyes, one by one. He shuddered. "My beautiful girl."

The warmth of his voice wrapped Philomena in bliss.

He groaned aloud. "No. It must not be like this. You are no milkmaid. I cannot bear to let you go. I long for you. But not today, like this, in hiding."

Tears sprang to Philomena's eyes and trickled down her cheeks.

Hugh kissed them away and smiled. "Salt. You taste of heaven, my dear Philomena."

Still, he held back. Philomena was bereft. She yearned to give herself to Hugh, to let the man she loved do whatever he wished. Her body ached for him. No matter that he did not trust her. His body was close to hers, his voice murmuring in her ears. Every nerve in her body tingled.

Hugh turned aside, picked the blanket from the floor and arranged it, tenderly, across her shoulders. "I was wrong. Please forgive me. I did not realise—" He broke off and stepped away. "What shall I do?" He spoke as to himself.

He turned back. "There is only one thing for me. Perhaps I am a little mad. I do not know. All I know is what I feel for you, beautiful Philomena. Strange girl, I know nothing of you, but I know I love you."

His words echoed in Philomena's ears. She could not speak but gazed, hardly daring to breathe, into that beloved face. The silence stretched into an eternity.

At last, Hugh spoke again. "Philomena, will you be my wife?"

She cried out. Her hands flew to her mouth. Whatever she had expected, it was not this. She stared at Hugh, aghast, her mind in turmoil. Would he truly make her his wife, to live in this beautiful place with him for the rest of her life? Her head swam, intoxicated with delight.

Philomena opened her mouth to reply, to shout agreement to the heavens, but no words came. She reeled. What of her terrible secret? For a moment, one wonderful, brief moment, she had forgotten. Reason returned, with a flood of despair and desolation.

Heart bursting with sorrow, Philomena shook her head. "No, Hugh, I cannot marry you."

She longed to tell him the truth. Every inch of Philomena's body screamed at her to tell him of the dreadful secret, but she bit back the words. She could not bear to say, "I cannot marry you because I am already married." Hugh had forgiven her a great deal, but no one could overlook such wickedness.

She grew hot with shame. She had told Hugh nothing but lies and he had forgiven them all. He had excused her for dressing in men's clothes, travelling alone like a woman of dubious morals. He had pardoned her for disobeying his direct commands.

She could never tell him of her shame. She must spare him such pain. He would soon recover from his love for her. Such a man was a magnet for young, pretty girls from aristocratic families in search of a suitable husband. Hugh would be better without her. She must let him go.

Tears flooded Philomena's face as she sobbed. She struggled to speak, but words deserted her. She shook her head wildly, her throat raw with weeping. Through a mask of tears, dimly, she watched Hugh's face. She ached to see him so white, so shocked. She reached out and dragged her soaking dress back on, too distressed to fasten the buttons.

Hugh grasped her hand. "What is it?" he cried. "Tell me what ails you."

Philomena shook her head and pulled herself from his grasp. "No," she wept. "I cannot…" She cried out in pain as her heart broke. She darted away, running as fast as she could, leaving Hugh, the man she loved, staring after her, pain and despair spread over his dear face. She threw the door of the summerhouse wide open and escaped into the wild weather.

As she ran, sobbing, memories flooded Philomena's head. That dreadful day in London, the day she tried so hard to forget, that haunted her dreams, played again. Still a child, parted from her father, wondering why he had deserted her, she trembled in the church. Samuel tried to calm her, promising that nothing would harm her while he was alive. Tears stood in his eyes.

The terrible, unknown stranger with the cold green

eyes took one of her hands. The clergyman, well paid, wrote the names in the register and signed it. The stranger signed his name. Philomena did not speak a word. Samuel spoke on her behalf, marrying her at the age of eleven to an unknown, cold stranger.

Why had it happened? Who was the stranger? Why had he married her? Even now, Philomena understood only that she could not marry Hugh, although she loved him with all her heart and knew he loved her too. Hugh loved her enough to defy convention, ignore the disgust of his family and marry her. He offered her everything, and Philomena had to refuse him.

Chapter Twenty-One

Hugh, burning with pain and fury at Philomena's rejection, urged Thunder into a headlong gallop, away across the fields, urging the horse to race faster and harder. He had no desire to overtake the woman on her return to the Hall. The rain had long stopped, but the sky was grey and bleak, echoing Hugh's mood.

What was wrong with her? What more could he offer Philomena than a home in one of the greatest houses of the land, a life full of ease and pleasure? What other unknown woman, with a mysterious background and an unlikely story of relatives in distant parts of the country, could even imagine such an offer?

Yet she had refused him. She had not even done him the honour of concocting a reason. Resentment overwhelmed Hugh. He would have done with her. There were plenty of other women in England and he would find one far better than Philomena. He grew hot remembering that foolish offer of marriage. He should have bitten his tongue. What in the world had made the Master of Thatcham Hall behave like a love struck idiot?

Philomena had bewitched him, where all other women had failed. She had taken advantage of his good nature and set a trap. Hugh had fallen headlong into the snare. He closed his eyes, dizzy and sick. What a fool he was.

Since his ill-fated essay into matrimony, many prettier, wealthier, more eligible girls had sought to win Hugh's hand. He had withstood their smiles and curtsies with ease. He had learned his lesson. Once, he had allowed himself to fall into Beatrice's trap, hoodwinked by her charms and flattery. Furious at himself for such a lack of judgement and appalled at the tragic consequences, he had vowed never to wed again.

Then, like an innocent child, as simple and naïve as John, he had opened his heart to Philomena and she had turned away: a cruel rejection of such a gift. Hugh ground his teeth. She had taken him in completely. With so much charm, such a generous mouth, and such blue eyes fringed by black eyelashes, she had ensnared him.

It was not just that unique face, though, that had beguiled Hugh. Philomena was a breath of fresh air. She dared to disagree with him. While all around treated him with obsequiousness, Philomena alone teased and scolded. An ironic twinkle lit her eyes as though she was always on the verge of bursting into laughter. She made fun of Hugh and showed no deference to any ancestral pride. Surprised at first, angered by such a lack of respect, Hugh had rapidly learned to love her.

Unlike every other woman, she cared nothing for her beauty. Philomena never simpered. She behaved as Hugh's equal in every way that mattered, despite her dubious past. Hugh had begun to believe that at least one woman in the world was untouched by greed and selfishness. The scars left open by Beatrice's treachery had begun to heal.

He was a fool: more than a fool, for trusting

Philomena. He had not even waited to uncover the mystery of her past. He would put her from his mind.

Hugh gave the horse his head. He rode wildly; half hoping that disaster would strike. He urged Thunder on to jump higher and wider over fence, hedgerow and gate. The horse, ever sensitive to his master's moods, hurtled through the countryside. Hugh would put as much distance as possible between himself and Philomena.

At last, even Thunder began to tire. He slowed to a trot. Hugh reined him in and let him rest. The air smelled clean and fresh now, cleansed by the bluster of the storm that had driven Hugh and Philomena to the summerhouse. The fields sparkled, grass green from that winter's rain. Wintry tree skeletons kept watch, bare branches triumphant, as pale rays of sunlight stole through the cloud. Hugh's heart rate slowed and the heat of his fury cooled. As resentment evaporated, it abandoned him, unprotected, to the painful creep of self-reproach.

Philomena's response to his kiss had been honest. Her lips had trembled, finally giving way. Hugh had not mistaken the soft smile in her eyes. He knew she cared for him. For a moment, the sweetness of that remembered kiss overwhelmed Hugh. Philomena, the woman he had believed he would never find, was real and honest. Whatever her reason for rejecting him, it was no scandal of her choosing.

The ache in Hugh's chest eased. Here was a chance to act. He would not let Philomena slip out of his life without a fight.

For a year, he had borne bitter frustration. He had stayed silent on the manner of Beatrice's death, allowing rumours to spread unchecked. Muldrow lived unpunished, poisoning the countryside with lies. Hugh yearned to fight back, to restore his reputation, but could not, for the sake of John and of his dead wife.

Here, though, was a battle he could join with honour. Philomena had suffered some unknown catastrophe. Hugh did not doubt that, now that the first fury had faded. She would not or could not explain her misfortunes, so Hugh must discover the truth for himself. He would not abandon her. He would overcome his damaged pride, unravel the secrets of her past and destroy the unseen obstacles that kept them apart.

Hugh frowned as he stroked Thunder, the horse's neck damp with sweat and rain. He tried to piece together the small clues Philomena had dropped about herself. She spoke well and could read and write. She had claimed an uncle in Bristol. Hugh found it hard to believe in such a person, who if he were as respectable as Philomena claimed, would never have allowed his niece to travel, unprotected and dressed in man's clothes, across England. Nevertheless, it was a starting point. Hugh would begin his search in Bristol. He would set off that very evening.

All anger forgotten, filled with relief at the prospect of real action, Hugh returned to the Hall to throw together a bare minimum of possessions. To keep the destination private, for he would encourage no further gossip, he refused all Martin's requests to accompany him and told no one of his plans.

Hugh spent several minutes with pen in hand, composing a short note, before slipping quietly downstairs to the housekeeper's room. "Mrs. Rivers," he said. The housekeeper's jaw dropped. Aware that his heightened colour and blazing eyes revealed restless agitation, Hugh took several slow breaths.

"Is all well, my lord?" the housekeeper asked.

Hugh held his face impassive. "Please give this note to Miss Philomena."

Mrs. Rivers pressed her lips together. A trusted servant in the house since Hugh was a boy, she had helped him to avoid his father's temper many a time. The housekeeper's loyalty and good sense had extricated Hugh from all manner of scrapes.

She knew when to keep her counsel. "Of course, my lord." She took the note. "Is there anything else I can do for you?" Her eyes widened. She could always see through Hugh. He was tempted to share his despair and, as so often in childhood, drink a soothing cup of hot chocolate in the neat, tidy parlour.

No. He must keep his purpose secret. He must not reveal his feelings for Philomena. "There is nothing. I will be gone a few days."

He turned back at the door. He wanted to tell Mrs. Rivers to keep Philomena safe at the Hall until his return but could not find words that would not give away his feelings. "Watch over John," he muttered and hurried away, leaving Mrs. Rivers shaking her head, her face thoughtful.

Chapter Twenty-Two

Philomena climbed the stairs, slow and heavy with despair. She did not know what to do. How could she ever face Hugh again? What must he think?

She leaned back against the door of her tiny room. Her head pounded. She wanted to sleep, to forget everything that had happened this afternoon, but it was impossible. Hugh's face, pale and shocked, forced itself into her mind.

Philomena paced, restless, back and forth from the door to the window, one hand at her mouth. She chewed at her nails until her fingers bled but hardly noticed. What should she do? She could not leave. Her heart would break.

Philomena's thoughts grew wilder. How could she stay here, at the Hall? Perhaps she should throw herself at Hugh's feet, beg for forgiveness and offer to become his mistress. She covered her face in shame. She had thrown his proposal in Hugh's face and had run away. How could he ever forgive her?

What could she do? What could she say to return things to the way they had been? Questions whirled through Philomena's aching head, but she had no answers.

She had been happy here at the Hall. Hugh returned some at least of her feelings. They had laughed together and argued as equals. Such memories: she'd tried to hope for nothing, but, oh, the warmth in Hugh's eyes when he smiled at her. She should never have imagined it could lead to happiness. Why had she galloped so heedlessly to disaster?

At last, exhausted, with no more tears to cry, her heart drained to the dregs, Philomena lay on her bed and fell into a restless, fitful sleep. She dreamed again of the train derailment, of Hugh appearing to rescue her, ending the whirl of fear and confusion. She dreamed that Hugh walked with her, arguing and teasing. She dreamed Hugh's arms were around her, his lips warm on hers and his body pressed to her breasts.

She woke to a robin singing outside. Sunbeams slipped through the curtains, but no answering joy entered Philomena's soul. The world was a black hole of hopelessness and desolation. Dully, she rehearsed painful words to say today. She would ask to see Hugh, explain that she could not marry but would be his mistress. What man could refuse such an offer? Philomena cared not a fig for her reputation. It would hurt to leave the Hall, but maybe Hugh would find a cottage somewhere. She could see John from afar, watch the child grow and give Hugh everything he wanted: anything, except marriage.

Philomena would never forget that wonderful offer of marriage, but surely, Hugh would be pleased to avoid a connection that must disgust anyone who had the master's best interests at heart. Her head ached, but with a plan in mind, Philomena felt strong enough to begin the day's work.

First, she must see the Dowager, to receive instructions. She never entered that lady's presence without a shiver of nervousness. The servants all dreaded the Dowager's sharp tongue. Each had at one time or other received a scathing rebuke. Whether triggered by the sight of a table less than perfectly polished or a meal undercooked, the Dowager's remarks never failed to hit home. Even John held his tongue in her presence, for anything the Dowager considered idle chatter incurred a tart retort.

"I see you have been spending time in the kitchen," she commented yesterday, eyebrows raised. "Perhaps a few moments learning your letters would be of more benefit."

Philomena privately believed that a four-year-old child should spend his time in play and leave reading and writing until later.

As she completed the necessary preparations for the interview, checking for a mark on her apron, a smut on her nose, or the escape of yet another wayward curl, a knock sounded at the door. Philomena turned, betrayed by the heat in her cheeks. Of course, it could not be Hugh. She smoothed the front of her apron and opened the door.

Mrs. Rivers handed her a letter. "For you, my dear."

Philomena turned the paper over in a trembling hand, wondering what it could contain. There could be no good news. There was sympathy in the housekeeper's voice. Unwilling to look directly at Mrs. Rivers, Philomena muttered "Thank you," and closed the door in the housekeeper's face.

Her fingers fumbled as she opened the letter. Dread filled her heart.

"*Dearest Philomena,*" it began. Hot blood rose to her cheeks. Her eyes ranged over the letter, too full of tears to read at first. Shaking, she sat on the settle before the fire, composed herself and read.

"*Dearest Philomena,*

I write in haste. I cannot explain myself. I can only offer my heartfelt apologies for my behaviour yesterday. If I misunderstood your feelings for me, I deeply regret my stupidity. If, as I pray, I did not, then I must find the cause for your rejection. My vanity will not allow me to believe that a simple dislike was at the root of such an action.

I will not burden you longer with my presence. I leave at once for Bristol, where I mean to find the relative who should, I believe, undertake your care. I pray that I may discover the reasons for your refusal of my hand, in learning more of your parentage and upbringing.

Perhaps I intrude where I have no right. Forgive me for this, my dear Philomena. I cannot continue in ignorance, and you tell me nothing. Perhaps with this step I may find a way to overcome the obstacles, unknown to me, that stand between us. Please believe that I will never force myself upon you. I have behaved inexcusably but will not do so again. When I return home in a few short days, I hope to bring with me a greater understanding of the reasons for your distress.

I can bear to waste no more time. I leave at once. Please know that I am now and will always remain,

Your most humble servant,

Hugh, Lord Thatcham."

Philomena sank onto the chair, the letter clutched in her hands. Should she laugh or cry? One thought only rang through her head. *He truly loves me.* For a moment, she gave herself up to the joy of that knowledge. Her cheeks burned and tears prickled her eyes.

Slowly but surely, reality intruded to dull the edge of such unexpected joy. Hugh would find nothing in Bristol but more evidence of lies. Philomena had no connection there. Hugh would find that she was not the woman he believed her. Then, what would he imagine? Surely, his love could not survive yet more proof of her depraved character.

Her head swam. She could not think. What should she do? A stark choice lay before her. She could wait for Hugh's return, dreading to see disappointment and disgust in his face, or she could leave, now, pretending that these past days at the Hall were no more than a dream.

Aware of time slipping rapidly away, her thoughts still in turmoil, Philomena readied herself for this morning's interview with the Dowager. She would make decisions later.

Chapter Twenty-Three

The Dowager Lady Thatcham had taken a small morning room for her exclusive use. There she wrote notes to wide acquaintance, organised future visits, and shared plans with friends for their daughters' activities during the London Season. From this room, snug in the weak winter sunlight, she summoned the cook to agree the menus for the day, gave orders for the maids to stoke up the fire in the room to an intense heat, and complained to the housekeeper about the servants' clatter on the back stairs.

Philomena entered quietly and curtsied, demurely. Tears had left her eyes red and sore. The Dowager looked up, through her lorgnette. Philomena suspected she wore such an item to intimidate the servants rather than to correct poor eyesight.

"Good morning, Philomena."

"Good morning, your ladyship." Philomena held her breath.

"I have sent for you this morning to explain some changes that are to take place in the Hall. Selena and I will soon leave, in order to visit my cousin. We do not intend to return to Thatcham Hall this spring but will go directly to the London house, for Selena's season."

Philomena nodded. She was glad the Dowager was going, not least because John would find life more comfortable. Her iron discipline irked him. He would miss Selena, however. Philomena sighed. Poor John, so often left behind as people moved on.

"We have a small change to make in our arrangements, however," the Dowager said. "Yesterday, my son found it necessary to leave the Hall at short notice in order to undertake a visit he suddenly recollected." The Dowager's pinched lips left Philomena in no doubt that she disapproved.

"Selena and I must, therefore, remain here a while longer." The Dowager removed her lorgnette before she continued. Her eyes darted from side to side. Could she be uncomfortable? "As we will be here longer than we intended, I will have time to make some more appropriate arrangements." She turned from Philomena to look out of the window. "I plan to appoint a governess for Master John. He is too big to remain in the care of a nursery maid."

Philomena started, but the Dowager held her hand up to call for silence. "Please do not waste my time with hysterics. You possess no qualifications as a nursemaid, and although I admit we have been surprised and pleased with your work, it is time Master John began a proper education with a governess. She will supply all the care he needs and give lessons at the same time."

"Yes, your Ladyship," Philomena's voice trembled. She fought for control. She would sooner die than weep in front of this woman. "I-I shall be sorry to leave, but I understand."

The Dowager paused for a long moment, as though making her mind up. "My dear, please understand me." Her voice sounded unusually uncertain. "I will be honest with you, because you have served well. I have seen some attachment growing between my son and yourself." She raised a hand to forestall any protest. "I do not entirely blame you," she added. "My son is partly responsible. That is of no account. You must realise that any—er, liaison between the two of you would be entirely inappropriate." She leaned forward a little, in emphasis. "It cannot be allowed to continue. I must, therefore, act while my son is away, in his best interests."

Philomena's head buzzed.

"I do not know where he has gone," the Dowager continued. "He is a grown man and has male pursuits. I do not enquire into them. Men must be free to come and go as they wish." She turned away again, her face a little pink. "He has taken a sudden fancy for travel. Who knows why that should be so?" She coughed, recollecting herself. "However, all you need to know is that Lord Thatcham is gone and will be away for some time."

Philomena, numb, said nothing. The Dowager stood, rigid, gaze fixed on the view through the window. Philomena had twisted the front of her apron into a ball. She forced her hands to relax until the cloth fell back into place. She smoothed away the damp creases, trying to breathe steadily. The silence in the room lengthened.

"Now, I will allow you a few days to make your arrangements." The Dowager gave ground first. "You will want to continue on your way to your uncle."

She never believed the story, Philomena acknowledged. Still, she could not hold that against the woman. It was, after all, a lie and Lady Thatcham was no fool.

The older woman continued. "I am a little surprised that the uncle in Bristol has not responded to your letter. However, that is your concern. I will begin the search for a governess at once. I have already heard of a suitable woman." Her voice gained in assurance. Any momentary uncertainty gone, she became once more the Dowager, confident and important. "She is a little older than you, as is far more acceptable in a household where the master is without a wife. Please make yourself ready to leave within the week. You may go."

Philomena turned to leave without a word, but the Dowager called her back. "There is one thing I wish to know. When you arrived here, had you any knowledge of Thatcham Hall and its inhabitants?"

Philomena, outraged at the suggestion, took a moment to collect her thoughts. Did the Dowager believe she had deliberately found a way to the Hall, in the hope of capturing a rich and noble husband? If it were not so ridiculous, she would have laughed aloud. Instead, she clung fast to her dignity, for soon that would be the only thing left. She shook her head.

"Mmm," the Dowager murmured. "There is something about you that reminds me a little... I felt that perhaps we had met before...but no, I must have been mistaken. That is all."

Philomena fled up the back stairs. The Dowager's words had at least removed any need to make her own decision as to whether she should remain at the Hall. She must go. There was no choice. Blinded by tears of regret that she could hold back no longer, she hardly noticed as she cannoned into one of the under housemaids, knocking a pitcher of water on to the stairs. The pitcher bounced down the treads, spinning noisily as it came to rest in the centre of the hall, water pooling around it.

"Whatever's the matter?" the maid cried. "Why, look what you've gone and done, Miss Philomena. Here. Wait a minute."

Philomena, too desperate to care what should happen to her now, ran headlong back to the nursery. She threw the door open, rushed past Alice and John, ignored their startled exclamations and shut herself into her little sitting room, leaning back against the door to prevent anyone from following. Alone again, she sobbed harder than ever. So, this was how it felt to have a broken heart. If only she had never left home.

Later that morning, Selena visited the nursery, her face pale. She took one look at Philomena, who had recovered sufficiently to sit listlessly by while John scribbled on table and floor, and ran to her, arms outstretched. "My dearest Philomena..." Selena took Philomena's hand. "Mama has told me you are to go." Her eyes filled with tears, which threatened to trickle down her face.

Philomena rose, setting Selena aside. "Please do not cry. I have gained command of myself now, but I fear I am not yet strong enough to bear the sight of your tears."

Selena frowned, puzzled. "But all was well, was it not? I do not understand why my Mama insists on a governess for John, nor why Hugh has taken it into his head to disappear at such a moment. Why, I am sure he would never have allowed Mama to act in such a way, if he was here."

Philomena forced a smile. "I cannot stay here forever." She kept her tone calm. "Your family took me in when I needed help, and it is only right that I leave now to continue my journey."

Hugh's sister looked hard into Philomena's face. "I can see that you do not mean those brave words, but I salute you for them. Mama does not understand. I mean, she is from a former age, and Hugh went off in such haste last night... I do not know what is wrong with everyone. Everything was so happy. Hugh had even stopped scolding me. Whatever happened?"

Philomena could only shake her head, wordless. Selena opened her mouth as though she would speak further, but Philomena met her eyes steadily. The younger girl subsided and sighed.

"Let us be practical," said Philomena, desperate to avert further tears or disloyal reproaches. She did not wish Selena to be tempted to make remarks about her own mother that she would later regret.

"I have a few days to pack and to say my farewells to John. We must think of John above all, you know, to make sure he remains happy."

"He will not be happy without you," said Selena, stoutly. "Nor will Hugh—" She caught herself, paused a second and continued, choosing her words with care. "I know Hugh has come to think a great deal of you, as I have, but in a different way, of course."

Even in the midst of her distress, Philomena managed a watery smile. Selena was as naïve and innocent as though still in the schoolroom. "Your brother has been most kind," Philomena managed, her voice calmer now.

Selena shook her head. "No, I will not allow that. Hugh is never kind. At least, perhaps he is sometimes kind to others when he is not cross and scolding, but not to you. I believe he is truly fond of you, Philomena, and so does Mama, and I know that is why she wants you to leave."

The set of Selena's jaw made it clear that Philomena need not trouble to argue.

"If only Hugh had not taken it into his ridiculous head to run off to Bristol," Selena murmured. Her eyebrows rose in exasperation. She looked so like Hugh that Philomena had to turn away, fiddling with a vase of dried lavender on a nearby table. Her fingers, shaking and clumsy, broke off half a dozen stems. In her distress, she hardly noticed as they showered her apron with tiny fragrant flower heads.

"What business he had in the West Country, I do not know." Selena shook her head. "I suppose he is off to find some more complicated machines to thresh the wheat or dig the earth or some such ridiculous nonsense." Selena's delicate little nose wrinkled. "Hugh used to disappear like this often when Beatrice was alive, but since you came, he has appeared almost content." She could not know how her words sliced Philomena's heart like knives.

Unable for the moment to speak, Philomena slipped into the next room. She busied herself replacing John's crayons in their container and sorting his drawings into neat piles until she was sufficiently collected to speak.

She turned back to Hugh's sister, determined to avoid a rift between Selena and her brother. "Dear Selena. You have been so kind to me. Please trust me now when I say that this is for the best." Her voice broke a little, but she squared her shoulders and continued. "I cannot reproach your mother for attempting to prevent a liaison that would be most unsuitable. I know I must leave. I am glad that Lady Thatcham's plans have made it possible for me to go at once."

Selena snorted. "What nonsense, to say you are unsuitable, just because you are not a member of a great family. We are not living in the eighteenth century, you know. Why, no one cares about that sort of thing any more. Worrying about rank or money only leads to unhappiness. Look at Hugh himself." Selena grew pink with indignation. "No one could have been more unsuitable for Hugh than Beatrice. Why, she shared none of his interests and made him thoroughly miserable, despite coming from one of the best old families. I am sure Hugh wished he never married her. Although she was very beautiful and rich, I would far rather have you for a sister and I care not who knows it."

Selena subsided, cheeks aglow. She blew her nose noisily into her handkerchief and allowed Philomena by degrees to comfort her. A little older and far wiser than Selena, she tried in vain to explain that differences in birth did matter and that any relationship with a nursemaid would severely damage Hugh's reputation. The words she spoke rang true, though each echoed in her own ears like a funeral dirge.

Chapter Twenty-Four

"John," Philomena said. They were alone in the nursery. "Your grandmamma has had a happy thought."

John stopped painting his picture of Thunder and looked up, frowning. "What thought?"

"Well, I have to go away for a little, like Papa, and your Grandmamma has asked a Miss Smith to come and teach you some new things."

John's frown deepened. "I don't want you to go away."

"Oh, just for a while," Philomena kept her voice calm and cheerful. "Soon, Papa will be back and you can tell him all the new things Miss Smith teaches."

John thought for a moment and then smiled. "I'll tell you as well, Miss 'Mena." He dipped his brush in purple paint and began to layer it in long strokes for Thunder's mane. Philomena turned away. He must not see the pain in her face.

When the Dowager made a decision, no time was lost in its implementation, and the day of departure soon came. Miss Smith, the new governess, would arrive after Philomena left the house, for which Philomena gave thanks. She could not bear to meet the person who would take her place in John's life.

Philomena was to travel by train, but this time with a first class ticket to Bristol. The Dowager, to the astonishment of the butler charged with procuring the ticket, insisted the nursemaid must travel in comfort, although her benevolence did not stretch to the provision of a companion. Unwilling to listen to servant gossip and determined not to ask questions, the Dowager knew nothing of Hugh's plans. Selena remarked that she hoped Philomena would run into Hugh in Bristol and that he would bring her back to the Hall. Philomena kept her own council.

The coachman was to drive Philomena to the station and see her safely onto the Bristol train. Philomena, though, had other ideas. Each night since the Dowager had ordered her from the Hall, she had lain awake, deciding what best to do.

She realised that her escape from London had been rushed and poorly managed. The result was confusion and unhappiness. She had left with insufficient resources. She could not regret the hasty actions, for she would never forget either John or Hugh. She struggled to hold back tears at the thought of a future without them. Those few short Christmas days of utter joy would stay in her memory forever. Once the first pain had passed, she would remember them with happiness.

Once she had left the Hall, she would be strong. She would not jump, eyes closed to the consequences, into another mad adventure. Sadder and wiser than just a few weeks ago, Philomena had devised a new and more sensible plan.

She would not to go to Bristol, after all. She knew nothing of the city. She suspected it had become her goal just because it was a long way away and the railway line led there. Philomena had thought herself in command of her destiny, but she had made a muddle of her escape. She would think more carefully in future.

Her only happiness had been here at Thatcham Hall. She could not remain here and so she would return to the city she knew. She would make a successful life for herself in London.

It was true that Joseph still lived in London, but Philomena knew the city well enough to avoid him. In any case, he had rushed off to Bristol. Philomena was as likely to run into the man there as in St. Giles or Seven Dials. She must not bump into Joseph while alone and friendless in a strange town. London was a bigger city, and she knew it well. She could far more easily lose herself in the familiar streets and narrow passages of the capital.

Even so, she could not escape Joseph forever. She shrugged. She had a new plan. Joseph surely knew the truth of her strange wedding. Until she encountered Hugh, she had blocked the marriage from her mind, determined to live happily alone, needing no man in her life. Now, she felt less confident. A small voice in the back of her head spoke to her. *Once you uncover the truth of the marriage, you may find a way to overcome it. Perhaps it was not legal, after all. Or perhaps the man with the cold green eyes is dead.*

Philomena tried not to listen to that voice. She could hardly bear to imagine her joy should she discover the marriage was a trick. Why, she would be able to return to Hugh and accept his proposal. *No.* She must not allow herself to imagine that day could ever arrive. Still, she would return to London.

The more she considered it, the more sensible it seemed. She would stop running away. She would go home to London, seek out a way to manage Joseph, and find out the truth of her past.

She could find something to hold over Joseph, to make him tell the truth. She could handle him. Why had she ever been terrified of him? She was more than a match for such a poor specimen. Fear of Joseph was nothing compared with the misery in her heart.

Philomena had a little money now, saved from her wages at the Hall. In fact, she had more now than when she left London, for the Dowager had insisted on giving her a parting gift. She could not accuse Hugh's mother of lack of generosity.

Philomena had a suspicion that the Dowager was a little in awe of her son. She would want Hugh to know how reasonable she had been in his absence. Philomena laughed bitterly at the thought.

Next day, she left the house quietly and unobtrusively, and on arrival at the station, she insisted the coachman leave her. He argued. "Her Ladyship said to see you on to the train, and that is what I shall do."

His will was no match for Philomena's, however. She easily persuaded him that he would endure a long and dull wait before the train arrived. He could spend a far more interesting morning with a certain young girl of his acquaintance in the village. Succumbing to temptation, Ince left Philomena to wait by herself, safe in the presence of the local stationmaster.

Philomena found a quiet corner in the waiting room and sat until the London train arrived. Unobserved, she slipped aboard.

Chapter Twenty-Five

Hugh arrived home, tired to the bone, angry and defeated, coldly furious to have failed in his task. He had found no trace of Philomena's uncle. The trail had turned quite cold.

No one came out from the Hall to greet him. Used to a cheerful welcome from the servants, he was surprised to receive little more than a perfunctory curtsey from Mrs. Rivers and a courteous bow from the butler.

"Is something amiss?" he asked Martin as the valet followed him up to his room. "Where is my mother? Or Miss Selena? And John? Are they away from the house?"

Martin stared at the floor and shuffled his feet.

"Come on, man," said Hugh, growing anxious. "What's wrong? Tell me, now, or I'll find another who will."

"My lord." Martin avoided his master's eye. "No one is ill, but there have been some changes while you were away."

"Good God, I've only been gone a few days. What can have happened in that time, in my own house?" Hugh peered at Martin and saw anxiety in the familiar face. "Come on, man. Has John been stealing from the kitchen again?"

Martin, still shifting from foot to foot, took a

breath. His words tumbled over one another in his haste to get the matter over. "Master John has a new governess, my lord, who arrived yesterday. Miss Selena is a little upset."

Hugh stared. "What of Miss Philomena?" His heart raced. "Is she also upset?"

Martin swallowed, his adam's apple jerking nervously. "She's gone, my lord," said the faithful valet, backing away as the thunder gathered on his master's brow.

"Gone." said Hugh. "Gone? Come, man, be clear with me. I do not understand. Where has she gone? Who with?" He glared.

Martin pursed his lips, his mouth firmly shut.

"Oh, no matter." Hugh strode to the door and bellowed, "Where is Lady Thatcham?"

The sound echoed along the corridor and down the stairs to where the Dowager sat in her drawing room, pretending to read. Only her fingers, flicking the corners of the book, betrayed her agitation.

"Well, Mama?" Hugh burst in without preamble, his voice cutting the air like a knife. "What is this I hear?"

"Good morning, Hugh. Please show a little more respect." His mother peered up at him through her lorgnette, her cheeks unusually pink. "I collect you have heard that I have succeeded in finding the perfect governess for your son. She is, at this moment, giving John a lesson in arithmetic. The temporary arrangement made with the young woman to whom we offered succour at Christmas was no longer necessary, so Miss er, Miss Philomena has left us." Her voice faded.

Hugh, shaking, was too angry at first to speak. He

fought for control. "A governess." The word reverberated with disgust. "How dare you appoint a governess for my son without asking my permission?"

The Dowager rallied and stood, raising herself to the height of her tiny frame. "Your sudden disappearance left me with no alternative but to take charge of such affairs. I merely chose to make an appropriate decision on behalf of my grandson." She removed her lorgnette. "I should think you would thank me," she finished, with dignity.

Hugh bit his lip. This was his fault. He should not have travelled so importunately to Bristol. He must put aside his fury, though it threatened to engulf him. He clenched his hands and kept tight command of his voice. "You have interfered with my life once too often, Mama. I have ever remained mindful of the respect due to a parent, for my father's sake and for your own. I have allowed you to meddle in my affairs in ways that reached far beyond reason."

He moved closer, staring his mother down until she could no longer meet his eye and looked away across the room. "This is my house, however. You have over-reached yourself for the last time. For the future, you will stay out of my affairs, or you will no longer be welcome at Thatcham Hall." Hugh turned on his heel. The Dowager watched, speechless, as he left.

From Selena, he learned the full story. "She has gone to Bristol," she told her brother, her voice trembling.

"Bristol." Hugh spat the word. "I was there today. Damn the place, I wish I had never heard of it."

"She has an uncle there. I'm sure all will be well."

Hugh snorted. "Uncle, indeed. There is no such

uncle. I scoured the city, and no one knows of Philomena or her fantastical relative. Whoever the child may be, she has no connections with that city."

"Well, wherever she is, she has plenty of money. Mama gave her a generous gift."

Hugh raised an eyebrow. It seemed that Philomena had managed to charm even his mother.

"All will be well with her." Selena was still talking. "You know how clever she is. She will find work, perhaps in a great house like this, and is sure to find another family that esteems her, as they should. Though, I am sad to think we will never see Philomena again."

Hugh, unable to speak another word on the subject, left the room.

The cruellest thorn in his heart was the knowledge that he had only himself to blame for this disaster. Had he remained at the Hall, trusting Philomena, she would still be here. What a fool he was, undeserving of the happiness that had been so close. Philomena had slipped through his careless fingers.

Hugh tried to tear his thoughts away from her, but Philomena's face shone bright in his mind. The memory of her dimples tormented him. How hard he had worked to make the child smile against her will, for the pleasure of seeing them appear. He recalled the feel of Philomena's body, held all too briefly. Remembering the touch of her lips, he closed his eyes, overcome with anguish.

Was he destined never to know the happiness of a loving home life? He had tried marriage once, with Beatrice, and it had resulted in naught but pain and, worse, in his wife's death. The only happy outcome of his married life was their son, John. How would he face the long days here at the Hall, with no Philomena to smile at them both in the warmth of the nursery?

Hugh cared nothing for her background, for the lies or the false address Philomena had supplied. Whatever, whoever she was, he needed his love beside him. Life was nothing alone.

He sent for the coachman. Ince visibly quaked, twisting his hat around in nervous fingers.

"Miss Selena tells me you saw Miss Philomena to the train," said Hugh. The man's hands began to shake "There is no need to be afraid. Just tell me that she set off safely for Bristol."

The silence stretched out for long moments.

"Oh, my lord, I am sorry." Hugh could hardly make out Ince's words; the coachman's voice shook so. "She would not let me see her on to the train, my lord. She sent me away. I am sorry. I was wrong, and—"

"You do not know whether or not she went to Bristol, if I understand you correctly?"

"That's right, my lord."

Every bone in Hugh's body ached with weariness. The coachman's confession meant that no one knew where Philomena had gone. He sighed. "You may go," he said.

Ince made himself scarce, hardly believing his good fortune in escaping Lord Thatcham's famous wrath. Hugh trudged up the stairs to the nursery, which he supposed should be called the schoolroom, in future. He pushed the door open.

John turned and beamed. "Hello Papa. Miss 'Mena's taking a holiday. Have you seen Miss Smith? She's in Miss 'Mena's room." He came to the door and whispered in his father's ear. "She smells funny."

Hugh put his arm round his son. He must not give up hope. Philomena was out there, somewhere, on her own. He would find her. He needed her and so did John.

For many days, Hugh searched fruitlessly for some trace of Philomena. He found no clue. He left the Hall to scour the country. He took the train once more to Bristol but achieved little beyond offering delicious encouragement for the wagging tongues of that city. They found great entertainment in the spectacle of a handsome aristocrat on such a wild goose chase, asking constantly after an unknown woman.

Martin, saddened by his master's loss of interest in hunting, faithfully reported all the information available from the servants' hall. This was little enough, beyond a description of Joseph, culled from the single visit to the back door of the Hall. That was the only clue Hugh had. He turned it over in his head, but try as he might he could find no help in it. The appearance of a strange man searching for Philomena simply deepened the mystery.

Slowly, reluctantly, Hugh realised he must waste no more time searching. He had neglected his duties at Thatcham Hall for too long. For the moment, he would wait, but he would never give up. One day, somehow, he would solve the mystery that was Philomena.

The year drew on. At last, the cold, February winds became only a memory. The fields around the Hall blossomed with a spring in their step. The snowdrops from the path Hugh had walked with Philomena were long gone. Crocus, daffodil, and tulip took their place, in the long progression of the seasons. Hugh spoke coldly but politely to the Dowager, and she left the Hall on the long-delayed visit to her friends, taking Selena with her.

The time was fast approaching when Selena would enter into society. Hugh promised to join her at his London house as soon as was reasonable and pay for a ball in her honour. She threw her arms around him. "You are the kindest brother in the world. We will have such a merry time in London that you will soon become happy again, I promise you."

Chapter Twenty-Six

In Cadogan Square at the start of the Season, hustle and bustle engulfed Hugh's London house. He sighed as daily deliveries of ribbons and lace filled the rooms while posies of flowers overflowed the vases. Selena appeared to possess an ever-growing band of admirers. Mrs. Bramble remained at Thatcham while a famous French chef concocted banquets of rich food. The man condescended to Mrs. Rivers and flirted with Selena's maid, but the butler, Mayhew, forbade complaint amongst the servants. "No self-respecting family can give dinners or dances in London using their country cook," he pointed out.

It did not take Hugh's sister long to recover from the distress at the loss of Philomena, in the excitement of her first London season. Hugh smiled at her. "London agrees with you."

She gave a little skip and linked her arm with that of her cousin, Lucy. "There is so much to be done here in town that my feet hardly touch the ground."

"Indeed. What plans have you, then?"

"Tomorrow I have a fitting with Mistress Matilda, who is making my gown for the Fancy Dress Ball at the Palace. Then we must walk in Hyde Park, to take the air, you know, before dressing for the dinner and ball at the Marchant's house, though I am sure Angelina Marchant's ball will be the dullest affair in London."

Lucy, in possession of a smaller fortune than Selena, nodded obligingly. After all, the Dowager Lady Thatcham had agreed that Lucy should share Selena's own ball.

Hugh took little interest in the forthcoming event. Gritting his teeth, he wrote bank drafts to pay for the arrangements, hiding horror at the expense. He promised to attend, though with a heavy heart, but insisted on wearing last year's coat. "You will be the centre of attention," he told Selena, "and few will care how inelegant your poor widowed brother may appear beside you."

Selena laughed. "Indeed, you know you will be the main attraction of the ball, brother. All the young ladies of my acquaintance are a-flutter at the thought of dancing with you."

Hugh made himself as scarce as possible. Business appointments and Parliamentary sittings ate into the greater part of each day. He dined often at the club. There was little to interest him in the activities of the cohorts of fresh-faced young ladies, hardly distinguishable one from another. Hugh bowed when he encountered them in the house and assisted them into carriages after a morning visit, but the blushing giggles failed to charm him. How insipid and dull they were in comparison with Philomena. They had not one tenth of Philomena's intelligence, wit, or humour.

"Thatcham, I do believe you are becoming ridiculously middle-aged," scoffed Lord Hadden, as Hugh declined another invitation. "These days, you spend more time in the House than the ballroom. People are beginning to talk."

Hugh shrugged. "Let them. I have never cared for

gossip, and I have no plans to start now. I find Parliament a more congenial place than any other through this endless season."

"Well, you may not care that you are becoming a prize bore, but perhaps you should consider your sister." Hadden took a pinch of snuff and sniffed, holding the jewelled box out to Hugh.

Hugh shook his head. "How so?"

Hadden narrowed his eyes. "I will just draw to your attention that Miss Selena has many admirers and you may not approve of them all." He took a step back. "It's no good looking at me like that, my dear fellow. I tell you only for your own good. Your charming and beautiful sister is in a way to taking London by storm. The most level head in the world can, as we know, be turned by too much admiration from the wrong quarters." Hadden snapped the snuffbox shut and tucked it into the pocket of his waistcoat. "You have only to observe how the young men gather around Miss Selena in Hyde Park to see for yourself, even if you refuse to attend evening engagements."

Hugh, more disturbed by this conversation than he would allow his friend to see, resolved to take more account of his sister's activities. "Do you walk in the park this afternoon?" he asked as they breakfasted the next morning.

"Oh yes. Lucy and I propose to take the air." Selena blushed. "Lucy's mother will accompany us, of course."

"Well, you may tell your friend's mother, that unless she wishes to walk for her own health, she may hand you into my care, for I plan to see the sights myself."

Selena blushed more deeply. "Oh. Oh," she stammered. "Are you sure you would want…I mean, I thought you disliked parading through crowds. I'm sure you said as much the other day, when I suggested you accompany us to see the balloon flight."

Hugh raised his eyebrows. "I have changed my mind and would be proud to accompany my sister on her walk." His voice discouraged argument.

"Oh, then, thank you. I will send a note to Lucy."

Selena smiled, but the smile did not reach her eyes. "I am sure she will be pleased, for I believe she has a little tender spot in her heart for you, dear brother, if the truth were told."

"Well, then, I will endeavour to disabuse her of any such feeling and restore her heart to robust health." He smiled. "Let us drive up Rotten Row in a carriage. An hour or so of my company will be bound to cure your friend of any foolish infatuation."

Selena blinked. Hugh suspected that she would need to write more than one note, recounting the sudden change of plan. He supposed that the recipients of these notes might be men Selena preferred to keep away from her brother's notice. He must keep a closer eye on his sister in future.

A spring sun shone so brightly that no lady would dare venture out without a parasol. Selena and Lucy took trouble with their appearance, and Hugh had to admit that both looked charming. They wore bonnets embroidered with spring flowers and embellished with bright ribbons. Selena had on a new walking dress. Her choice of rose pink enhanced her blossoming beauty and her delicate complexion glowed with pleasure. Her friend, in more dashing yellow, provided a perfect foil for Selena's delicate figure.

Hugh drove the carriage sedately behind a pair of matched chestnuts. The sun had brought many young people out to take the air, so progress was slow. Every acquaintance must be acknowledged and a few words bestowed on the ladies' favourites. Hugh maintained a perfect demeanour of affable brotherliness, while only an occasional twitch of the lips betrayed any secret amusement. He would have enjoyed a conversation with Philomena on the occasion.

"Oh," Lucy exclaimed. "I do believe that is Mr. Muldrow over there, with that group by the elm trees. Look, Selena, do you not see him? He is looking this way."

Hugh glanced at his sister in time to see her dig her elbow into her friend's ribs. "Look, there is Major Cornwell." Selena spoke loudly and pointed in the other direction.

Her friend, a little slow on the uptake, finally took the hint and turned her attention to a group of officers. Their proximity to the carriage forced Hugh to halt and engage in a few moments of conversation. Selena quickly established that all parties except Hugh had seen the latest play, and that the ladies were breathlessly awaiting invitations to attend the young Queen's Fancy Dress ball.

The conversation turned to newspaper accounts of the latest political arguments. The officers were keen to hear Hugh's opinion as a member of the House of Lords, on the demands of the Chartists for all men to have a vote.

"If that were their only demand," Hugh said, "I would find it difficult to condemn them, for I do not believe that the gentry I see here in their finery, with nothing in their heads but flirting, have any better sense than a poor man who labours all hours to feed his family."

A shocked silence fell. Selena fluttered her fan. "Oh, take no notice of Hugh. He is out of sorts today and will say anything to start an argument. Is that not so, Hugh?"

Hugh flicked the reins, nodded at the officers and trotted on.

"Brother, we will have no acquaintance left at all if you talk so," Selena scolded.

Hugh kept his counsel. Philomena would have entered with spirit into a debate on this or any other subject. His short speech, designed to shock the self-satisfied officers out of their complacency, could have come directly from her mouth. Such thoughts of Philomena teased him daily.

As Hugh, Selena, and her friend passed on, nodding and smiling, they became aware of a cacophony of noise. The elegant carriages of the gentry turned towards Hyde Park Corner in a bid to discover the source of the excitement. Hugh took his barouche to within a safe distance of the excitement, where he drew the horses to a halt, mindful of the carriage's cargo of young ladies.

A rowdy mob surrounded a rough wooden platform. Feelings ran high.

"A secret ballot, that's what we want."

"And the vote. A vote for all, that's what we need, not just for the rich. It's time we had a fair say."

Workers in coarse jackets and heavy boots, every one of them with a cap on his head, shouted, pushed and shoved, their worn clothes in stark contrast with the elegant uniforms of the nearby soldiers. Over-decorated, expensive young bucks sauntered carelessly around the outside of the crowd, tossing insults.

One of the mob, a red-haired lad of eighteen or so, turned his attention to a foppish youth with a tall hat and tightly cut trousers. "You're naught but a bunch of toffs and dandies."

The boy lobbed a stone accurately at the other's hat. It flew from the dandy's head and landed nearby in a puddle. "Well, I'll be damned," said the dandy, dropping his elegant air to put up his fists and land the ginger lad a facer. The lad was no slouch with his own fists and set about the dandy with a will.

Delighted, others nearby joined in, aiming their fists, sticks and stones at the younger of the gentry around them while less excitable gentlemen stepped back to check that no ladies were in danger.

The young bloods were glad to show off their prowess to the ladies who took the air in the Park. In their enthusiasm, they mistook the ladies' horrified shrieks for encouragement and the mill grew, until cut heads and bloodied noses were everywhere. Hugh had enjoyed the spectacle at first without feeling the smallest desire to join in, but now matters looked as though they may be getting out of hand.

Leaping down from the barouche, leaving the ladies at a safe distance, Hugh ran to a group of officers that included Major Cornwell, his recent acquaintance. "We must calm them down before there's real bloodshed."

The man nodded, and they moved into the fray together. Hugh grasped the arms of one of the more energetic young bloods. "You're scaring the ladies," he hissed into the young man's ear, as he pulled him away. "For God's sake calm down or this will turn into a riot."

The younger man, surprised to see Lord Thatcham, the elusive and celebrated aristocrat, recollected where he was, dropped his fists, and blushed crimson.

"Pull your friends away. You're making yourselves ridiculous," Hugh said.

The man hesitated, as though about to argue, but decided he would prefer to obey Lord Thatcham.

The officers, led by the major, exerted a similar calming effect on the other combatants. It took just a few moments to gain control of the mob, for the sight of so many red coats and shining spurs soon overcame them.

As the mill grew quieter, whistles rent the air and half a dozen peelers arrived, targeting the youths and avoiding inconveniencing the gentry as far as possible. The rout ended with a general escape of any who could get away. The ringleaders, including the redheaded lad, too excited to recognise what was happening until too late, were marched off to cool their heels in gaol and await a visit from the magistrates.

Hugh saw that the mob was under control, dusted off his coat, and searched for his hat. His jacket was torn. He touched his lip to find it was bleeding and swelling rapidly. Invigorated, he returned to the barouche where Selena and Lucy giggled excitedly, not at all frightened.

"Lord Thatcham," breathed Selena's friend, Lucy. "How very brave you were. Why, we were sure you would be knocked unconscious at any moment."

Hugh laughed aloud, excitement still pumping

through his veins. He had not enjoyed himself so much for weeks. A sudden movement behind the carriage caught his attention. A woman appeared among the trees at the margins of the park, a shawl obscuring her face. She took an uncertain pace forward, as though she would run towards Hugh, but then stopped, hesitated and half-turned to leave.

Hugh's breath caught in his throat. Waves of hope quickened his pulse. He dropped the reins of the carriage, careless of Selena's indignant cries and ran forward a dozen paces. Now he was close enough to see the woman clearly. Her shawl slipped back, revealing a face framed by curling black hair. Hugh did not know how long he stood, transfixed, aware of nothing but Philomena's face.

Selena called to him. Fleet as a startled deer, Philomena turned back into the shadows and was gone.

Selena's voice, insistent, called Hugh back to the present and a sense of what was proper. "Brother, it seems your manners have quite deserted you," she cried, retying the pale green ribbon on her becoming pink bonnet. "Lucy and I will take the cold if you do not convey us home, at once."

Hugh came to his senses. He could not leave his sister and her friend stranded longer in the barouche. Reluctant, yearning to chase after Philomena, he jumped into the carriage, setting the horses to a fast pace. Ignoring his sister's excited chatter, he turned his head as he drove, struggling to catch a glimpse of Philomena. He caught a brief glimpse as she ran in the shadow of the trees, too far away to reach.

Hugh took the ladies straight home, too full of hope to talk. Lucy was speechless in her admiration for his valour in the face of the riot, but unfortunately, Selena was not. "Hugh," she cried, as she alighted, "I declare I do not know whether you are a hero or simply as great a hooligan as the rest. I know that you have some sympathy with the demands of the Chartists, but I did not know you were one of them."

It was useless to argue the rights and wrongs of the case with such a featherbrain as his sister, so Hugh contented himself with a warning that should Selena carry tales to the Dowager, he would immediately cancel the ball and ban his sister from attending any of the next week's routs.

Chapter Twenty-Seven

Philomena fled back to her lodgings, shaking. *He is here.* She had believed she was learning to forget Hugh, but when she saw him in the park, so tall and commanding above the crowd, she longed to throw herself into his arms.

Life with Hugh is just a hopeless dream. Philomena tried to remain calm. She had found work as a dressmaker, using the remains of the Dowager's money to buy materials. She was slowly making a name, working at the trade she knew so well. For London dressmakers, the Season meant a flurry of activity. In a whirl of cutting patterns, making up calico models and redesigning gowns to hide a debutante's thick waist, clumsy ankle or thin shoulders, Philomena hoped her broken and battered heart would heal. She had no time to mope.

She rented two rooms, using the last of her money to furnish one suitable for receiving customers. The room was elegant enough for a Duchess and the Duchesses liked Philomena. She was not afraid to voice an opinion, but her manner was so gentle and tactful that she caused no offence. She had a talent for persuading young girls and their formidable mothers to avoid the showy but often almost-unwearable patterns displayed in the popular La Belle Assemblée magazine.

The debutantes prized Philomena's finished

garments as a result. Several awkward young ladies attending Queen Charlotte's Ball would benefit from the new dressmaker's careful cutting and stitching, which would allow them to make their curtsey with the minimum danger of toppling ignominiously to the floor before Her Royal Highness.

Philomena often bit her lip to hold back laughter as the Duchesses and their spoilt daughters fussed over the most sophisticated shade of puce for ribbons, the superiority of Nottingham over Brussels lace or the latest designs.

Today, a burst of sunshine had tempted Philomena out of her rooms. The fog had lifted for once, leaving the skyline sharp all the way to St. Pauls. Philomena gazed longingly out of the window. It was a lovely day. How beautiful it must be at Thatcham Hall. The sun would dapple the woods where she had run with John and quarrelled with Hugh. She sighed and her eyes filled with tears.

This would not do. Philomena raised her chin and wiped her eyes. She would allow herself a holiday, today. She would go for a walk, enjoy the sunshine, and watch the gentry in their new clothes, showing off to each other.

She soon found herself in Hyde Park, where a crowd of Chartists waved their fists and shouted. She stood well back from the crowd and wondered whether Selena had yet arrived in London to enjoy her first Season.

Thoughts of Selena led naturally to memories of Hugh, so vivid that when Philomena first saw him she believed herself still to be daydreaming. She gasped and stared harder. It was no dream. She would recognise Hugh anywhere. As he stood, one hand on a hip, the other flicking his whip idly, memory took Philomena straight back to those days at Thatcham Hall. Just so had Hugh stood outside the kitchen on Christmas morning, talking to John.

Philomena watched Hugh wade in to break up the fight, calm and authoritative, oblivious to the loss of his hat and so much more dignified than any other man nearby. Fair hair fell over his brow in the untidy manner she loved. Philomena knew she should run but could not persuade her limbs to obey. Instead she remained rooted to the spot, one hand to her mouth in sudden fear as a burly fellow swung a heavy stave towards Hugh.

Hugh turned, parried the blow, grabbed the stave from the man, and shook him by the arm. The attacker shrugged and fell back. Philomena glowed with pride. When the constables arrived, she longed to run to Hugh. She took a step forward, then, coming to her senses, retreated. She must not let her love catch sight of her.

Nothing had changed. If she approached and tried to rekindle their acquaintance, she risked exposing Hugh to insult and derision. Philomena was a humble dressmaker, secretly married to a man with cold green eyes. She was not a suitable acquaintance for Lord Thatcham. The best way to show her love was to keep out of Hugh's sight and his life.

She hesitated a moment too long. Hugh saw her and ran forward. For a moment, their eyes met and held. Philomena's first glance at his dear face told her that he loved still her. If only she could hurry forward, reach the safety of his arms and remain there forever.

The longing choked her. She must not give in. She clenched her fists until sharp nails dug into her flesh, then turned and fled, blinded by tears.

She shut herself into the cosy rented workroom and sobbed, unchecked. Hugh was here. He was in London. Her love was so near and yet so far away that despair overwhelmed her. Philomena closed calico curtains across the window and collapsed on her bed. The sight of Hugh had destroyed the tiny bubble of tranquillity she had constructed. Her broken heart, that had slowly begun to heal, ripped apart once more. Philomena knew beyond all doubt that without Hugh, life would never be more than a sad, desperate battle. She would find no peace.

Chapter Twenty-Eight

Selena, pretty in her favourite shade of pink, descended the stairs to meet her brother. Hugh had agreed, just this once, to escort her with the Dowager to Miss Angelina Marchant's ball, on the strict understanding that he would leave early to spend the remainder of the evening at his club.

Selena's eyes shone with happiness. "Dear Hugh." She slipped her hand through her brother's arm. "We will have such a delightful time. Angelina will be so excited when she sees that I have actually persuaded Lord Thatcham to attend that she will introduce me to all the most attractive men."

Hugh eyed her, frowning. "I think perhaps you need no more gentlemen to add to your tally."

Selena had taken to the London Season like a duck to water. Hugh feared that such feverish enjoyment hovered dangerously close to behaviour that would allow the chaperones to label his sister as fast. Selena's colour was a little high, her laughter shrill, and her eyes slightly too ready to lock onto those of the most dashing cavaliers. She laughed and Hugh shrugged. The Dowager would be present this evening. His mother's eagle eye would surely allow no excessive flirting.

The ballroom was crammed. Hugh counted over three hundred guests squashed into every corner of the Marchant's house. Tomorrow, he supposed, the guests would describe this Ball as "a dreadful squeeze", affording it the highest possible compliment for such an evening.

An accomplished, if reluctant, dancer, Hugh circled the floor with a succession of over-excited young ladies. Their skirts, which grew wider at every ball, swished against each other as they waltzed sedately or, more daringly and certainly more energetically, danced the polka around the room. How soon could he make his escape?

Miss Henrietta Hay, his current partner, was hot with the excitement of the dance and with the distinction of dancing with the most eligible man in the room.

"Perhaps you would like an ice." Hugh led her out of the ballroom. As they turned into the passage to the refreshment room, a pink gown whisked through a curtain that led outside to a small balcony. That dress was familiar.

Hugh excused himself to Miss Hay and followed the pink dress, swishing the curtain abruptly, to confirm his fears. Selena stood much closer than was appropriate to Mr. Arthur Muldrow.

Hugh's sister gasped, taking a step away from Muldrow. "Oh, Hugh," she whispered, cheeks pinker than her dress. Her hands fluttered at her neck. "What are you doing here? I mean, why have you followed me?" Selena tried to smile but her lips trembled. "I simply came to feel the cool air as it is so hot in the ballroom."

Hugh looked from one to the other. A heavy weight settled somewhere in his chest and two words echoed in his brain. *Not again*. Hugh hid his agitation, his face and voice impassive. This was a public place, and Lord Thatcham must avoid embroiling his sister in a scene that would make Selena the subject of some of the juiciest gossip of the season. "I believe you would feel cooler if you were to eat an ice, Selena. Please join Miss Hay and myself."

Selena's eyes widened.

"I say." Muldrow interrupted, his face an unbecoming purple. "Miss Selena may surely do as she pleases. Her mother is present, you know."

Hugh looked him up and down in silence. He did not dignify the man with a reply but took Selena's arm and escorted her away.

His sister fumed at his side. "Hugh, let me go," she muttered, through stiff lips. "You are hurting my arm."

"I do not wish you to spend time with that man." Hugh, released his hold on her. "He is not to be trusted."

"We were doing nothing wrong." She tossed her head.

Hugh smiled, hiding his fury behind lazy hauteur. "My concern is to make sure that remains the case." He offered his arm to Miss Hay and smiled, glad for the first time that his partner's head would be empty of any thought but dresses and balls. "Now, let us enjoy one of Lady Marchant's spectacular ices." Miss Hay's face lit up.

Selena's sulks did not last long. She maintained a cold silence while they ate ices, but Miss Hay's exclamations of amazement at the number of titled names on Selena's dance card soon enabled her to remember how much she loved to dance. She returned to the ballroom. Hugh relaxed a little. Perhaps the preference his sister had shown for Muldrow was less entrenched than he feared.

He could not explain his hatred of Muldrow to his sister. Selena knew little of the manner of Beatrice's death, and Hugh preferred that she remain blissfully ignorant. He felt certain that Muldrow had enticed Beatrice to the Manor on that day, not so much for love of the beautiful Beatrice, as to pay Hugh back for the past.

Hugh's dislike of the man had begun long before his marriage, when they were at Oxford together. Muldrow, as befitted a near neighbour, had been included in Hugh's card parties. One day his extreme good fortune at the table caught Hugh's attention. He watched the play more closely. All was not as it should be. Muldrow shot his cuffs a little too often and his luck at those moments made it apparent that he had additional cards secreted up his sleeve.

"Muldrow," Hugh had said, his voice dangerously quiet. "Your luck improves with every hand." Muldrow looked up at him. Hugh stared hard at the man's sleeve, one eyebrow raised.

Muldrow's hooded brows had lowered. His face flushed an unpleasant shade of purple and his eyes flickered from side to side. "Oh. Can that be the time? I must be on my way."

Hugh rose from his seat. "Surely not," he drawled. "Why, young Mr. Dunsmore here has had an unfortunate evening of it. Surely you will remain and allow him to recoup some losses if he can."

Muldrow heard the menace in Hugh's voice and blinked. He smiled, but his eyes were narrow slits. "Perhaps I will remain for another hand or two. My appointment can surely wait a few moments."

"Indeed." Hugh hooked his boot into a chair. He pulled it across and sat close by Muldrow's side. "Cut me out of this hand. I wish to observe such expert play at close quarters."

Hugh's friends glanced at each other, hearing the dangerous undertones in his voice. Muldrow had no alternative but to play on. Hugh, legs crossed, observed him closely. Strangely, Muldrow's luck changed. Dunsmore, a young member of their set who could ill afford large losses at cards, recouped his stake and won an equal amount.

Hugh decided he had made his point. "I believe you needed to leave?" he remarked to Muldrow, his voice casual.

The man scrambled to his feet. "Er, yes. Best be off, don't you know," he muttered, making for the door.

The room remained deadly quiet until he left, but as the door closed, laughter followed him into the night. From that day, Mr. Muldrow had no place in Hugh's circle of acquaintances.

Once returned to their homes, situated within ten miles of each other, the two men could not entirely avoid one another. Hugh maintained a cool, polite demeanour when meeting Muldrow but preferred to avoid him where possible. Beatrice, though, had struck up a friendship with Muldrow's sister soon after her marriage to Hugh. She spent more time at Fairford Manor than Hugh wished and resolutely ignored every hint as to Muldrow's character.

Hugh, wishing his bride to enjoy her new life at Thatcham Hall, allowed her visits to continue. If only he had forbidden the connection. The consequences to

Beatrice proved disastrous.

Watching Selena twirl happily around the room in the arms of one admirer after another, Hugh began to relax. He retrieved his hat and gloves and left, hoping to enjoy the cool night air on the short walk to his club. One or two other escapees were leaving this and other parties, some passing on to the next—others, like himself, searching for peace and quiet.

Hugh had gone only a few steps when he caught sight of Muldrow, walking briskly a few yards ahead. Relieved to see the man putting distance between himself and Selena, Hugh slowed his pace, having no desire to catch up. In any case, the evening air was pleasant. The fogs of the winter and early spring had given way to light summer breezes. These could not entirely lift the London stink of cabbage, horse and excrement, however, and Hugh hoped a cigar would counter the worst of the smells. He stopped at a corner to light up, pulling the smoke gratefully into his lungs.

Ahead, Muldrow also stopped and leaned on a lamppost. The gas light gleamed yellow. A smaller, thinner figure joined him. Something about the attitudes of the men disturbed Hugh. They peered around, their glances hurried, as though checking no one else stood nearby.

Hugh slipped into the shadows, away from the light of the gas lamps. The street had grown quiet. He was near enough to hear Muldrow's voice but could not make out the man's words. He trod quietly closer, keeping in the shadows, curious to know what was going on.

The newcomer was not dressed in evening clothes. He wore a labourer's fustian coat, heavy boots, and a flat cap. Muldrow and the thin man seemed an unlikely pair. Hugh, closer now, held his breath and strained to make out what they were saying.

"Have you found her?" asked Muldrow.

"Yes, sir," the other replied. "I know where she's at, all right. You just say the word, Guv'nor."

"Have you the plan clear in your mind?" Muldrow shot another glance behind him.

"Don't you worry about that." The thin man sniggered. The hairs on Hugh's neck stood up at the sound. "She'll get what's coming to 'er, won't she?" He hawked and spat into the gutter.

Muldrow stepped away. "That's enough. Get out of my sight and don't come near me in the street again. I don't want you seen with me."

"Now, my lord, don't you be like that. I'll be needing some blunt to set things in motion, won't I?"

"Here," said Muldrow. "This is all you'll get for now. The rest's for when I have her safe."

He strode away. His companion stood a moment longer, flicking coins over in his hand and biting one with his teeth. He half turned and Hugh caught a glimpse of his face in the lamplight. A bush of unkempt hair hung down over a low forehead. The man's mouth, open to bite on the coin, showed a gap where the front tooth should be.

Recognition struck Hugh like a hammer blow. The man matched the description James, the footman, had given of a strange visitor to the Hall at Christmas. Thin, with long hair and a missing tooth. Hugh could not doubt that this man was the same one who had called at the Hall asking about Philomena. Hugh had no further details. He had assumed the man had taken a fancy to the nursemaid on seeing her in the village.

Could there be a link? Philomena was in London. The strange man was also here and seemed, by all that was incredible, to be plotting with Arthur Muldrow.

Hugh's cigar burned unnoticed in his fingers as Joseph wandered away into the distance, whistling. What could this mean? Why should Muldrow be meeting with this man? Was Philomena really the "her" they discussed?

No name had passed Muldrow's lips. The thin man had simply said he had found "her." Hugh's heart thudded. If indeed they were referring to Philomena, she must be in danger. Hugh's hands tightened into fists. He had never discovered the truth but he knew there was a mystery associated with Philomena's former life. The thin man must be part of it.

What could Muldrow possibly want with her? The mystery of Philomena seemed deeper than ever. Hugh could not begin to see any pattern that fitted the facts. Nevertheless, one truth stood out starkly, so clear that Hugh's head ached with shock.

If the thin man planned to kidnap Philomena, Hugh must find her first.

Chapter Twenty-Nine

Philomena looked forward to a busy day. The balls and dances of the night before had been hard on the debutante's dresses. While their own maids could clean the gowns, mend small tears to the lace, or sew a ripped hem, several young girls wished to return their dresses for Philomena to repair serious damage. Others, especially the thriftier among them, wanted creative alterations so they could wear the same dress again without attracting derision.

Philomena had no time today to spend on thoughts of what might have been if she was a lady and Hugh was not an aristocrat. She was glad to be busy; the demands of the ladies and their fond mothers drove the memory of Hugh's adventure in Hyde Park quite out of her head.

This morning, she was engaged with a young lady who had been one of her first customers. Philomena enjoyed her visits for the girl was always full of gossip from the night before.

"Well, Miss Philomena," she began, watching intently as Philomena held a selection of different coloured ribbons against the bodice of a blue silk gown. "We had such a crush at the Marchants' ball last night. Everyone was there. I declare, I tasted six flavours of ice, and I danced every dance." Young Miss Everett smiled, shyly. "In fact, I even danced with Lord

Thatcham. He was in attendance for once. He was by far the most handsome man at the ball, of course. He attends very rarely, you know; for he is only lately out of mourning for his wife."

She sighed, luxuriously. "Lord Thatcham is so romantic. Everyone wonders who will catch him. You know he must have another wife before too long. He has but the one heir."

Philomena turned her face away. It cut her to the quick to hear of Hugh dancing with young ladies. How foolish she was. She knew he was in London with Selena for the Season. Of course, he would accompany his sister to the occasional ball. Miss Everett was right. He would outdo everyone else. Hugh would be taller and far more handsome than the rest, and he would never titter or jostle like the callow youths.

Philomena kept a tight hold on her emotions and ordered her hand not to shake. "I have heard of Lord Thatcham." She kept her voice low and calm. "I believe he has a sister who comes out this year?"

"Oh, yes, Lady Selena is such a great friend of mine." Miss Everett beamed. Philomena wondered how closely this friendship connected to Hugh's eligibility as a suitor. She wondered whether he had any interest in this fluffy young girl.

For a second, her spirits faltered with jealousy of this silly, wealthy girl. What had she done to deserve her comfortable, sheltered life in London Society? Why should she look forward to a prosperous future? It was the slightest accident of birth that Miss Everett was a lady and Philomena a poor dressmaker.

Philomena shook her head, trying to clear it of such thoughts. She would not become jealous. Her own life, after all, was far from unpleasant, apart from her heavy heart. She enjoyed needlework, had funds enough to live comfortably and had made many new friends. Those friends were far more suitable than the aristocratic Lord Thatcham and his family.

Miss Everett chattered happily, not noticing her dressmaker was distracted or that her fingers shook as she pinned the hem of the dress. Only a word or two penetrated Philomena's thoughts. "Lady Selena..." and "Ripped her dress..."

Philomena concentrated as the girl rattled on. "It was quite shocking. Lord Thatcham was so angry that he positively reprimanded Selena. He is very fierce, of course, despite being so handsome." The girl frowned. "Perhaps he would not be such a very good husband, after all."

"Surely he was not angry because Lady Selena tore her gown?" Philomena ventured, ignoring a pang of guilt at encouraging gossip.

"Oh no, it was to do with Mr. Arthur Muldrow. Lady Selena, you see, has a special fondness for him, but her brother dislikes him. Lord Thatcham saw them together and took her straight away. It was the most diverting thing I have seen in my life." She giggled, delighted. "But what I was going to say was that Lady Selena is meeting me here. I told her all about you and the tiny stitches you use, and she said she had once known someone who sewed like a fairy and that she was sure no other would manage nearly as well."

Miss Everett paused for breath. "So I said that, of course, you were every bit as good, and Miss Selena said she did not think you could be and then she asked me all about you. I told her what you look like, Miss

Tailor, for you are much prettier than the other dressmakers."

Miss Everett paused again, leaving Philomena open mouthed. She dropped a ribbon on the floor and bent to pick it up, her mind racing while her fingers fumbled. Before she had time to speak, there was a knock at the door.

"Oh, I believe that is Selena, now," said Miss Everett. "Do let her in."

Philomena had no choice. Half running, half-reluctant, she opened the door. Selena jumped into her arms with a shriek of joy. "Oh, I prayed it would be you. Dear Philomena, I am so happy to have found you!" There were real tears in her eyes as she held Philomena by both hands. "How could you come here and fool us all into thinking you had gone to Bristol?" Selena said, laughing. "You are so very wicked. I must give you another hug."

Philomena, very aware of Miss Everett's round-eyed astonishment, gently removed Selena's hands and closed the door. "I am pleased to see you," she said, and then whispered in Selena's ear. "Pray take care. I am not a suitable companion for you."

Selena laughed aloud. "Not suitable! Why, you are an old friend of our family, and I do not mind that Lucy knows it."

Philomena, aware that she had not long before been encouraging Lucy to gossip about Selena's family, wondered how she would extricate herself from this situation. In truth, she was as delighted at this meeting as was Selena. She felt for Hugh's sister as if she were her own. The loss of such a friend, who cared nothing for the difference in rank, compounded Philomena's misery at leaving the Hall.

"Come, Lucy." Selena took her friend's arm. "Philomena is a companion of mine from long ago. I told you she was the best dressmaker in the world. Was I not correct?" Miss Everett, her eyes wide as saucers, found nothing to say. "We must be off," repeated Selena.

She turned smoothly to Philomena and winked. "I have a dress that I would like you to alter for me." Her voice was heavy with emphasis. "I will bring it over myself, later today."

The girls left Philomena in a state of confusion. She had no doubt that Selena would return as promised, and her spirits leapt at the prospect of renewing their friendship. For several minutes, Philomena paced around the rooms, hands twisting together. She could not sit still.

She bit her nails with anguish. She must not spend time with Selena. She must forget Hugh. They could be nothing to each other. The Dowager had been right to separate them. They were worlds apart. It was best that she had left the Hall. She had escaped a life as Hugh's mistress, a life that would make her an outcast from every society except the very lowest and would bring shame on him.

Philomena longed to see Selena again. She would explain that she could not renew their connection, except as her dressmaker, and would allow Selena to treat her only as she would any other former servant.

Other clients had appointments that day. Philomena discussed their needs with half her attention, for her mind was in turmoil. She begrudged every moment spent with the plain Miss Down and her even plainer mother, designing a dress to conceal the girl's enormous hips. "The current fashion for many petticoats under your skirt will flatter your tiny waist," Philomena said, abstracted but tactful. "See, I will make the bodice a little longer and the neck a little lower, the better to show off your elegant shoulders. There, how charming you will look."

Miss Down left more satisfied than ever. Philomena sat alone, waiting for Selena's return. The hours ticked around. She imagined Selena, surrounded by a group of admirers, forgetting her promise. *Will she never come?* Philomena's head ached. She applied brown paper soaked in vinegar, to her forehead, but felt no relief from the pain.

She lay on her bed in her tiny room for so long that when the knock sounded at the door, she had decided that Selena would not come. She could hardly drag herself up to open the door.

Selena saw at once that her friend was not well. "Why, Philomena, what is the matter? You are ill. Come and sit, and I will make you a salt pack. Our nurse used to give it to Hugh and myself whenever we had the headache. Not that Hugh ever had the headache, I remember, but he often had cuts and bruises and once he broke an arm when he climbed the old oak tree and fell out of the top branch. Mama was sure he was dead, but Hugh was up again next day and riding his pony."

Chattering happily, Selena bustled about. "I have given my maid Alice the slip and come in a carriage by myself. I told Mama I was to be with Lucy. Lucy will keep my secret so long as no one asks her anything about it, for she is exceptionally stupid, as you must see. Still, she is a good friend, even if she does talk about Hugh all the time, and we can all see that he has no interest in her at all."

Philomena roused herself enough to nod and smile.

"As for Hugh—" Selena sat to watch Philomena sip from a cup of water. "Are you feeling better?" she asked, interrupting herself. Philomena nodded and held the linen bag of ice and salt against her brow.

"Now, what was I saying? Oh, yes, Hugh. He is so disagreeable now. Why, I thought he was bad-tempered enough before, but that was as nothing. Since he came back to the Hall the day after you left, he has been like a bear with a sore head."

Selena stopped a moment and giggled. "I saw a bear dancing in the Park the other day. I wonder if he had a sore head."

A glance at Philomena showed her that her friend was in no mood for jokes. "Yes. Hugh is so unkind about you. You know, I did think that he liked you when you were with us at Christmas. Sometimes, he even became civil to me and to Mama, but after you left, he talked of nothing but lies and false addresses and how you must be no better than a thief."

Heedless of the pain her gossip caused, Selena prattled cheerfully, turning the knife in Philomena's heart. It was hard not to cry out with the pain. Could Hugh hate her so? He had not seemed to, in Hyde Park. He had started forward with such enthusiasm. It might mean nothing. Perhaps Hugh had been shocked rather than pleased to see Philomena.

Philomena asked after John. He remained in Hampshire, she heard, with the governess. "John does not like Miss Smith," Selena said, "but Hugh said that is because he is not used to her and because she makes him work hard at his lessons. Hugh says John will soon be cheerful again. I must admit, Hugh often spends half the day with the child when he is at the Hall, just as he used to when you were there. Hugh will send for him to visit, soon."

Philomena, claiming her headache had quite disappeared, steered the talk around to the fashions of the day. Selena need not know of the misery in her heart.

Selena clapped her hands in delight at the pretty workshop, thrilled to find her friend building a successful business. "I suppose we cannot meet quite as we used to, but I shall make sure all my friends come here for their gowns, so you may become as rich and famous as you deserve. That will be good, will it not?" She beamed.

"It will be wonderful." Philomena hesitated. How best to ensure Selena was not forbidden to visit? "I expect you will not tell Hugh I am here, will you?" It was bad enough to hear of his anger. Philomena could not bear to lose Selena as well.

Selena pouted a little, but agreed. "I will like to have a secret from Hugh, for he is so cross. He has taken such a loathing for Arthur Muldrow, you know, our neighbour, and I have no idea why, since he was fond of Mr. Muldrow's father and never cared whether or not his money all came from trade. I am afraid Hugh has grown very old and boring, these days. I do not like it at all, if you want the truth."

Selena blushed prettily when she mentioned Mr. Muldrow. Philomena wondered why Hugh held such dislike for the man. Should she warn Selena against making a liaison with someone her brother detested?

No, she did not dare. She did not want to lose Selena's goodwill so soon after meeting her again. "Your brother is a man and sees things rather differently from women."

Philomena bit her tongue, annoyed to hear herself excusing Hugh's behaviour on the grounds of sex. How differently, indeed, how tartly she would have spoken, had she been talking with him in the nursery.

She had longed to hear news of Hugh but now, as his sister left to return home, Philomena wished Selena had told her nothing. *Well, I have learned my lesson.* She would make her own life, here in London. She would be perfectly happy with people of her own class. How foolish to ever imagine that Lord Thatcham, the head of a noble English family, could care for someone so lowly. The Dowager had been right to send her away. Wiping away tears, Philomena opened the bottom drawer of her dresser. Inside, she kept a drawing John had made. She planted a kiss on the picture and tucked it away, safe under a pile of linens. She would not look at it again.

Next day, true to her word, Selena sent a parcel containing two gowns, along with a note, full of innocent deception, childish delight and exclamation marks.

"My dear Philomena,

I am sending these to you as I promised, for you to alter them. I will leave you to plan the alterations because no one else has such good taste! I will be unable to visit for a few days, as Mama was very angry with me for venturing out alone in a carriage! I found myself hard pressed to prevent her from keeping me at home altogether! I declare, if Mama were not worried I would never find a husband she would prevent me from attending any entertainments at all! Hugh was horrid and agreed with Mama, just as I expected. I can assure you I have said nothing to him about finding you: he does not deserve to know any secrets!

Please send the gowns back when they are done and make sure the account is very large indeed. Perhaps you should make it in a different name, for we do not want our little secret to be discovered, do we?"

Philomena smiled. She shook out the dresses and set to work at once. Selena would be the belle of the ball if her stitching could make her so.

Chapter Thirty

By late in the afternoon, all Philomena's young ladies and their mothers had returned home to prepare for the evening's receptions and balls. Philomena settled down to an hour or so of needlework. She liked to finish the gowns herself, despite having a small army of girls living nearby, each well able and willing to undertake piecework. The clever use of a needle could be the difference between misery and comfort to such young women.

There was little time to spare. The evening would soon fall and the light grow dim. Philomena did not wish to ruin her eyesight by undertaking too much close work by gas light. She made a few stitches on a gown she was completing in readiness for a lady's maid who would arrive to collect it early the next morning.

She turned the skirt over. Oh, Lord. Where were those ruffles? Several pieces were missing. How could that have happened? There was no time to lose. Philomena's growing reputation depended on reliability as much as talent. She must retrieve the missing sections at once.

She slipped on a woollen shawl against the chill of the cooling air and exchanged cotton slippers for stout boots. She must run the three streets to find Cherry, the young seamstress whose neat stitching enabled her to sew the most elaborate of broderie ruffles.

The distance to Cherry's lodgings was further than Philomena had remembered, and the light was fading fast when she arrived. Cherry shared a room with three other girls. Philomena caught a whiff of cabbage and urine. This part of the city reminded her of that former life, lodging with Samuel and Joseph. She would leave as soon as possible.

Cherry was hard at work by the light of a tallow candle. Her stitches were fine and neat and the completed piece already lay in a basket ready for delivery. Philomena, a tart rebuke for tardiness on her lips, held her tongue. The tiny room was uncomfortably crowded, although it contained only one rough bed, shared by the four girls, and a mix of assorted chairs. Philomena spied a large hole in Cherry's stocking.

One of the other girls was anointing her face with crude white. No doubt, her living depended not on sewing but on something far earthier. Philomena shivered. Would she have ended up in such a life, if she had offered herself to Hugh without marriage?

"There you are, me darling," the girl cried to Cherry. "You'll be joining me in my game if you keep forgetting your sewing."

"Indeed she will not," Philomena retorted, but the girl crowed with laughter.

"Just you wait a few months. There's better money to be had on the game."

"Give up, do," said Cherry. "Miss Philomena don't want to 'ear your nonsense."

Philomena set off home to find the daylight quite gone and the streets dark. Gas lamps were the only illumination. Pools of eerie yellow gleamed through the murk that had descended this evening, matching

Philomena's mood. She shivered. This was no time to be out alone in this district. Glancing to either side, gripping the parcel of ruffles tight to her chest, she slipped down the street, keeping close to the houses, her head bent.

Philomena quickened her pace, heart racing. She was used to London streets. Why was she suddenly so nervous? She came to a crossroads and stopped, puzzled. Where was she? Turning round, she retraced a few steps, but recognised nothing. She pulled the shawl close. There was no need to panic. She would come to no harm. If she followed this street, it was sure to lead to a more familiar part of town.

Philomena's feet slipped on the damp streets and black mud clung to her boots as she stumbled across the road. She passed a public house. Ugh! It stank of beer and tobacco. Raucous laughter spilled out as the door swung open. On an impulse, Philomena looked up at the sign over the door. *The White Hart.*

No. Surely not. She was back in the one part of town she needed, above all, to avoid. Joseph had frequented this same public house. Philomena shuddered, kept her eyes on the ground and started to run.

A couple of youths tumbled into her path. "'Ere," said one to the other, clutching him by the shoulder. "Look what we've found." Boozy with drink, neither was quick enough to stop Philomena as she pushed past, the shawl hiding her face.

A third youth lurched into the street, singing tunelessly. "Dear ol' Bessie, don't you leave me now," he bawled. Thin and scrawny, he was barely able to walk for the drink. "Why, that's a nice piece of arse!"

Philomena, her heart sinking, knew that voice at once. She'd heard it many a time as Joseph rolled home late at night. *No, it can't be.*

There was no mistake. "Oi, you," Joseph shouted again. "Get back 'ere, you, if you know what's good for you."

One of his mates pitched forward and spewed the contents of his stomach into the gutter, spraying Joseph's boots liberally with vomit. Cursing, Joseph grabbed the culprit's jacket, and Philomena seized her chance, running as fast as a pair of tired feet would carry her, successfully putting a street between them. Even as she stumbled round a corner, out of sight, Joseph shouted again. "I know where to find you, don't worry."

Philomena's chest heaved with sobs, her face soaked with tears of fear and horror. Did Joseph truly know where to find her? What would become of her, if he did?

If only she could run to Hugh and throw herself on his mercy. But she dare not. He had loved her once, enough to offer marriage, but he had not forgiven her. Selena had made it clear. Hugh had dismissed Philomena as a simple, foolish female. She had entranced the Master of the Hall for a while with lies and falsehoods, at a time when there were few other ladies around to take an eligible aristocrat's eye, but now he was done with her.

All Philomena's fear of Joseph returned, as vivid as though the wonderful Christmas interlude at Thatcham Hall had never happened. Who could help her? Was she quite alone? Perhaps she could ask Selena for help?

She shook her head. No, she had made a new life

here. The business brought in enough money to live on. There was no need to run from danger and difficulty. After all, she had returned to London determined to make Joseph tell the truth about the secret marriage. She had escaped his clutches once before. The horror of seeing her tormentor in the flesh and hearing that uncouth voice again had been shocking, but at least, now, Philomena had found her enemy.

She peered through the gloom before entering the lodgings, anxious to make sure there was no sign of Joseph. He had not followed. Maybe the threats were empty words and he did not know where she lived.

Her shivering stopped. Joseph was as dangerous now as he had been before, but Philomena was stronger. An independent woman, making her own way in the world, needed no help. It was time to face up to Joseph. Philomena began to make plans.

Joseph was dishonest. He had cheated customers in the past, and there had been other clues to his duplicity. How could he afford several pints of porter each day, and amass so many kerchiefs to sell and pockets full of loose change? He gambled, it was true, but was too stupid to win honestly. Philomena was convinced he picked pockets—or worse.

A scheme formed itself. To catch Joseph in some criminal act would give her a weapon. She would threaten to inform the peelers, and force Joseph to tell the truth. At last, she would find out the identity of the man with cold green eyes, and be free of Joseph, forever.

As Philomena planned, she sewed, the tiny needle dipping rapidly in and out of the delicate tissue. She loved sewing Selena's gowns. Service to Selena felt like a service to Hugh. Every stitch Philomena made was a gift. She worked hard, late into the night, to complete the dresses. She shook them out, thrilled to imagine Selena wearing the elegant, soft blue costume to the next ball.

She packaged the gowns, folded neatly in tissue, into boxes tied with pink ribbon. Cherry would call round the next day and deliver them.

Chapter Thirty-One

Hugh and Selena did not quickly forgive one another after the Marchant's Ball. Hugh spent the whole of the next day away from the house but did not explain his errand to Selena. Dark circles hinted at his lack of sleep and the bruise round his eye, the result of the mill in the Park, quickly turned yellow.

He glowered at breakfast, hardly touching the bacon or kidneys.

Selena was the first to speak. "I am not a schoolgirl anymore. There is no need for you to be so rude when I talk to Mr. Muldrow. Surely, I may choose my own friends."

The footman retreated to the end of the room to pretend he could hear nothing of the conversation.

"You may," Hugh raised an eyebrow, "whenever you like. Of course, that would mean leaving this house. Do you have somewhere pleasant to go? I would have imagined all your acquaintances to be in London at this time of the year, but perhaps we can find a distant cousin who would enjoy your company in her declining years."

Selena scowled.

"You have only to say the word," said Hugh, "and I will set Mama to the task of finding someone."

"You are not at all amusing." Selena pushed her food around her plate. Hugh allowed his to remain untouched.

The Dowager, though puzzled as to why her two children insisted on arguing, joined in. "Do not play with your food, Selena. It is as well that we will dine alone, tonight, for you seem to have forgotten how to behave."

Selena glared but said no more. Her own ball was fast approaching, and she was relying on her brother's generosity to ensure the event was suitably splendid. She must not annoy him.

Hugh found his sister changed. Was she becoming spoiled? He preferred not to believe that to be true. He loved Selena, and usually found her nonsense amusing. She had been kind to Philomena at Christmas.

Selena took him aside later, interrupting a planned escape to his club. "Dear brother…" She twinkled so sweetly that Hugh could not resist smiling briefly in return. "I am sorry to have offended you. I see that you dislike Mr. Muldrow. I am sure I do not understand you at all, but nevertheless…"

Selena held up her hand in an imperious gesture learned from their mother, forestalling Hugh before he spoke. "Nevertheless, I will obey you and spend no further time with him. In any case, he insists on wearing a most unbecoming mustard coloured cravat." She giggled. "Anyway, dear brother, I wanted to tell you about the delightful time I spent the other day. You had gone to see some horses, I believe, and so I went out with Lucy, to the dressmaker."

"How interesting." Hugh made no attempt to hide his complete lack of interest.

"Yes, you would indeed find it so if I were to tell you what happened," Selena teased.

Hugh looked at his sister with suspicion. "What have you been up to?"

"There is no need to be so distrustful. We did nothing of which you could possibly disapprove. But I wonder whether you can guess who we met?"

Hugh groaned. Would she never tire of these childish guessing games? "Her Majesty the Queen?"

She giggled again. "Oh Hugh, you are ridiculous. No, someone we know much better than that."

"One of your old school teachers, perhaps." Hugh wished to put an end to the conversation. "Please tell me at once, for I agreed to meet James Hadden at the livery stables, and I do not mean to be late."

"Oh, nonsense." Selena diverted onto a new track. "You are ridiculous, insisting on arriving everywhere on time. I declare, half the world laughs at such an insistence on punctuality."

"More fool them. Now, are you about to explain, or shall we forget this conversation?"

"Oh no, for you will be so very pleased when you hear what I have to say. But you must not tell Mama, for perhaps she would not like it overmuch." Hugh frowned and Selena hurried to finish. "I have visited Philomena. That is all I wanted to say."

Hugh, the air knocked from his body, turned to the piano beneath the window. He leaned on the instrument for a moment, waiting for the jangle in his head to subside and his wild pulse to slow. Selena's words seemed to echo through the room. She had seen Philomena. For a moment, Hugh could think of nothing else.

Selena continued, her tone peevish. "I thought you would be interested. After all, you liked Philomena as much as I, and so did John, for that matter. I thought you would be pleased to know where…" Her voice faded away at the sight of her brother's face. Her eyes opened wide with shock.

Hugh fought to appear calm. Selena stared, her eyes slowly filling with tears. "Oh, poor Hugh." Her voice was full of compassion. "I did not know. I mean, I thought Philomena was just John's nursery maid."

Hugh's voice cracked. "Yes, that is true."

Selena put her hand on his arm. "I should not have told you," she said, half to herself. "I promised I would not, and I have broken my promise."

"I saw her, you know," Hugh said. "In Hyde Park. Philomena was there."

Selena took one of his cold hands and stroked it. "My dear Hugh, what can I do? How can I help?"

He swallowed hard and forced a smile. "Tell me where she is, I beg you."

"There's something else." Selena sounded nervous. "You see, she works as a dressmaker."

Of course, she would be making a way in the world.

"I left my dresses with her to alter. I thought you would want me to." Selena's eyes were huge.

Hugh managed a smile. "Very well, I will not be angry with you. What happened?"

Selena grinned, relieved to see her brother recover some composure. "The dresses were delivered this morning, and when Alice and I took them out of the boxes—by the way, I shall be magnificent at our Ball. Philomena is so clever—but I am wandering from the point. When we took out the dresses, something else fell out of the box." She reached into her reticule and drew out a small object. She handed it to him.

Hugh weighed it in his hand. The brooch was heavy. Made from gold and fashioned in a style from twenty years ago, it bore a miniature portrait on the front. The portrait depicted a young lady with bright golden curls and shining blue eyes. He met his sister's eye.

"It could almost be a portrait of Philomena, could it not?" said Selena. "The likeness is very strong."

Hugh shook his head. "No, the style of it is too old. In any case, why would Philomena carry her own portrait? However, you are right. It does seem to have a look of her. If the hair were but a different colour—black, like hers."

"I know who it must be," said Selena.

"Who?"

"It must be her mother. Look, the lady in the portrait is wearing a dress like Mama's, so that would make her the right age, wouldn't it?"

Hugh considered. "How can this be her mother? Philomena is of no family who would own such a brooch. Why, she was brought up by some old uncle, or so she said…" He knew so little about her. "Certainly, Philomena is no great lady like the one in this picture."

Selena hopped on one leg. "Isn't it the most delightful mystery? Philomena must come from a wealthy family, but she never said so. Why could that be? Even now, she makes her own living. What can have happened?"

Hugh shook his head. He had no more idea than Selena.

"The odd thing is," Selena went on, "I think I've seen this picture, or one very like it, before, but I'm sure Philomena never showed it to me. I would remember, wouldn't I?"

Hugh stared hard at the picture. "No. I am quite sure I have never seen this before." He took out a kerchief and wrapped the brooch carefully. He put it in his pocket. "It's valuable. We must return it to her."

His heart leapt at the prospect and Selena grinned. "I will allow you to have that pleasure, although I did promise not to tell you or Mama of her whereabouts. Philomena may be angry."

Hugh shook his head. "When will you learn that you must keep your promises?"

"I would never want to stand in the way of your happiness." Selena gave a cheerful giggle. "Even if it does mean I must break a very small promise. I did it for your sake, you know. Now, you must remember how kind I have been and stop plaguing me about my friends."

With that, Selena thrust a scrap of paper into Hugh's hand and ran happily upstairs, conscience apparently quite clear, to try on more dresses. Hugh studied the paper. Selena had written Philomena's address in a round, childish script.

Hugh took the stairs two at a time, hardly able to restrain a shout of glee. Instead, he bellowed at Martin to come at once and help him dress, for he had some important business. "And Mayhew," he shouted to the butler, "send a message to Lord Hadden to say I will not arrive at the stables today, nor will I attend the club tonight, after all."

Chapter Thirty-Two

The fog of terror clouding Philomena's brain cleared as she rehearsed a new plan. She was more than a match for Joseph. There was no need to give up her independence or appeal for help from anyone. She looked with pride around her tiny rooms, prettily decorated with swathes of the loveliest materials she could afford. She had created this small world unaided.

She opened the dresser drawer, to look once more at a few cherished mementos. There was the picture John had drawn, with a small stick boy next to a larger figure, a depiction of Philomena and himself. She had vowed not to look at it, but such a promise proved impossible to keep. She wasted long moments smiling at the childish drawing.

There, too, was the small kerchief John gave her at Christmas. Philomena buried her nose in it. It smelled of the nursery. Blinking away tears, she moved on, searching among the paper and ribbons in the drawer for the precious brooch. She was sure she had left it there, but it had vanished.

Philomena tried to remember the last time she saw the brooch. She felt around the seams of dresses and undergarments; she had sometimes sewn the brooch into clothes for safety. She searched the rooms. This did not take long, for there were few places where the brooch could be hidden. At last, she had to admit that it had gone.

Philomena missed her treasure terribly. She had always kept it safe. She knew it must be valuable, but would never sell it. She loved it, fancying that the lady in the miniature looked a little like her. Samuel, seeing the likeness, had probably bought the brooch cheaply, through one of his shadier acquaintances. Philomena sighed for the loss, but given her current predicament, she had no time to waste on a missing trinket.

She would need all her courage to carry out her plan. Philomena had an unreasonable fear of the dark, ever since that dreadful night in the cutting when the train was derailed. She could overcome any number of frights while the sun still shone, but the scheme she proposed would need the cover of darkness.

As the days passed, and there was no sign of Joseph, she felt bolder. Joseph was, after all, a man not an ogre. Dishonest and crude, he had nevertheless never managed to harm her. He was not a monster, like those in Hugh's ridiculous stories for John, but a weak and rather stupid human being. All she had to do was find some hold over him, and that should not be too hard.

He was dishonest. Once or twice, Sam had questioned him about the kerchiefs and purses that appeared and disappeared. The punishment for theft was hanging or, more often these days, deportation. "I will not visit you in prison before they send you away, neither," Sam told him.

Philomena would use Joseph's weakness against him. Her first task was to find a disguise that would allow her to approach close to Joseph without being recognised. She checked her appearance in a little gilt mirror near her bed. Her hair had not grown too long.

She could easily pass for a boy, as before. Dressing in a man's garments helped her feel safe. No one looked twice at a youth in the streets by himself, while a woman alone would be a target for whistles and worse. Philomena ventured out to find the items she needed. Her first stop was Petticoat Lane.

"Now I wonder what a nice young lady like you would be wanting with a pair of breeches," asked the clothes' seller. Philomena, dressed as drably as she could manage in a brown dress and colourless shawl, turned over the old, worn garments on the stall, using the tips of her fingers. "What have you got?"

"What about this 'ere pair, nice and clean. Come from one of the best houses. I can let you have it for a shilling."

"A shilling?" Philomena shook her head. "I'll give you nine pence."

"Eleven pence and I'm putting my poor children out of dinner tonight," said the old man, piteously.

Philomena stood firm. "Ten pence, and that's the most I'll give you."

"Ten pence ha'penny?"

"Oh, very well."

After half an hour of bartering, Philomena had all the clothes she needed. Her skin crawled throughout the transactions. She was terrified to look round in case Joseph appeared behind her. Several times, she sensed he was close, but when she turned, there was only an unknown street hawker or crossing sweeper.

Philomena relaxed at last when she arrived home. She tried on her new clothes and suddenly, she was Phil again: a young lad setting out on adventures. "Watch out, Joseph," she said, and laughed aloud. "I'm coming for you."

She waited, sick with excitement, until darkness fell. She felt invincible in the disguise. She pulled the worn cap down over her brow and banged the door of her lodgings. Affecting a mannish swagger, she strode back to the street where she had encountered Joseph. At least, this time, she was prepared.

She hesitated at the door of the White Hart. Did she dare go in? This was the best place to find Joseph, but she had never entered a public house before. She sniffed. The smells of ale and tobacco seemed strangely enticing. She would never dare to enter such a place in her own clothes, but today she was not Philomena, the dressmaker, but Phil, the labourer. She could do anything a man could.

Plucking up every ounce of courage, Philomena lifted her chin, pulled her shoulders back, pushed the door open and strode inside. No one even glanced at her. She found a seat on a wooden settle in a dark corner and sat, watchful, not sure how to behave.

She need not have worried. A girl a few years younger than herself arrived with a tray, shoving greasy locks of hair behind one ear with a grimy hand. "What can I do for you?" she asked, grinning. There were sores round her mouth and her eyes watered.

Philomena gulped. "Get me a pint," she growled, imitating the calls of the nearby drinkers.

"Anyfink else?" The girl leered. She was looking for more business than waitressing. Philomena waved her hand, dismissively. "Get a move on about it," she barked.

The girl wandered away, grumbling. "All right, all right, keep your 'air on mister." She brought the pint soon enough. "That's tuppence."

Philomena threw the coins on to the girl's wooden tray. "Here's a farthing for you."

She sat in silence, feeling safely invisible in the gloom. So, this was what the male population did? Curious, she watched the other drinkers in the room from the corner of her eyes. Three working men at the nearest table, caps discarded on the table, clicked dominoes. A group in a far corner flipped greasy cards on the tabletop while one or two loners sat quietly, like herself, watching the world. An aged man with a long grey beard settled nearby and nodded at Philomena when she glanced in his direction. Nobody else acknowledged her presence at all.

There was no sign of Joseph. Philomena took a small sip of her beer. Lord, what a taste! She'd known nothing like it. There was no need to take the disguise that far, surely. She wondered what to do. She could not sit for hours with a full glass, and there was no knowing whether Joseph would even turn up tonight.

She jogged the glass on the table and slopped half of the contents on the floor, where it soaked into the sawdust. That should do it. Satisfied that a half-empty pot was more convincing than an untouched glass, Philomena waited.

The girl came round again. "Drink up, then, me darlin'," she encouraged. Philomena raised the glass in salute and kept her mouth firmly closed. From here, she could see everyone who entered or left. Time dragged. She wished she had thought to bring a book, to help the time pass. After an hour, she was sleepy with boredom. Perhaps she had made a mistake. Maybe Joseph did not come here regularly, after all. Still, she would wait a while longer. The room was warm and, now that she was used to them, the smells of beer and pickles had become friendly.

At last, a familiar voice cursed outside the door. Heart pounding, Philomena sat back in the shadows, keeping her face down as Joseph lurched in along with the same two cronies, jostling for a seat.

"I thought you wasn't coming, tonight." The serving girl leaned close to Joseph. "You ain't been in for two days."

"Looking for me, was yer?" Joseph grabbed the front of the girl's dress. "Let's 'ave a look at those little apples then, shall we?"

Philomena waited for the girl to slap Joseph's face, but she just laughed. "Same old Joseph," she leered.

"Give us a kiss, darlin'."

"Not now. Later on, maybe. Or maybe not." She flounced away. Joseph slapped her behind and cackled.

The three newcomers downed two mugs of beer each in quick succession. They talked quietly. Philomena had to listen hard at first to catch their words. As the beer took effect, though, they got louder, not caring who heard them. They boasted of deals that they'd done that day. Philomena did not believe half the tales of making £1 each. Five shillings was more likely, and that would be a good day's profit. She wondered what they were selling, and what had happened to the tailoring business Joseph had inherited. Probably, it had failed. He had no idea how to run an honest establishment.

Joseph hawked to clear his throat, and his cronies leaned in. "I've got a job on. A big one. I'll be out of town a few days, but I'll be well paid."

"What's the game, Jo?" one of the cronies asked, but Joseph shook his head.

"Never you mind. You ain't sticking your nose in that one. But there's somefink else I mean to do first." He looked over his shoulder and lowered his voice further. Philomena strained every nerve to hear. "There's an 'ouse round Paddington way. The family's gone to the country. One of the brats took ill and they've all scarpered right out of town. I 'ear there's only a couple of servants in the 'ouse, and they'll be drinking their master's wine tonight." Joseph cackled. "So let's get over there and see what we can find."

Philomena held her breath. This was better news than she had dared to expect. Something was about to happen, this very night. Joseph had gone from petty theft to full-blown burglary. Poor Sam would turn in his grave if he knew. If Joseph were caught, he'd be deported, or worse. Plenty of thieves were hanged every year for such crimes.

Still, that was Joseph's problem. Philomena would follow him and find out where he hid his booty. This was just what she'd hoped for. She'd get enough information to prove Joseph's crimes and then threaten him with the police unless he told her about the man with cold green eyes and agreed to leave her in peace.

Philomena slipped out of the drinking parlour, making sure to attract no attention. She was almost invisible: a youth of few means wandering home for supper. Rain fell relentlessly. Philomena was glad of that, for once. Passersby had no desire to stop and stare in such weather. They scurried past as though Philomena did not exist.

Joseph had described the house he planned to

target. She would get there first and find a hiding place. It was easy to find. One of a row of elegant townhouses built in the reign of George the Third, the back of the house was hardly visible from the street.

Philomena walked to the end of the road, turned left, continued for a few more minutes and turned left again into a narrower, unlit road. Here, the yards and gardens of the houses ended. Counting carefully, she established which back entrance led to the house Joseph planned to rob.

The gate was closed, but it was low. Glad of her breeches, so much more convenient for climbing than a skirt, Philomena scrambled over the gate and landed on the other side, a little breathless. Outbuildings lined one side, surrounded by bushes. Amongst them, gloomy in the shadows of a range of trees, were the privies, various tool sheds and a greenhouse.

Philomena wriggled between the two thickest bushes she could find. She scratched both hands and face painfully in the process, for one of the shrubs bore vicious thorns. It must be a raspberry or gooseberry bush. A pity there was no better hiding place. Still, at least she could hide here, unseen unless an observer brought torches and searched carefully. All she had left to do was to wait.

This waiting was a dull business. A thrill of adventure had buoyed Philomena at the start of the escapade, but now it waned. The scratches on her face hurt and she was hungry, but there was nothing to eat. No fruit hung on the bushes at this time of the year. She should have filled her pockets with food earlier.

Very few lights shone in the house. Candles flickered and died as servants left the main rooms and retreated to their quarters for the evening. The time ticked slowly by. A church clock chimed ten times. Nothing happened. In the distance, the dull roar of London never ceased. The noises of the night were quieter than those during the day, but were unrelenting all the same. Coaches clattered round the streets, splashing through mud and puddles, while cabbies hallooed for business. In the distance, a steam train hooted.

The damp seemed to rise slowly up her legs, seeping through the thick hob-nailed boots. At a price of just two shillings a pair, they had seemed a bargain, but now Philomena suspected that some problem with the seams had exasperated their previous owner into selling them for half their worth. Still, she had no alternative but to wait. Her legs ached from standing, but sitting on the wet ground would only add to her misery.

The clock struck again. The weather obliged with a sudden downpour, soaking the top half of Philomena's body. Sorely tempted to forget the whole idea, Philomena had to summon all her fortitude. This was her one chance to get the better of Joseph. She would not admit defeat now. Her anxiety had melted away to wretchedness. The scratches on her face ceased to hurt but her frozen fingers began to ache. At last, the final candle in the house went out as the last servant went to bed. Now all was quite still.

She heard a murmur from the street. The voices, quiet at first, grew louder, accompanied by the clang of boots, loud in the night. If this was Joseph, she feared for the success of his venture. Frenzied shushing noises convinced her that this was indeed the burgling party, full of beer and bravado. "Climb the gate," hissed one voice, "and open it for us."

"Nah. You climb it." They jostled and sniggered.

Another voice articulated carefully. "Smitt, you climb it." That was Joseph. Philomena recognised the sneer. Smitt, who she supposed to be a junior member of the team, obeyed, scrambling awkwardly over the gate that Philomena had climbed. There was much huffing and cursing. Philomena made herself as still and small as possible. She need not have worried. Joseph and his cronies were too busy trying to tread quietly, to notice her.

They passed the clump of bushes where Philomena hid and tiptoed round the house. The two at the front carried lengths of metal. These must be jemmies, intended for opening windows. The third to pass by was Joseph. He carried an empty sack over his arm.

All was quiet for long minutes. The gang had sobered a little. Philomena needed to know where they would hide their ill-gotten gains. That meant following them after the robbery. This would be a trickier task. She must keep near them to avoid losing them in the dank night, but to follow too close would put her in danger of discovery. She hesitated. Should she remain in position, or slip away to the street and pick up their trail as they left?

She waited too long. The gang returned to make their getaway. The sack over Joseph's shoulder joggled and clanked, its weight a sign of their success. No sound came from the great house as the gang made good their escape. Philomena let them pass, close by in the dark. Her palms were sticky and her heart thumped. She set off in pursuit, half-running, half-creeping.

It was a struggle to keep up as the gang ran through the twists and turns of London alleyways. Philomena's boots, at least one size too big, slipped and slithered on the pavements. It was hard to breathe and her chest hurt, but she must keep in sight of them. They turned into a narrow lane, but at first Philomena, exhausted and panting, ran past. After a few steps, she realised they had disappeared. Panicking, she skidded to a halt and turned to retrace her steps.

"Ha!" Someone grabbed her arm. "Thought we didn't see you?" He twisted her arm up behind her back. Terror flooded through her and she kicked out.

Her captor swore. "Give 'im a good kicking, mate," called a voice.

Philomena struggled with all her strength. Joseph had hold of her. Twisting and turning, she tried to pull her arm away but his grip on it was too tight. She feared her arm might break and braced herself for the promised kick. The cap flew off her head.

"Wait a minute." Joseph spun her around. She tottered, off balance. He grasped the front of her collar and heaved, pulling her face close. It was just like the day she escaped from London. She closed her eyes, stomach churning. This time, Joseph had the advantage. She would not defeat him so easily, tonight.

Still, no blows came. Philomena opened her eyes again. Joseph, his face red, his mouth opened in a leer that displayed the full glory of a set of rotten teeth, with the familiar gap at the front, grinned at her. His breath was foul. "Now, what piece of luck is this?" he sniggered.

Chapter Thirty-Three

Hugh, suitably dressed to visit a lady, breathed hard. His heart beat faster. He fought to stop himself running through the streets to find Philomena. He must maintain some dignity. He would see her soon and find out the truth, if he had to shake it out of the woman. Then, he would make sure she never left him again. He laughed. Philomena would doubtless tie him in verbal knots and leave him as confused as ever.

His carriage arrived. Leaping into the driver's seat, Hugh gave the matched chestnuts their heads through the streets. He paid little heed to the mud thrown up by the curricle wheels, until a succession of oaths from passersby persuaded him to drive more temperately.

His love of driving a racing carriage at dangerous speeds was no reason to cover every unfortunate merchant or clerk in town in a spray of muddy water. Philomena would take him severely to task if she knew. He reigned in the horses and drove in a more decorous manner.

Soon, the carriage entered the less salubrious area of Spitalfields, where Philomena lived along with many other dressmakers, milliners and lace-makers. Lord Thatcham's arrival in a spanking carriage with the family coat of arms painted on the side caused little comment. The residents were used to seeing the carriages of the wealthy arriving to discharge young ladies and their mothers for fittings.

Hugh rapped on the door at the address Selena supplied. His heart raced as the door opened, but his hopes were soon disappointed. An elderly, wizened woman squinted up at him, scratching at sparse grey hair with bony fingers.

"Miss Philomena Tailor?" Hugh enquired.

The woman looked him up and down, but her expression did not become any more cordial. "Second floor. But she's not in."

Hugh stopped, one foot raised to enter the lodgings. It had never occurred to him that Philomena would not be there, looking as pretty and self-possessed as ever. "When will she be back?" he enquired.

"Who knows?"

He drew himself up to his full, considerable height. "I am Lord Thatcham." He glared. "I wish to know her whereabouts at once."

"I'm sure you do." The old woman regarded him from top to toe once more, unimpressed. Hugh supposed she was familiar with calls made by various gentlemen to the inhabitants of the rooms—inhabitants who often walked the fine line between respectability and disgrace.

He had an idea, reached into his pocket and offered the woman a sovereign. "This is for you, if you can help find Miss Tailor. I can assure you I have only her best interests in view."

"I'm sure you do," the woman repeated, but her eyes flickered with a greedy light. She held out a thin claw.

Hugh pulled his hand back. "Information first."

The woman capitulated. "She's gone out and she

won't want to be found, unless I miss my guess."

"Why would you say that?"

The woman cackled and scratched her head again. "There was a young man left the rooms a while ago. I didn't see Miss Tailor leave, I must be truthful, but the rooms are empty." She kept her eye on the sovereign that Hugh held tantalisingly out of reach.

"What young man? Where did they go?"

"I just saw him leaving. He went that way." She pointed to the right. "Then I went to call on Miss Tailor, to see she was well."

Or to find out what was going on. Hugh's pulse quickened, but he nodded and moved the sovereign a little nearer to the crone's outstretched claws.

"She was gone. It's not like that Miss Tailor to go out in the evening. Not like her at all. Not without saying when she'd be back. I keep a respectable house here."

Hugh relented and dropped the coin into her hand. Philomena had gone, and if this woman was telling the truth, had left in company with a young man. Joseph? If so, Hugh was too late. Joseph had found her first.

He must find Philomena and rescue her. There was no time to waste. Who knew what Muldrow would do when Joseph delivered Philomena? Whatever the connection between the three, there was no doubt she was in danger.

Hugh leaped back into the carriage under the watchful gaze of the old woman, cursing under his breath. A line of occupants peeped through grimy windows to admire the smart carriage and exclaim at the dashing good looks of the noble driver, but there was no sign of Philomena.

He flicked the reins. The horses picked up a rhythm at once. Hugh would not hold them back, now—not for deep puddles or angry pedestrians.

Philomena was gone and so was Joseph. Joseph had done the job as instructed. Hugh sweated. Why had he not acted sooner? He should have searched Philomena out, the moment he knew she was in London. Now, the poor thing was in Joseph's clutches. Hugh shuddered. Knowing Muldrow, a dreadful fate awaited Philomena.

How had Joseph persuaded her to leave? The mystery was deeper than ever, but only one thing mattered. Philomena was in danger and Hugh must rescue her.

Hugh's first stop was Muldrow's London lodgings. Heavy hammering on the door brought Muldrow's butler. A sharp rebuke died on the butler's lips when he saw the titled gentleman at the door. "Mr. Muldrow has returned to his estates, my lord."

He eyed Hugh's apparel. An approving smile suggested the butler wished his own master had half the address and a quarter of the style of Lord Thatcham. "Mr. Muldrow set off early this morning for Fairford Manor. He will no doubt have arrived already. Will your lordship be pleased to leave a message for his return?" The butler raised an eyebrow, clearly hoping for a clue to the business that had put Lord Thatcham in such a flurry.

"You may tell him—" Hugh stopped. He would not make Philomena the talk of the town. That would not help matters. Whatever the truth, he must avoid alerting Society. He handed his card to the butler. "You may tell your master I called and will call again in connection with a certain matter."

The butler, disappointed, bowed Hugh out of the house. Back in the curricle, Hugh whipped up the horses for a night ride up to the shires.

Chapter Thirty-Four

Philomena, imprisoned in Joseph's clutches, soon gave up the struggle. The rest of the gang had disappeared with the loot from the burglary. Philomena could not see where it went. She clenched her jaw until her teeth ground together. So much for all her plans: Joseph had outwitted her this time. What did he have in store for her? She shuddered, imagination running wild. She would pay the wretch back one day.

Joseph bundled his prize into a carriage round the corner. Philomena opened her mouth to beg the driver for help, but Joseph thrust his hand over her face, crushing her lips painfully against her teeth. Her blood tasted of salt.

Joseph sneered. "You'll get no help there." He wiped his nose on his sleeve and cackled. "Did you think I didn't recognise you from the start? Sitting there with a pint of beer, like some floozy. Why, you're no lady, for all your airs and graces."

So, Joseph had known she was there all the time. Maybe he'd left her out in the rain deliberately, as a punishment. Furious, Philomena jerked a hand free and clawed at Joseph's face. Two long scratches blazed on his cheek. Joseph cursed and clenched his fists. Philomena winced, braced for a blow, but it did not come. Joseph contented himself with tying her hands together. He wrenched the rope tight. Her fingers throbbed.

Joseph could never have planned this alone. Where was he taking her? He lived in London. It made no sense: Joseph had no carriage. Unless… Panic struck. Joseph knew about the secret marriage. She had always suspected he did. Now, he was acting under direction. The man with the cold green eyes had a plan for Philomena. God only knew what would happen to her now.

She lay squashed in a corner of the carriage. With every bump and jolt, her body slammed into the wooden sides, but she would not cry out. She bit her lip. She must think. How could she outwit Joseph and escape? There must be a way.

Philomena's mind raced ahead. The carriage must stop along the way to feed and water the horses or exchange for a fresh set. She would get a message to the innkeeper.

It was dark. Philomena lost track of the time. She spoke to Joseph, hoping for clues, but he replied only in monosyllables. "Joseph, surely there's no need to keep me tied up," she said, in a pale, wilting-female voice.

Joseph grunted. "Can't trust you."

"Even if I promise to be good? Couldn't you just loosen the rope a little? Look, it's hurting my arm."

"Well," Joseph weakened. "Maybe…"

Philomena's heart leapt, but Joseph changed his mind. "I got my instructions. Don't you try no tricks."

"Instructions?" Philomena tried for more information. "Who's giving you instructions, Joseph? I thought this was your plan."

"Never you mind," he growled. "You'll find out soon enough."

Philomena shuddered. Her husband was behind this, she was certain. Who could he be? The shadowy figure in the church had worn a hooded cloak. She thought hard and remembered cold green eyes. The stranger's fingers were long and pale, with white fingernails. A green emerald glinted as icy hands grasped Philomena's wrist and forced a plain gold ring on her finger. She shuddered. The stranger, her husband, was the bogeyman of nightmares. How many times had she wakened, shivering, in the early hours of the morning, panting with fear, dreaming of those cold green eyes?

For hours it seemed, the carriage thundered through the dark before drawing up at last at a turnpike. Philomena struggled to sit, bracing herself on her elbows, determined to scream and shout at the top of her lungs as soon as anyone approached.

"Don't you make a sound, now," Joseph hissed. "I've got a musket here, and I'll use it if I have to."

To Philomena's horror, he pulled out an old-fashioned pistol from under the seat and pointed it, waveringly, at her. "It's all right," she gasped. "I won't make a noise. Just don't point that thing at me. Your master will be angry if I arrive with my head blown off."

Joseph saw sense and put the pistol away. Philomena trembled with fear. Joseph could not be trusted with a pistol. There was no knowing what he might do. A manservant came out to the coach and whispered to Joseph.

"There's food and drink on its way," Joseph said. "You'll take it in here and don't you make no noise."

Philomena nodded. A basket of bread and cheese

appeared, along with bottles of beer. Joseph loosened the ropes around his captive's wrists to let her eat. Philomena was ravenously hungry and still cold and wet from the hours spent in the gloomy London garden. The bread was stale but at least it filled her stomach and staved off for a while the headache that threatened to overwhelm her.

Then, they were off again. Philomena wriggled herself into a more comfortable position, decided she could do little to help herself until they arrived and tried to pass the time in sleep. Yet sleep eluded her. She closed her eyes, fearful of bad dreams, but instead, thought of Hugh, of Thatcham Hall, and of John. Memories of the wonderful time at the Hall helped her stay calm. No matter what happened now, she would always have those. She could bear anything, so long as Hugh and John were safe. At last, Philomena sank into a dreamless sleep, oblivious at last to the jerking and jolting of the carriage.

The sky was lighter when she awoke. She saw Joseph clearly. It must be five o'clock or so in the morning. The light hurt her eyes. A roaring ache had taken hold, hammering in her head. Philomena closed her eyes again. The hammers quieted but did not stop. Her clothes seemed tight and hot. She could hardly breathe. The carriage stopped. Philomena slid forward and crashed against the side.

"Right." Joseph yanked her upright. "Here we are, just like I promised."

The door of the carriage flew open. An arm slid through and grasped Philomena. With a thrill of fear and disgust, she recognised the elongated nails and etiolated fingers of her nightmares. It was just as she had feared. "No," she cried, shrinking back.

The grip on her arm tightened, nails digging in to flesh. "Come with me, wife. You are home at last. What could be more charming?"

The man with the cold green eyes tugged Philomena out of the carriage. She tripped on the step and only her captor's grasp prevented her from falling. She saw the face she dreaded.

"Yes, my dear, we will deal happily together," said Mr. Muldrow. "Just as soon as you learn who is master here."

Shivering, Philomena stumbled into the Manor. She saw no servants. They must be about their business in other parts of the house, lighting fires and preparing the breakfast. How strange to imagine normal life continuing. Philomena's own life was over. There would be no escape from this man. She was at his mercy.

Hot tears pricked her eyes, but she blinked them back. She would not let him see her distress. "I am a little tired from the journey." She fought down a sob. "Please allow me to go and change my clothes." Her voice faltered. She had no luggage: no clothes to change into, no hairbrush, perfume or any everyday item.

"There are clothes a-plenty in your very own room, my dear," said Muldrow. "Make yourself at home. We have plenty of time ahead in which to become acquainted."

Renewed hope sprang in Philomena's heart. There must be a way out of this horror. She must remain calm and think carefully. She peered from side to side.

"If you imagine you can escape, my dear, may I

advise against it?" Muldrow poured cold water on her hopes. "I am not a fool. My servants are almost as loyal to me as those at Thatcham Hall are to their master. I would make life extremely hard for any servant who shows disloyalty. My household has instructions to keep you in sight at all times." Muldrow smiled, his green eyes gleaming. "Some, like our friend Joseph here, are armed. I suggest you find a suitable gown, my dear, wash your face and join me for a late breakfast within the hour." Muldrow twirled his watch on its chain. It caught the light, blinding Philomena.

She struggled, knowing it was hopeless.

Her captor's hands gripped more tightly. "I fear we will have to teach you a lesson or two in ladylike behaviour, my dear," he murmured.

****

Hugh's curricle sped through London's streets. His mind raced, calculating as he drove. Joseph's drive to Reading would take several hours, even with the fastest of horses. No horse could pull a coach at a gallop for forty miles. The wretch would stop to bait the horses from time to time, and they would need to walk a little, to recover from the bursts of speed.

Hugh's own curricle was small and light and the fit chestnuts raring for a gallop, sick of the stultifying pace of London in the Season. As Hugh whipped the horses faster, determined to overtake and rescue Philomena, an idea struck. The railway: why had he not thought of that? Each half hour in a railway carriage would take Hugh further than two hours in the curricle. He would arrive at Fairford Manor well before Joseph. Hope mounting, Hugh steered towards the terminus at Bishop's Bridge Road. Even if he had to wait an hour

253

or so for a train, there would still be time.

The station clock ticked slowly onward. Hugh cooled his heels on the platform. Such lack of action was unbearable. He paced urgently, up and down, head spinning. What a fool he'd been. Damn his stupidity: why did he not seize good fortune when it was there for the taking? At Christmas, Philomena transformed the Hall with a wicked, bubbling laugh, cheerful smile and endless good sense. Why had Hugh let her go?

Philomena was in danger, and Hugh could have kept her safe. Only he could prevent certain ruin. He still understood nothing. Why had Muldrow arranged for Joseph to kidnap Philomena? What connection was there between the two? Muldrow hated Hugh, but why did he want Philomena? Philomena remained mysterious. Who was she?

If only Hugh had forced her to tell the truth. He never believed her stories, but he let anger and hurt at such dishonesty blind him. Philomena was in trouble, and he had not helped. An uncle in Bristol, indeed! A child could have seen through such a tale.

One thing was certain. When Hugh rescued Philomena, he would discover the truth. He cared nothing for secrets from her past. Whatever she had been before, she was now the woman Hugh loved and needed. He would find her and never let her go again.

Hugh longed to leap into action but could do nothing. He'd pinned every hope on the train. It was too late to follow by carriage, but what was happening to Philomena? Hugh prayed that the speed and wild jolting of the carriage, as it raced along the dirt roads of the countryside, would prevent Joseph from harming her. At least Joseph was working for Muldrow. He would need to deliver the goods in one piece to his master.

At last, when Hugh felt he might go mad at any moment, the train arrived. He leapt on, heart pounding, and watched the countryside race by. The engine sped through England, unbelievably smooth and fast.

After little more than half an hour, the train huffed pompously into Reading station. All that remained was for Hugh to hire a coach to take him the short distance to Fairford Manor. He leapt to the platform. A mob hemmed him in. "There he is," someone cried. "Grab him before he gets away."

The village constable grasped Hugh's arm. A couple of heavy-looking thugs stood nearby. Angry, Hugh shook the constable away. "What's the meaning of this, Stephens? Can you not see I'm in a hurry, man? Get out of my way."

The constable stood, foursquare, in front of Hugh, the labourers panting at his side. "Excuse me, your lordship, but I've a warrant here for your arrest."

"What? Don't be ridiculous. Arrest for what?"

"A very serious offence, my lord," said the constable with lugubrious satisfaction.

Hugh took an impatient step forward. The heavyweights each grasped an arm. The mob, excited, urged the constable on, for the villain might try to escape and, with luck, force a fight. At a distance stood a group of his own cottagers, mouths agape at the sight of Lord Thatcham in custody.

Hugh took a deep breath and glowered at the constable. "Explain yourself, man." He glared at the constable's thugs. "There's no need for your men to hold on to me."

Stephens shook his head. "I'm afraid you have to

come with me, my lord. There's been a complaint laid against you."

"What sort of a complaint, man, for God's sake? I've more important things to worry about than arguments over rights of way or a neighbour's sheep. I'll deal with it later. You know where I live, after all."

"I'm sorry, my lord," murmured the constable. "It can't wait. The charge against you is murder."

Hugh, dislodging his captors with the impatience of a dog shaking off water after a swim, stopped dead. "Murder? What murder?"

"Well, my lord, I'm afraid it's for the murder of your wife."

Hugh, stock still, felt the blood drain from his face. "My wife? Lady Beatrice?"

"That's right, my lord, so if you come along quietly, we'll get things sorted out as quick as we can."

The constable's round, pleasant currant bun of a face bore the unmistakably resolute expression of a man who knows his duty and is determined to carry it out. His two helpers grinned broadly. This was the most exciting thing to have happened for years.

Hugh saw he would gain nothing from causing more excitement. He would prefer to keep any further spectacle to a less public arena. "Very well, Constable." He spoke through a rigid jaw, fighting down panic at the waste of time. Philomena's danger grew by the moment. Somehow, he must extricate himself from this tight spot as soon as possible.

He fought for calm. "We must clear this up at once. Shall we visit Lord Wrighton, my fellow magistrate, to discuss any evidence? I suspect there is none, for of course, I am quite innocent."

Muldrow must have instigated the case simply to gain time for his purposes toward Philomena.

"Thank you, my lord. That will clear the matter up, I'm sure." The constable shifted uncomfortably from one foot to the other. His uneasiness convinced Hugh that no trumped-up evidence existed. If the consequences of delay had not been so serious, Hugh would have felt sorry for the official, torn between the normal obsequious manner towards the gentry and his role as defender of the law. Stephens' face was scarlet. He did not know whether to stand firm, with folded arms, or lean forward deferentially.

Their arrival by carriage at Lord Wrighton's property did not bring the simple end to the matter Hugh had expected, for Lord Wrighton was away from home.

"He has gone to London, my lord." The housekeeper, Mrs. Barns, addressed her remarks to Hugh rather than to the constable. She had long been familiar with Lord Thatcham as a regular visitor and friend of her master.

"Then we must send for him, at once," said the constable.

"For God's sake, man." Hugh was losing his temper. He spoke firmly. "I shall go home to Thatcham Hall tonight. When Lord Wrighton returns, send for me at once. You have my word that I will return."

Stephens hesitated, licked his lips, head on one side, and then nodded. "Very well, my lord, as you give your word." He stood back.

Hugh's journey by train had left him without immediate transport. The constable would doubtless draw the line at lending the carriage. Hugh turned to

Mrs. Barns, whose eyes could open no wider if she were to use matchsticks. "Mrs. Barns, as you can see, there is a misunderstanding. Be good enough to send round a horse, would you?"

"Oh. Yes, sir," she murmured. "That is…" Her eyes flickered from Lord Thatcham's face to the constable and back. Finally, deciding she would prefer not to antagonise such a powerful man as Lord Thatcham, she curtsied and ran off, full of excitement, to spread the word and obey his commands.

Hugh winced. Mrs. Barns would spare no details. The Thatcham name and reputation would soon be in tatters. He would worry about that another time. The carriage carrying Philomena to the Manor would arrive within the next hour. Hugh must get himself out of this predicament. He dashed off a note on a page from his pocketbook, folded it, scribbled a direction and thrust it at the constable. "Give this to my solicitor."

"Yes, sir." The constable, now thoroughly regretting the whole business, took the note and departed.

In minutes, Hugh was galloping towards the Manor, cursing the wasted time. He would not be able to forestall Philomena's arrival.

Chapter Thirty-Five

At Fairford Manor, the housekeeper took Philomena to a room on the first floor and threw the door open. "Mr. Muldrow had it decorated, special, a few years ago."

Philomena, shaking with anger and fear, stared. The room was a bower of pink and white. Yards of netting surrounded the four-poster bed, and silk roses and satin swags draped themselves over the posts. Every chair was decorated, each piece of furniture finished in white painted curlicues, as though in the Palace of Versailles. It was a monstrosity.

"It was intended for Lady Beatrice, of course," said the housekeeper, small black eyes fixed on Philomena. "But she never used it."

Philomena gasped. "Lady Beatrice?"

"Oh, yes. The master had it all ready, just to her taste."

"Wait a moment," stammered Philomena. "Surely you cannot mean Lady Beatrice of Thatcham Hall?" She blushed. What could Lady Beatrice have been to Mr. Muldrow? The idea of Hugh's wife here, at Fairford Manor, with another man, was shocking. No wonder Hugh hated Mr. Muldrow.

The housekeeper smiled but her lips were tight. "My master had intended Miss Beatrice Cobbol, as she was then, for his wife, but she preferred Lord

Thatcham." She laughed. "Who could blame her? They were never suited, though."

She leaned closer to Philomena and whispered, like a conspirator. "People do say that she used witchcraft to bewitch Lord Hugh, and that once she was safely married, she turned back to Mr. Muldrow for—Now, you choose something nice from these clothes," she said, changing the subject.

Philomena, standing stiff as she tried to stop her body trembling, put out a hand to steady herself against the wall. At any other time, she would have laughed at the thought of Lord Thatcham and Mr. Muldrow as romantic rivals. She pushed the information to the back of her mind. She must concentrate on escape. "No, I won't be changing my clothes."

The housekeeper shook her head. "It's no good displeasing him, my dear. He can be cruel when he's angry. Just you do as you're told and all will be well." She turned to leave.

"Wait a minute," Philomena called, panicking, but the woman was gone.

There was no way to escape. Philomena would obey Muldrow's instructions for the moment. She sifted through the wardrobe and lighted on a pale green gown. The sleeves were loose. She would remain as unrestricted as possible, ready to make an escape. The waist was uncomfortably small, but there was no corset, so Philomena breathed in as far as possible and hoped the stitches would hold.

Head held high, Philomena descended the staircase to the dining room and made her entrance, her eyes searching for any way of escape. She was surprised to see Joseph seated at the table. Mr. Muldrow laughed.

"Come in, my dear. You look ravishing. I believe that to be the correct term."

Butterflies swooped in Philomena's stomach at his sneer.

"Sit here," said Muldrow, "between me and this good friend of mine."

Joseph did not attempt to get to his feet at Philomena's entrance but looked her up and down and winked. His insolent gaze lingered on her breasts. She wished she had not chosen such a low-cut dress.

"Joseph will be joining us, tonight," said Muldrow. Joseph took a gulp of wine and belched unpleasantly. "It will be just the three of us. Will that not be charming?"

Philomena, seeing she had no alternative, took her seat in silence.

"Drink your wine," said Muldrow. She shook her head. She must not become intoxicated. She must keep her wits about her. Muldrow sighed. "Really, my dear, do I have to force you?"

He took a position behind Philomena and grasped her chin. He leaned forward. His sour breath made her gasp. His voice hissed, soft and menacing in Philomena's ear. "You will do as I tell you or find I can be less kind and generous. I am sure you have known this day of reckoning would arrive, one day. This time, Lord Thatcham will not prevent me having my wishes."

"Lord Thatcham? What has he to do with this?"

"Oh, plenty." Muldrow linked his hands together and cracked his long fingers. "Did you think you were my only prize?" He laughed, and in a swift movement tipped the contents of Philomena's wine glass into her open mouth. She spluttered and coughed as the liquid burned. For several moments, she gasped for breath and could not speak.

"It will do no harm to let you into some of my secrets, my dear, now that I have you all to myself. " Muldrow smiled. "I have waited a long time for this moment, and I believe I shall enjoy myself extremely." He snapped his fingers and the butler appeared at the table. "Fill the wine glasses, then leave two bottles on the table. Bring the dishes here, and then you and the other servants may depart for the evening." The butler left the room.

"You see, my dear, I pay my staff well, and they obey my commands. You need look for no help from them. Indeed, I would advise you to enjoy the evening and get to know our friend on your right once more. You will be spending time with Joseph, later."

Philomena felt sick. Joseph leered at her, spilling red wine on an ill-tied cravat, winking and re-filling his glass with enthusiasm.

The butler and footman brought laden platters to the table. Philomena's mouth was too dry for food. The wine had already made her head swim unpleasantly, and she feared that whatever she put in her stomach would return before long. There seemed to be no way out of this predicament. She must play along and keep alert, ready to grasp any opportunity for escape.

"Now, where was I?" Muldrow leaned back in his chair and tapped his right hand on the table. A green ring glinted against the white skin of his hand. He twirled his wine glass so that it gleamed in the light from the candles. "Drink up, my dear. It really would be too much of a bore to have to use violence. I am sure you will enjoy your time here far more if you have taken wine. On the other hand, perhaps you wish to remember every moment of your encounter with a clear head. We are certainly anticipating it with the greatest of pleasure." Muldrow reached across and stroked Joseph's hair.

Philomena's stomach heaved.

He leaned forward, his face close. "Remember, you cannot escape. By morning, you will no longer be a virtuous maiden. Your cavalier, Lord Thatcham," he spat the name with venom, "will want no more of you. You will be damaged goods, just like dear Beatrice. Oh—" he smiled, his eyes flashing green—"how I enjoyed the game with his wife. Did you know, my dear, that Beatrice was visiting me on the day of that unfortunate accident? I did not let her in to the little secret of my friend Joseph's presence here, of course. The foolish woman thought she would be here alone with me."

Muldrow sipped from his wine glass. "Revenge is very sweet, is it not?"

"Revenge?" she whispered.

"Oh, yes. It took many years to find a way to punish Thatcham for disgracing me at University." His lip twisted. "My father taught me well, but Thatcham caught me out. Well, I was young in those days. It takes years of practice to become invincible as a card-sharp, you know." With a swift movement, Muldrow tossed the remainder of his wine down his throat. "In any case, I digress. We were discussing plans for the evening. You, my good friend Joseph and me, all together. How very charming it will be."

Philomena could not keep the horror from her face.

Muldrow laughed at her distress. "Any child, of

course, will carry the Muldrow name, although Joseph, who has a finer liking for ladies than I, may in fact have to—er, complete the task on my behalf, tonight. My pleasure will be in observation. That will be our little secret, of course. As you know, my dear Philomena, we were married in church, quite legally.

"If you are not immediately found to be with child, our friend will remain here with us at the Manor and there will be many more enjoyable episodes until you present me with an heir."

The full horror of her situation burst upon Philomena, and she trembled. She clutched shaking hands together, digging sharp fingernails into her own flesh. She fought sudden dizziness. *I must stay calm. That is my only hope. Oh, Hugh, if only you were here.*

As the thought of Hugh, Philomena felt some strength return. Hugh would never panic, no matter how dire the circumstances. She must be strong, escape from this vile beast and find her love once more. She would keep him talking. "Why did you choose me?" She struggled to sound confident, but her lips trembled so that the words were hardly audible.

"Why did I marry you?" He laughed, his voice as soft and smooth as satin. "Oh, how delightful. You really do not know? Well, this is better than anything I had hoped for."

Muldrow winked at Joseph, who guffawed. "Tell 'er, then guv. It's such a neat little tale."

"Ah, very well. The story begins, my dear, with your father. You remember the man? No? Perhaps that is just as well. He was a fool, although a wealthy one. Your dear father imagined himself to be a very fine fellow, with this house and its grounds, all inherited from his own father."

Philomena swallowed. "This house?" She was bewildered. "What can you mean?"

"Yes, my dear. Your father owned this house but did not value it. He wagered it at cards and, sadly, being such a fool, he lost. To my father, in fact, whose knowledge of cards was exceptional and whose ability to win against the odds was sometimes suspected but never challenged."

"You mean he cheated."

"Oh, those are such harsh words. Skill at cards is a family trait. As I said, it requires years of practice." Muldrow sneered. "Let us just say, my father gave fate a helping hand. In any case, your papa found himself signing the house over that very night. Fairford Manor became the property of the Muldrow family. Of course, no one knew how my father came by the Manor. The story put about was that he made a fortune up north, in a cotton mill."

Muldrow pulled a kerchief from a pocket and wiped his brow. "Unfortunately, my mother was never, in fact, married to my father, for she had contracted an earlier marriage." He sneered a little. "Yes, my dear, I am a bastard. I am not, actually, a Muldrow, although I have always used that name. The fact is not widely known, but, alas, it could one day come to light. We could not risk that, for the Manor would pass to a distant relative of my father. In order to ensure I had full title to the Manor, my father conjured up an ingenious plan. You have no male relations. I married you and could tear up the legal document signed by your fool of a father. I own the house, now, because you are my wife. Is that not delightful?"

Philomena rocked back in her chair. Was it the wine that made her head swim? Could it possibly be true, that the Manor House belonged to her father?

"Oh, please do not bother with that foolish, feminine swooning." Muldrow chuckled. "Surely you have realised I have no interest in females except when they offer the opportunity to cause pain to my enemies. However, I want this house, and since you and I married, it is mine."

"Yours?" She shook her head, still confused.

"You are my wife," Muldrow thundered. "We married, and the marriage was duly witnessed. Make no mistake about that."

Philomena's heart sank. She had not imagined it, then. She was truly married to this monster. She closed her eyes. There was no way out.

"However," Muldrow continued, "I am informed that the marriage must be—er…" He twirled his side-whiskers and tapped one finger on the table. "How can I express this in a style that will not offend your delicate ears, I wonder?" He frowned. "There is nothing for it but to be blunt. The marriage must be consummated to prevent any danger that it could be annulled."

Muldrow's words rang in Philomena's ears. At last, she understood what he meant. Horror struck cold into her heart. Muldrow would keep her here in captivity until she gave birth to a child by Joseph, which her husband would claim as his heir. Philomena's skin crawled as she imagined Joseph's hands on her body.

Beneath the revulsion, though, a tiny flicker of hope shone. He had spoken of annulment. Could such a marriage be overturned? Divorce, a long slow process involving an Act of Parliament, was granted no more than two or three times a year. Philomena knew nothing of annulment. What did the word mean? Was there any, faint chance that she could escape this terrible fate?

Philomena took a long, slow breath, determined to conceal a sudden lift of spirits. Her tormentor laughed, his voice a high-pitched titter. "I see you did not know the truth of your position. To put it in a nutshell, our marriage is legal, but there is one tiny flaw. Until we have—er, finalised the process, if I may put it that way, it is just possible for a minister of the church to grant an annulment."

"How does that work?"

"You hardly need know. Soon, despite reluctance on both our parts to undertake such an act together—" Muldrow's eyes roved over Philomena, his nose wrinkling in distaste—"Joseph will act on my behalf. All three of us will find something to delight us. I will secure you as my wife, and these very elegant apartments will remain in my possession."

Philomena's heart pounded. This was too much to take in. Her head swirled with a thousand thoughts. There might be a way out of this hideous situation, a way that would lift the curse. She could be free of this dreadful marriage, free to marry where she willed. Free to accept Hugh's offer.

She must not faint. She lowered her head, letting the blood return to her face. Her tormentor mistook the gesture.

"You are wise," he said, inspecting his green ring. "Give in gracefully and all will be well." He sighed. "We will do our best to take pleasure in the episode. Joseph and I have enjoyed such incidents before, although I have to say, never with such a charming young lady.

"Sadly, Beatrice could not benefit from our attentions. I could not let her see that I had no interest in her. My purpose was simply to punish Thatcham." He smiled, and the cruelty in his face horrified Philomena. "Poor Beatrice had to die, I am afraid. She was a beautiful woman but a very poor rider. All it took was the sound of a hunting horn nearby. The horse reared, and Beatrice lost control. Luckily, her neck was broken, so there was no need to complete the task by hand."

Philomena closed her eyes. This man's depravity knew no depths. Poor Beatrice, indeed, and poor Hugh. Had Lord Thatcham known his wife had left him for Muldrow? Even so, he could not have imagined that Muldrow had arranged Lady Beatrice's death. The man was cruelly deranged and corrupt.

"Now, be sure that my servants will give evidence of tonight's event, so that there will be no mistake." Muldrow, tiring of his explanations, stood up and pulled the cord to summon the housekeeper. Philomena glanced around, hope turning to panic.

"Come, my dear. Make yourself ready for Joseph. If all goes well, you may remain in comfort as the Lady of the Manor. I am sure your friends will enjoy watching your children growing up so close by. Everyone at Thatcham Hall seems to have become fond of you, have they not?"

"I will not allow you—You can't…" Philomena stumbled to her feet, blinking hard to keep tears of rage from blinding her. She was alone, in the power of this evil man. Joseph continued to drink in silence throughout Muldrow's triumphant explanations, a sneer on his face. He allowed Muldrow's caresses with every appearance of enjoyment.

Philomena's legs shook, but with an effort of will, she remained upright.

"Now, do not distress yourself, wife." Muldrow brushed an imaginary speck of dust from his waistcoat. "I am a most considerate husband in many ways, as you will find. Once we have dispensed with the necessary—ahem—activity, we will go on very well together, I am sure. You may retire for a while and weep to your heart's content. I believe young ladies invariably feel better when they have indulged in a few tears."

Muldrow held out a lacy handkerchief. Philomena dashed it away. She would not cry in front of this monster.

"I will attend you shortly, in your room," he continued. "My housekeeper will look after you in the meantime. I would not want to leave you alone. You are far too fond of disappearing."

Philomena stalked from the room with a straight back and chin held high. She would not let Muldrow see her terror.

The housekeeper was waiting outside to take Philomena's arm.

"Make our guest ready for bed," commanded Muldrow.

As Philomena reached the room, the housekeeper dropped her hand. The woman peered up and down the passageway, her face furtive, then pushed the door shut. "This is your chance. If you want to get away, go now."

Philomena stared. "B-but they'll know you helped me."

The woman shook her head. "I'm past caring and that's the truth. I thought I could sit back and let it happen, but I can't. I remember you, Miss Philomena, when you were but a tiny baby, before your mother died and your father, Mr. Stanton, went off to London with only a nursemaid to look after you." She shook her head.

Philomena sat on the grand four-poster bed with a thud. "You knew my mother?" she whispered.

"Oh, yes, she was a most elegant and gracious mistress. We all loved her dearly. It was a sad day when she died."

The woman crossed the room to the opposite wall and gestured towards a painting. Philomena gasped. "Is that my mother?" She ran to the portrait, her heart leaping. She saw fair hair, as in the lost brooch, neatly arranged in an old-fashioned style. The woman in the portrait had a wide mouth. A tiny, secret smile played across her face. Eyes, as blue and almond-shaped as Philomena's own, twinkled from the portrait as though the sitter shared a delightful joke.

"Yes, my lady," said the housekeeper. "Your mother, right enough. You lived here until she died and your father gambled away your inheritance." The woman sighed. "A sad man, your papa never had a sensible thought once your mother was gone. Broken hearted was Mr. Stanton. Said he would never come back here and he never did. Next thing, the Manor was signed over to the Muldrows. Your papa meant no harm, you know. You were only little, and all his money was gone."

She shook her head. "The master didn't live long after that. Once he went to London town, we heard no more, not even what became of you." She paced back and forth across the room. "We never saw the master or you again. I never forgot you, though, or your dear mother."

The housekeeper stared up at the portrait. "You look like her, you know. It brings her back, having you here. I don't pretend to understand what's going on, but I know Mr. Muldrow had you brought here against your will, and that's not right. I won't be part of it."

The woman turned back to Philomena and started to unbutton the back of her dress. Philomena resisted but the woman laughed. "I'll see you safe away from here, don't you worry. You change yourself back into those men's clothes and be off, the back way. I'll make sure Mr. Muldrow doesn't know you're gone for a good long while."

Philomena hesitated, her lip caught in her teeth. What would become of this woman if Muldrow knew she had helped in the escape?

"Now, there's no time for worrying," said the housekeeper. "You slip away from the back of the house. By the time Mr. Muldrow realises you've gone, he'll be too befuddled with his wine to give chase and so will that vagabond he's brought along to shame himself and you."

Chapter Thirty-Six

As the Manor came into view, Hugh slowed his horse to a trot, then a walk. The animal, not in the first flush of youth, was happy to slacken his pace. While still a field away, Hugh slid from the saddle, hooked the bridle to a gatepost near a drinking trough, and left the horse to enjoy a handful of hay.

The Manor was eerily silent. No servants called to each other in the yard. No noise came from the stables. No one spoke. Surely, Hugh had not made a mistake. Was this not where Joseph was heading with Philomena? If this was the wrong place, all would be lost. He must make haste.

Hugh hurried closer, slipping round a corner and halting by a window. The heavy drapes were drawn shut against the falling dusk but there was a narrow gap, where the curtains did not quite meet. A servant had pulled them carelessly across with a sloppiness that would never be tolerated at Thatcham Hall. Hugh peered in. He could see little except the end of a long table, but voices came from the other end of the room. Hugh heard the splash of wine into glasses, and bursts of raucous laughter.

"She'll have a night she'll never forget." The snigger was rough and uncouth. Hugh recognised Joseph's voice. "And now," Joseph went on, "it's time for the blunt you owe me."

"Just you wait until afterwards." Muldrow spoke coldly. "You'll get your reward, never fear." There was a sneer in the voice. "Once tonight is over, no one can touch me. The house, and the enterprising Miss Stanton, now to be known as Mrs. Muldrow, of course, will both be mine to do with as I please. Meanwhile, enjoy the rest of the wine while I prepare myself for the forthcoming encounter with the young lady."

The white heat of Hugh's anger all but overcame him. He would break through the window and give Muldrow the whipping he deserved. He took a breath. No. He must wait and find Philomena. He walked round the corner and along the side of the house, and met no one. All was quiet. Muldrow must have sent most of the servants away for the night.

Hugh turned a corner. There was the entrance to the kitchen. He slipped quietly up to the door and stopped to listen. Nothing. He tried the door. It would not move. He shook it, but the lock held. He walked on. There must be another way in.

Sure enough, a small door led to the scullery. Hugh rattled it. It was locked, but flimsy. It gave a little to his touch. Hugh gathered his strength, put a heel against the lock, and kicked forward with all his force. A crack rent the quiet, the lock splintered and the door swung open.

Hugh stepped inside, tense, ready to defend himself, but all was quiet. He slipped out of the scullery, through the kitchen and up the back stairs. Still, he met no one. At last, he burst through the servants' door into the house itself.

Muldrow stood in the hall, a lantern in one hand, a hessian-shod foot on the bottom stair. His accomplice was close behind. Muldrow's head jerked round.

"You!" The scoundrel grasped the banister, poised in mid-step. Cold green eyes flashed, angry, but he spoke smoothly. "How very unexpected. Perhaps you have come to rescue the young lady. If so, I am afraid you have sadly miscalculated."

Hugh ran at Muldrow as Joseph made himself scarce through the front door, but Muldrow's next words stopped Hugh in his tracks. "She is my wife, you know." Hugh froze in shock. "I will thank you to be off." Muldrow smiled at Hugh. "Perhaps you would be kind enough to use the front door?" He sneered. "Or, perhaps I should keep you here, for I believe the esteemed local constable is looking for you."

"Philomena is not your wife! She will never be so, by God, if I can prevent it, no matter what you have done." This time, Hugh did not wait for an answer, but landed his right fist squarely on Muldrow's jaw. Muldrow swung round under the force of the blow, tripped over the bottom stair, and fell heavily to the ground.

Hugh pushed past, taking the stairs two at a time. Muldrow thrust out a foot, and Hugh fell. In an instant, Muldrow snatched a knife from his sleeve and slashed it forward, aiming at Hugh's face, missing by a fraction of an inch. Hugh cursed himself for arriving unarmed.

He dodged back, then sideways. The blade slashed and glinted, inches from his face. Muldrow swished the knife, unskilled but vicious. Hugh ducked and swerved but his foot slipped on a rug and he fell, grasping blindly at the banisters. Muldrow slashed again. The blade whistled through the air and tore into Hugh's arm. Hot pain seared through him. Desperate, with a mighty effort he stood, gathered his strength and dived at

Muldrow.

A noise upstairs distracted Muldrow. He glanced up for a moment, and Hugh lunged. He grabbed the arm that held the knife and clung on, wordless, panting, as Muldrow struggled to free his arm. Hugh's limbs weakened. A cold wetness slithered down his sleeve.

Muldrow kicked out at Hugh's leg. In return, he sent a knee into Muldrow's groin that left the scoundrel groaning on the floor. His weight pulled Hugh from the stair. Hugh landed heavily on top of Muldrow, fingers locked into the man's linen shirt. Muldrow twisted under him. The linen ripped, Muldrow's arm pulled free, and the knife slashed through Hugh's waistcoat.

His strength ebbed fast. His breath heaved, and his head whirled. Summoning a desperate burst of energy, he kicked up at Muldrow. His boot located the man's elbow. The knife flew out of Muldrow's grasp and across the hall. It clattered to the floor. Hugh tried to follow it but could not drag himself up.

He clasped the banisters and heaved, grunting with effort, until he faced Muldrow. The scoundrel's lips drew back in a wolf's triumphant grimace. His eyes were small dark holes of malevolence. Hugh's strength was almost gone. He gathered for a final attack and took a long, shuddering breath into lungs that were ready to burst.

Something flashed before his eyes. A figure crossed the hall behind Muldrow, nimble as a mouse scuttling across the floor. It was Philomena. She was alive, at least. With renewed energy, Hugh grasped a heavy Chinese vase that stood on a table by the stairs. With a final ounce of strength, he crashed it down on the scoundrel's skull. Muldrow crumpled in a heap.

Hugh, aching limbs heavy, moved slower than honey pouring from a jar. He tried to take a shaky step forward but his leg folded. He slipped down, senses reeling.

Philomena frowned at him. "You'd better not be dead."

Hugh's lips twitched, even as his head spun. He laughed, lightheaded, remembering their first meeting. Now the tables were turned. "Don't you own any suitable women's clothes?" He closed his eyes.

Chapter Thirty-Seven

"Someone, lend me a hand," Philomena cried. "Lord Thatcham is bleeding."

Hugh forced his eyes open. "It is nothing." He felt helpless, as though he had spent a long evening with several bottles of claret. The feeling was not entirely unpleasant, though his right arm throbbed. "I fear you will be hard-pressed to remove the stains from this Persian rug," he murmured. "The rug, by the way, is no friend of mine. It caused me to trip at a most unfortunate moment. It almost ended the fight in Muldrow's favour."

He winced as Philomena raised his arm, checking the wound. "They say a good workman seldom blames his tools," she remarked with a smile. "I have never approved of duelling, but for one moment, I believed I should need to intervene and make use of the vase myself."

Hugh snorted, but his rejoinder turned to a grunt of pain as Philomena grasped his shirt, the front of which was rapidly turning crimson. She ripped away a strip of linen, exposing a gash of three inches or more in Hugh's chest. Her hand flew to her lips and her face grew pale.

"I believe all will be well," Hugh said, "If you will find something to stop the bleeding. Perhaps this good lady would be kind enough to help?"

The housekeeper had plucked up enough courage to descend the stairs carrying a bowl of water and a sponge. Together, she and Philomena made rapid work of securing a pad of cotton against the slash on Hugh's chest and binding the cut on his arm.

Slowly, Hugh raised himself to a sitting position. His opponent lay silent in the hall. Hugh leaned across to feel the man's pulse.

"Have you killed him?" Philomena asked. "I do hope so."

Hugh frowned. "I sincerely hope not. We will have difficulty explaining our behaviour if that is the case, thoroughly though the scoundrel deserves it." His frown disappeared. Muldrow was alive, at least. "He'll wake up soon, I'm sure, with a headache that will last for some time. We will just secure his arms with these bandages. We need to alert the constable."

Hugh thought for a moment, his mind clearing. "By the way, I am supposedly in custody with the constable myself. He is having a most unusual day." He laughed at Philomena's puzzled stare. Explanations could wait.

At that moment, the constable himself appeared.

"Stephens…" Hugh pulled himself up to his full height, holding firmly to the banister for support. "Your entrance is perfectly timed. I take it you delivered that note to my solicitor, who sent you here? As you see, we have the rogue neatly tied, beginning to stir a little, if I make no mistake."

Muldrow groaned. "Damn you, Thatcham. I'll see you in hell." Seeing the constable, Muldrow squirmed to a sitting position, his arms still secured behind his back. He smirked. "Ah, I see you have come to recapture your prisoner, Constable. How foolish of you to allow him to escape. However, there is little harm done. Please release me from these ridiculous bonds, remove Thatcham at once and leave me with my wife."

Hugh took a step forward. "She's no wife of yours, you snivelling coward. Nor will she ever be, no matter what wickedness you have planned for her." He turned to the constable, who looked from one to the other of the gentlemen, his face purple from the struggle to understand the situation. "Constable. There is more to this story than you know. With your permission, let us be seated like sensible beings and discuss this tangle. But first, we need to make sure that this devil cannot escape."

The constable scratched his head. "Well, I can't say as I understand any of this, but there's a complaint been made against you, Lord Thatcham, so I must take you back into custody until that complaint has been answered. The magistrate is on his way here. Your solicitor arranged for me to come first, once he read your note giving the particulars of this 'ere address." As he spoke, he loosened the bandages that secured Muldrow's arms.

"Oh!" Muldrow's face creased in fury. "So that's your idea of justice—to bring out one of Thatcham's old friends." Naked hatred flashed in the man's eyes. His cheeks reddened and his breath heaved. He cast a look of sheer malevolence at Hugh and clenched his fists.

The constable took his arm. "Now then, sir, let's wait until the magistrate arrives, shall we?"

Muldrow shook him off. "Get out of my house, all of you. I'll see you dead, Thatcham, and I hope it's on the gallows, though no doubt your friends will ensure you escape." He took a step forward, his face close to Hugh's. "You have always believed yourself to be so much better than me, with your Hall and your land and your riches."

Hugh looked into the red-rimmed eyes and feared for Muldrow's sanity.

"Things didn't work out so well with that little wife of yours, did they?" Muldrow said. Hugh stiffened. "Did she tell you how she came to me? Oh yes, she had had enough of you, and Thatcham Hall. She cared nothing for you." In the sudden silence, a clock ticked. Muldrow grinned.

Hugh spoke at last. "You are the scum of the earth, Muldrow. By your own admission, you attempted to steal my wife. I should have killed you last year when Lady Beatrice died on the way to be with you." Hugh spoke the words that had never before passed his lips. "Just tell me, you villain, was it an accident, or did you scare her horse deliberately, knowing she was a timid rider?"

Muldrow's teeth showed as his lips pulled back in a grimace of vulpine pleasure.

Hugh, seeing the answer in the man's eyes, took Muldrow by the neck and shook him. Muldrow's head rattled, and he spat in Hugh's face. "Oh, so clever. But it's too late, now. She is dead and buried." He laughed, cackling like a fool, his grip on reality slipping away. He was fast descending into real madness.

Philomena moved closer to Hugh, and he slid his arm around her waist, searching for the right questions to ask. He needed to know the full story of the man's deceptions, and his hold over Philomena.

"Why do you say this lady is your wife?" Hugh said, his voice quiet.

The constable, brow creased, shook his head in disbelief.

"So you know?" Philomena blurted.

Hugh's heart lurched. So, it was true. He had feared the worst, and he was right. Philomena was indeed married to Muldrow, Hugh's enemy. Hugh's arm slid away from Philomena and fell back by his side. His eyes closed. He could not bear to look at her beloved face. This pain was worse than the cut of any knife. Philomena could never be his wife, then. Every dream of love and married happiness was in vain.

Muldrow giggled and wiped his nose on his sleeve. "What a day it was when I caught sight of my dear wife in the village. Such good fortune! As soon as I heard the gossip, how the great Lord Thatcham had fallen in love with some waif from London, and I saw the wench, I knew who she was.

"What a gift. All my dreams came true. I would keep the Manor and stand by, year after year, watching you, Thatcham, yearn for my wife." Muldrow's words tumbled over themselves. "That I should take another woman from you—what a triumph, my dear Lord High and Mighty Thatcham."

Muldrow rounded on Philomena. "But you had to spoil it." Without warning, the man began to cry, snivelling into a sleeve. Hugh was transfixed. Muldrow had finally slipped into madness. "You little harlot, no better than your mother, spoiling all my plans."

Hugh turned to the constable. "I think we've heard enough. Take him away and lock him up. Make sure you keep someone on guard."

The constable led the weeping, shivering Muldrow away. The housekeeper decided discretion was the better part of valour and scurried away to the kitchens. Joseph had long ago made himself scarce. The constable could find him later. Hugh hardly cared, now.

At last Hugh was alone with Philomena. Her face paper white, she hung her head, eyes fixed on the floor.

"So you are indeed married," Hugh said.

She nodded. "I am sorry." Her voice was heavy with tears.

Hugh touched her arm and then dropped his hand. She was a married woman, no matter how disgusting her husband.

"I will tell you everything I know," she said, "although I hardly understand it all myself."

At first, Hugh could hardly make out her words, for Philomena sobbed uncontrollably as she recounted the story of her marriage to the man with the cold green eyes and green ring.

"Be calm," Hugh begged, grasping at straws. "Who knows, we may yet find a way through this infernal muddle, though I see no light in the tunnel as yet."

He listened, interjecting a question here and there, until Philomena reached the climax of her story. "So, Joseph brought me here, in a carriage, for my-my husband to—er…" Philomena covered her crimson face with her hands. "To make the marriage secure."

Hugh gazed at her for a long moment, frowning. What could she mean? An idea hovered for a second, just beyond reach. Then, in a moment of clarity, her full meaning burst upon him like sunlight after a storm. He grasped her hand. "You mean to say that no such event has yet taken place?"

Philomena looked in his eyes for the first time since she had begun the story. Tears streaked her cheeks. She shook her head. "He told me he would not—could not…" She took a deep breath. "Joseph was to undertake the task on his behalf."

"Ha!" Hugh stood and pulled Philomena to her feet. "Then, all may yet be well."

"No, no," she wept. "You have misunderstood me. I was married in a church. It is legal."

"But not consummated." Hugh laughed at Philomena's shocked gasp. "I beg your pardon. My choice of words is not appropriate for a lady, my love, but you will excuse me, I am sure, when I explain."

Hugh swung Philomena round by her hands, forgetting his wounds, until a stab of pain reminded him. He subsided on to a chair and shook his head. "You see, it is possible to obtain an annulment of a marriage, if it has not been—er, if husbandly duties have been neglected. It seems that the scoundrel is incapable of carrying out such duties."

"So that's what he meant." Philomena's eyes sparkled. "My husband spoke of annulment when I arrived here, but I did not understand."

"Please, do not describe Muldrow as your husband. By all that's holy, the wretch will not remain so for much longer. I sent a note to my solicitor warning of your abduction to this house. The lawyer's intervention brought the constable here. I will write once more and set proceedings in train to extract you from this so-called marriage. In exchange for escaping the rope for his part in the abduction that rogue, Joseph, will be keen enough to give evidence. My solicitor will help us move rapidly through the necessary steps, requesting

Parliament to end your association and return the Manor to your possession." He laughed and seized Philomena's hands.

Her tears dried on her cheeks. "Shall we really marry?" Philomena whispered, her face aglow.

"Indeed, we shall." Hugh pulled her into his arms.

Chapter Thirty-Eight

Philomena opened her eyes and nestled more closely under the covers. More than a year had passed since Muldrow had abducted her, and her memory of that horror was fading. Hugh threw back the embroidered bedspread that she had sewn before their wedding and leapt out. Philomena groaned. "I do not know why you insist on rising so early," she said.

Hugh smiled down on her, the stern planes of his face soft. "I will ride out for an hour before breakfast, but you must stay in bed until my return."

With an effort, Philomena rolled over and yawned. "It would be good to sleep a little longer. Our child is impossibly restless during the night. I believe he must be a boy, as active as John."

"Then you will need all your strength, soon." Hugh bent and kissed her forehead.

"Listen," she said.

Hugh paused as the whistle of the steam train carried through the frosty air.

"There goes the train to Bristol. Imagine, Hugh, if the train had been derailed elsewhere, rather than in Sonning Cutting? Is it not amazing that I should be thrown to the ground not ten miles from the Manor, my own rightful home?"

"Even more astonishing, my love, that I should find you there. How much has happened to bring us together. We must be the luckiest couple in the world."

Philomena struggled to sit up as a thought struck. "I have still never visited Bristol. Perhaps in the summer?"

"Do you imagine you may find relations there?" Hugh teased. "In any case, I think you may want to wait until the baby is more than a few weeks old."

"You know, in a way I envy Muldrow and Joseph. Both will soon be sent off to Australia to make new lives for themselves."

"I do not think they possess quite your sense of adventure, my love. They were lucky to be deported rather than hanged."

"All the same, there is something exciting about travelling to a new and unknown country."

Hugh's eyes brightened. Despite his happiness at Thatcham Hall with Philomena, he still longed for travel. "Then perhaps we should arrange our trip to the Americas." He sat on the bed once more. "I should like to see the machinery they use on their huge farms, and learn something of their agricultural practices."

He smiled. "Look at you," he said, lips twitching in the manner Philomena loved so much. "Your eyes shine at the thought. I see that our life together will never be dull."

Hugh bent to kiss her, full on the mouth, and Philomena responded to his caresses. He was gentle, these days, for the baby would be arriving in a few weeks. Philomena loved the way he controlled his passion. They had spent many exhilarating nights together, while Hugh raised her to the heights of delight with his ardour, but now he was all tenderness.

Later, as his head lay on Philomena's stomach, he

laughed. "I felt the baby move."

"Remember your mother joins us today," Philomena said.

Hugh shouted. "What a time to mention my mother."

"I must make everything ready. Your mama is not yet used to my presence in the family, although I do believe the inheritance of Fairford Manor, as an addition to your estates, helped to persuade her to accept the marriage." Philomena began to rise from the bed, all thoughts of sleep driven away. "Do you know what your mama said last time she was here?"

"Indeed I do. She wished you had been able to come out and enjoy the London Season before our marriage. If I remember correctly, you replied that it was impossible to 'come out' when you had never been in the schoolroom, and that you were proud to have worked all your life. It was not tactful."

Philomena giggled. "I was not thinking of that, but when we were taking tea, your mama admired my gown. I am afraid I could not resist explaining that I made it myself. She glared for a moment, over the top of her lorgnette, as you know she likes to do, and said, 'I suppose that at least my new grandson will be the best dressed baby in England.'"

****

"Papa," said John, as they strolled together in the woods, searching for a tree to cut down and take into the Hall. "Will you and Miss 'Mena tell me the story of Good King Wenceslas again, like before?"

Hugh looked down at his son and smiled. "You can ask her yourself. Here she comes." He nodded in the direction of the house as Philomena approached, her gait awkward. John waved.

Hugh stepped forward and took her arm. "I thought you were resting. You were awake early."

Philomena's cheeks glowed as she remembered the morning's pleasure. "I feel a little restless. I can't forget what happened at Christmas."

Hugh kissed her on the cheek. "No more can we. John was asking if you would tell him the story of Good King Wenceslas again tonight. And perhaps I will join you, to be sure you do not make mistakes."

"Miss Smith and I have read some Christmas stories today," said John, "but she makes me read parts of them myself and that takes too long." He ran off across the grass.

Philomena and Hugh walked on, hand in hand. "He still calls me Miss 'Mena," said Philomena, with a small sigh.

Hugh squeezed her arm. "Be content. It is quite right that John should still remember and love his mother. Beatrice and I did not do well together, but that was my fault and I would not have him forget her, even for you, my love."

They wandered arm-in-arm back into the Hall where fires blazed in every room. "Selena and the Dowager will be here tonight," Philomena observed. "I must go down to the kitchens to check all is well."

Hugh laughed. "And to see that the servants are comfortable?"

"I cannot forget how kind they were to me when I arrived here. They shook Joseph off my trail and kept me safe. To me, they will always be far more than servants."

As Philomena entered the kitchen, the hustle of

Christmas preparations stilled for a moment. "Master John is not here, my lady," Ivy volunteered.

Philomena laughed. "For once, I am not searching for him. I am come to thank you all for your kindness and to give Ivy and Tom my best wishes for their wedding."

Ivy blushed and giggled. "Thank you Miss Phil—I mean, Your Ladyship," she murmured.

"And now, I want to invite you all to come into the Great Hall to see the Christmas tree arrive. Truly, we will be as gay as Windsor Castle, this holiday."

Mrs. Bramble stepped forward, her hands pulling at her apron. "I know it's not my place to say so…"

Philomena laughed. "You may say whatever you wish to me, dear Mrs. Bramble."

"Then I would like to say that it was a good day for all of us at Thatcham Hall when you fell off that train, my lady, and we're all the better for it."

Tears burned Philomena's eyes. "You must not make me cry." She smiled. "Now, here is John come to collect us all."

John approached, solemn, with a package in his hands. "I want to give this to you today." He hesitated and fidgeted.

Hugh appeared behind him and rested his hand on the boy's shoulder. "John has a special gift for you. He has made it himself."

Philomena took the parcel. John had wrapped it in gold paper. Carefully, she untied the ribbon. The paper peeled away to reveal an oval, papier-mâché workbox decorated in pink and gold. Inside she found a pair of ivory handled scissors, a book of needles, a bodkin and a silver thimble. However, the tears that streamed down

Philomena's face were not due to the box or its contents. On a little card that rested on top, in childish, rounded letters, John had written two words that meant everything to Philomena. "For Mama."

Philomena's England

Philomena, Hugh, and the other characters in their story exist in our imaginations, but Victorian England in the 1840s was a very real and sometimes surprising place. Life upstairs in a Great House was very different from the world downstairs and both lifestyles were more comfortable than that of the average Londoner.

Great country houses, built by the old aristocracy several hundred years before the Victorian era, supported communities with as many as sixty estate workers and indoor servants. The Victorians enjoyed improving their houses. The wealth of the new middle class, based on mechanisation and factories in the north of England, allowed them to buy houses that previously belonged to the aristocracy.

Servants at the grandest and wealthiest houses bathed in the reflected glow of "their" family's importance. A butler managed the male servants, reporting directly to the head of the household. Responsible for the wine cellar and the silver, he enjoyed a position of authority over the other servants who addressed him as "Mr." Lesser servants were known by their surnames, except for the housekeeper and cook who used the honorary title of "Mrs."

Domestic servants ran the house from behind the green baize door. Maids took orders from the housekeeper, who communicated directly with the mistress of the house. Kitchen staff led by the cook prepared vast quantities of food, not only for the family upstairs but also for the staff, who ate in the servants' hall. Separate staircases allowed the family to avoid bumping into their servants unexpectedly.

The status of nursemaids and governesses hovered somewhere between upstairs and downstairs. They ate with the children, reported to the mistress of the house, and could exercise a little one-upmanship over the downstairs staff by requesting special meals for the children and themselves, brought up on trays.

Very wealthy young girls "came out" of the schoolroom at sixteen or so, to be presented at Court, at the Queen Charlotte's Ball in London. Magnificently dressed in white, they curtsied deeply to Queen Victoria herself, practising diligently beforehand for fear of toppling over. The London Season was their marriage market. Balls, dances, concerts and drives along Rotten Row in Hyde Park were opportunities to meet suitable husbands.

In Great Houses, dining took place around eight or nine o'clock in the evening. The family filled the long gap between lunch and dinner with a cup of tea and a biscuit, following the inspired example of Anna, Seventh Duchess of Bedford, in the early 1800s. This repast became the elegant "tea party" where the lady of the house poured tea from porcelain teapots into delicate cups for visitors.

At Christmas, the table in a Great House groaned under the weight of food, including turkey, geese, game, poultry, pork, sausages, oysters, mince pies, plum puddings, apples, oranges, pears, chestnuts, and cakes. The Victorians loved exotic fruit. They imported oranges and lemons all year round from Spain and tangerines from Tangiers. The expense meant that only the rich could afford them for their table.

Life for the underclass in London was less pleasant than in the countryside. The city was dirty, noisy, smelly and unhealthy, with black mud clogging the streets. A yellow fog of pollution, the notorious "pea-souper," often prevented the Londoner from seeing the hand in front of his face and provided cover for thieves.

Poor Londoners lived in cramped lodging-houses, sharing rooms and even beds. The Central Criminal Court, The Old Bailey, records many instances of Londoners turning a blind eye and deaf ear to quarrels, domestic violence, and murder.

Steam trains soon crossed England. The Great Western Railway took Londoners to Bristol and the West Country from 1838. Early on Christmas Eve 1842, a landslip at Sonning Cutting, near Reading, derailed the train. Several passengers died. As a result, the 1844 Railway Regulation Act set out improvements such as the provision of roofs on passenger carriages.

The Victorians enjoyed the novelty of photography. Fox Talbot, in 1841, patented a process that produced more than one copy of a photograph. As each exposure required the sitter to remain motionless for half a minute, many Victorian photographs seem stiff and posed.

The crayon, a stick of coloured wax, existed in Victorian England. The word, first used in 1644, derives from the French word for chalk, *craie*. Jane Austen mentions the fashion for drawing in crayon in 1813, in *Pride and Prejudice*.

Members of the Metropolitan Police Force, called "bobbies" after Sir Robert Peel, Home Secretary at the time, policed London from 1829. Outside the capital, most parishes had a single constable who kept order as best he could. Serious crimes like murder were punished by hanging, while lesser crimes could result in

deportation to Australia or New Zealand.
More English Victorian trivia can be found at:
www.fevesham.wordpress.com

A word about the author...

Frances Evesham writes, collects grandsons and Victorian ancestors, and drinks tea. She loves to walk in the country, breathe the sea air in Somerset, and read Jane Austen novels. One day she will clean the house, but not today.

She's worked in England and Belgium, as a speech and language therapist, a professional communication fiend, an intermediary in the criminal courts, and a road sweeper.

She writes historical romances, mysteries, and books about communication. That leaves just enough time to enjoy bad jokes and puns and wish she'd kept on with the piano lessons.

Thank you for purchasing
this publication of The Wild Rose Press, Inc.
For other wonderful stories of romance,
please visit our on-line bookstore at
www.thewildrosepress.com.

For questions or more information
contact us at
info@thewildrosepress.com.

The Wild Rose Press, Inc.
www.thewildrosepress.com

To visit with authors of
The Wild Rose Press, Inc.
join our yahoo loop at
http://groups.yahoo.com/group/thewildrosepress/

Lightning Source UK Ltd.
Milton Keynes UK
UKOW04f0741020614

232691UK00001B/9/P